DOLL SEED

DOLL SEED

STORIES

Michele Tracy Berger

aunt lute

Aunt Lute Books, P.O. Box 410687, San Francisco, CA 94141
www.auntlute.com

Cover design: Authan Chen
Text design: Sarah Lopez
Editorial: Emma Rosenbaum and Joan Pinkvoss
Production Team: María Mínguez Arias, Isis Asare, Sheree Bishop,
Shay Brawn, Bianca Hernandez-Knight, Evelyn Kuo, and Golda Sargento

Back cover author photo: Institute for the Arts and
Humanities, University of North Carolina

Supported in part by the San Francisco Arts Commission
and the Zellerbach Family Foundation.

Print ISBN: 978-1-951874-07-0
eBook ISBN: 978-1-939904-43-0

Library of Congress Cataloging-in-Publication Data

Names: Berger, Michele Tracy, 1968–author.
Title: Doll seed : stories / Michele Tracy Berger.
Other titles: Doll seed (Compilation)
Description: San Francisco : Aunt Lute, 2024.
Identifiers: LCCN 2024015766 | ISBN 9781951874070 (trade paperback) | ISBN 9781939904430 (ebook)
Subjects: LCGFT: Short stories.
Classification: LCC PS3602.E75443 D65 2024 | DDC 813/.6 — dc23/eng/20240408
LC record available at https://lccn.loc.gov/2024015766

10 9 8 7 6 5 4 3 2 1

ACKNOWLEDGEMENTS

I acknowledge and thank with joy, love, and gratitude:

The many teachers I studied with during 2010-2021 who were generous in their encouragement, discriminating in their feedback, and big-hearted in their vision of my potential as a writer.

Marjorie Hudson for nurturing me as I revised, organized the collection, and queried publishers. Thank you for the cards, gifts, homemade dinners, tea dates, phone calls and numerous ways you supported me as a friend and a writer. These special moments and invitations always came at the right time, lifting my spirit and helping me keep the faith. And, thank you for our special winter solstice ceremonies!

Val Neiman who generously gave her time to read an early version of the collection and provided crucial feedback. Thank you for suggesting the current order of the stories.

Nancy Bolish, Linda Johnson, Robin Whitten—the main members of a writing group simply titled "Writing Women" that met for over a decade. What we learned together about ourselves as writers and people was invaluable. I adore you and am eternally grateful for our years together.

Al 'Santa Al' Capehart for being my writing buddy since 2011. Our monthly meetings over the years have been filled with fun, laughter, support and a lot of chocolate! Gratzi, gratzi, gratzi.

Kelly Allgaier, Lynne Degitz, Kathleen Guidroz, Jodi O'Brien, and Jodi Sandfort, for being dear friends who have supported my writing life in meaningful and magical ways.

Rachael Herron who taught transformative writing classes during the pandemic and created the most amazing writing community.

The "BAMFS" group forged during the pandemic, evolving out of Rachael Herron's 90 Days to Done, 90 Days to Revise, and Grads online classes: William "Bill" Aperance, Lisa Fabish, Mary L. Hower, Nirmy Kang, Aylene Lambert, Susan Lee, Maria Olujic,

Heather Patel, Jason Poole, Rosie Stott, and Maile Topliff. Thank you for the care, the joy and tears, the vulnerable way we show up for each other.

The editors who originally published many of these stories.

Emma Rosenbaum for the care, attention and generative way you approached editing this collection. Your deeply considered questions and our conversations helped me to hold a bigger dream for these stories.

The entire team of Aunt Lute Books who made my dream come true. Thank you for seeing me. I am still pinching myself.

Melissa Hope Berger for having unwavering faith in me as a writer from the beginning. You are the best sister anyone could have.

Timothy Dane Keim for never making me feel wrong or judged by having chosen this often vexing, difficult, and sometimes soul-challenging artistic path. Thank you for reading every story in the collection (multiple times over several years—some even over a decade), for brainstorming titles, character details and plots, for knowing when to tell me to take a break, for bringing snacks and dinners at crucial periods and celebrating all the little wins along the way. Over the past twenty-four years, you have showered me with more support and love than I thought possible. Thank you. How lucky are we?

STORIES

NUSSIA

NUSSIA. I SAID HER NAME LIKE A WISH.

I was elated that our family was chosen to host Nussia, an alien child. My family was this regular Black family that owned a house in Parkchester, in the northern section of the Bronx. Nussia, well, Nussia was Fike (pronounced Fīkē).

The Fike landed on Earth in 1975. In 1976, the President announced a contest to build good relations between humans and Fike. The winner of the contest would get to host Nussia (pronounced Nōōsēä). Sixth graders had to write why their families should be chosen. The Fike and the President chose the host family. Nussia came to live with us toward the end of spring in 1978. I was thirteen. It was at a time when "firsts" for Black folks still mattered.

&

When my family found out that we'd won, my sister and I ran around the house shrieking. My dad put on some George Benson, and my mom opened the 1972 Burgundy. That night, my family toasted me, Lindsay Fields, and my sixteen-year-old sister, Virginia. We were each allowed to have a glass of wine. Mom wound up drinking several glasses that night.

It's strange how things work out. Even though Virginia helped me write the essay that won the contest, it was all my idea to enter it. We said silly things like the Bronx is a fun place, and that we would take Nussia roller skating at Skate Key, and to the Botanical Garden where she would be astounded by the variety of flowers. I also said that Mom made the best baked pork chops and potato salad. It was the kind of potato salad that's real sweet 'cause Mom used Miracle Whip, and put sliced green apples in it. I put in that our grandmother had been a "hoofer"—a dancer at the Cotton Club in Harlem in the 1930s (as she would say, "When Harlem was *Harlem*")—and was one of the adventurous Black expatriates who still lived in France.

I argued we were a family of pioneers, so hosting Nussia would fit right in. Maybe we were the best family chosen out of those that applied. Maybe not. I was, however, a sincere child when I wrote the essay. I wanted to have a best friend very badly.

♡

My sister and I sat up all night preparing and rearranging our dolls, games, and toys. We did everything over again as if to familiarize ourselves with who we were. I couldn't wait for Nussia to experience the newest craze, video games. We made lists of things our parents would just *have* to buy us in order to host Nussia properly. I wanted to play *The Game of Life* with Nussia, though I figured it'd have to be adapted for the Fike way of doing things.

I proudly hung up the acceptance letter amid an ever-growing collage of photos, articles, and pinups of Michael Jackson, Rod Stewart, and Shaun Cassidy that cluttered my side of the bedroom I shared with Virginia. I wanted to look at the acceptance letter every morning and evening.

Later that night, I sat in the foyer next to the phone, anxiously waiting my turn to call my favorite person in the whole world — my grandmother. I waited for what seemed like an eternity while my parents broke the news over the phone, watching as the newscasters did the same on TV from the White House. First, they called the pastor of our church. After that, they called Dad's lawyer, a reporter from the *Amsterdam News*, our doctor, and then all their white friends. Dad talked the longest; he paced back and forth with his hands wrapped around the snaky, yellow telephone cord. "My daughter, this family, an alien...can you believe it? Uh-huh, Lindsay's going to be able to write her own ticket. Maybe I'll even stop going to the racetrack," he said with a chuckle.

When I finally got through to Grandma it was very late. For at least five minutes, I didn't give her a chance to speak. She finally broke in with, "I'm so excited for you, baby. This is a big first for the family...for America...for America." Her deep voice crackled and several words echoed. The connection to France wasn't so great.

"I know, Grandma. I'm going to try to make Nussia real happy."

"I bet some white folks are eating their hearts out," she said, giving a real hearty laugh. Grandma was an "uplift the race" type of woman.

"But...you don't worry about that, you hear?" she said.

"Okay," I said.

"Those Fike are a good-looking group. Even the French are saying that. God knows we got enough ugly people in the world. We don't need anyone or anything else that hurts the eyes."

"Oh, Grandma."

☙

Nussia. I said her name until it became a song.

Soon after the decision, the exchange committee sent us pictures and information about Nussia and her people. I had read a lot about the Fike already, so I skipped most of the background on them being humanoid aliens. But I studied Nussia's picture. She was beautiful.

In the picture they sent of her, Nussia stood against the backdrop of the Black River Ridge, majestic mountains in the background and the sky dusted with yellow clouds, on the southern tip of her planet. Her blue tunic played off the deep amber color of her skin. Flipping to customs and traditions, I found more about their *surricille*, or head covering in English. The most striking characteristic of the Fike was the contrast between the iridescence of their surricilles and the darkness of their eyes. The surricille was made of thick cartilage, which covered the top of her head and came down to just above her eyes—the place where we humans have eyebrows. When I looked at her surricille, a peacock eye shimmered back at me.

Fike surricilles fall off in adulthood and are replaced by less luminous skin. This phase was called the Time of Awakening because Fike went out unprotected into their world. Their physical self was biologically and literally changed; they took on a different identity within their community.

Although our ages didn't correspond directly, Nussia was considered an adolescent by Fike standards; that is, an age when she was to practice under guidance from elders for the Awakening. She was making a great sacrifice by coming to Earth. I should have thought more about this fact, this price. At the time, I had no idea what she was giving up.

Most Fike had some telekinetic powers. I was hoping that when Nussia came, she would be able to make me levitate like I had seen other Fike do on television. They also could manipulate matter on a small scale. In the packet sent to us there was a letter attached from Nussia that I read over and over, especially the lines, "When I come to you, it will be as if Fike and humans had always known of each other. We will create a lasting friendship for us and our peoples."

The letter went on to talk about how much fun she was going to have on Earth, and how she was looking forward to meeting me and my family.

Mom helped me put together a care package to send back to Nussia with jacks, *Betty and Veronica* comics, and *Tiger Beat* magazine. I hoped she would love all the items in the package and know that I was taking care of everything on my end. My new friend was going to be great! Her coming to stay with us was going to erase how invisible I felt. Sometimes I would stand in front of a mirror and pretend I was introducing her to everyone. With her at my side, how could people ignore me? Yes, I had one or two friends at school, but I never was first on their (or anyone else's) list for parties or teams. I faded into the background easily. And, lately, Virginia and I weren't getting along so well. Teenagers can be mean.

℃

We only had two months to prepare! So much to do, including setting up Nussia's special sleeping chambers—a floatbed, which apparently was some sort of domed tank; get training in the eating habits of the Fike; and meet the Secret Service team that would work with us. My mother put the calendar on the fridge, and I marked off every day and task, closing in on Nussia's visit with big red 'X's.

℃

No one told us how tiring it was going to feel being the first family, the only family, a Black family, hosting an alien. Photographers camped out at the house. Soon my family appeared on every magazine cover in America. Within a matter of weeks they splashed our hopeful faces across the world.

There was Dad at his job as Bronx Lebanon's hospital administrator. Click. *People.* There was me at school answering a question. Click. *Time.* There was my sister helping Mom in the kitchen cutting up green peppers. Click. *Good Housekeeping.* There was my mom with her telephone headset on, plugging into the switchboard.

Click. *Life.* The clicks buzzed in our ears, and the flashes blinded us for days, stealing our lives away from us slowly. We lived through the negatives they left us.

I saw so many photographs of myself that I never had to look in a mirror. From every magazine cover, every newspaper article and news program, a short, flat-chested girl with a crooked smile and sleepy eyes always stared back at me. My mom would fix my wiry hair the same way—a part down the middle and two buns on either side of my head. I used to think of them as idiot dials. It was a different story when I looked at Virginia's picture. A tall, shapely sixteen-year-old with a small well-groomed Afro, perfect teeth, and high cheekbones smiled back at me. Every picture made her look like a model.

If it wasn't the press people that we tripped over, then surely it was the nest of Secret Service men stationed in our house and around our neighborhood. Their head of operations was a large man with the complexion of spit up grits, ears smaller than most rodents and mean, shovel-gray eyes. I always thought of him as "Mean Grits." Whenever he said my name, he drew the "Lind" out for an unbearably long time. *Liiiindsay.* I immediately disliked him and decided to avoid him as much as possible.

The press picked up and promoted every scrap of information about us. We moved like shadows in our own house. My sister said she wanted to be a doctor, but I knew the thought hadn't occurred to her until some pinched-faced reporter asked. Reporters portrayed us as an all-American wholesome family—a good old-fashioned popsicle that had been surreptitiously dipped in dark chocolate.

Mom played right into their hands. First, we needed a better vase for the living room, then a new recliner, then better china. Next, Virginia needed to go to the hairdresser more often to get her Afro shaped. I kept to myself while waiting for Nussia, seeing these changes in my family, not sure of what we were becoming. Were we just hosts for Nussia, or something else?

❦

The editorials started showing up just a few days after the announcement. These were pieces in *The New York Times, Washington Post,* and *The Wall Street Journal,* mostly tirades about how the Bronx wasn't a fit place for an alien child to visit. Even beyond the op-eds, we heard the phrases "affirmative action" and "charity case" everywhere on the news and radio shows.

My parents told Virginia and me not to open the piles of mail that greeted us after school, but I was *into* mail. Mom should have known that. I'd been mailing myself letters since I was six years old.

I only remember one letter. A manila envelope arrived with cheerful animal stickers of giraffes, monkeys, and lions on its outside. The envelope was addressed to me. I pulled out a posterboard collage from the envelope. On the posterboard were ripped out pictures of monkeys from *National Geographic* magazines. The makers hadn't been very concerned with accuracy. They had different types of monkeys, gorillas, chimpanzees, marmosets, and baboons cavorting together who would never live together in real life. Even I knew that. The primates had enlarged lips and genitals drawn over their bodies in red ink. The primates' penises jutted upward, and the scrotums were intensely swirled red circles.

The creators named each of the monkeys in the middle after someone in my family. These monkeys were placed around a picture of Nussia being boiled up in a big black pot. The forks in some of the monkey's hands were so big that the tines reached the top of the page. The speech bubble over Nussia's head read, "Help! Get me away from the niggers!"

A bubble over one of the other monkeys read, "You suuuuure gonna taste gooood."

I pulled the picture of Nussia up from the crude monkey collage and put her on my collage. I threw the rest of it away, and I didn't tell anyone about what I saw. I stopped wanting to go to the mailbox after that.

Nussia. I said her name like a prayer.

I asked God to please keep us all safe so we could welcome Nussia.

☙

When she came back to the States, Grandma became the spokesperson for the family. She took a hiatus from her traveling, finding that it was great to be back in the limelight. No matter what my mom did, she could not drag Grandma away from the reporters. Her height and commanding presence made people pay attention. Grandma was the calm in our storm. She'd never change. I took great pleasure in spending every moment I could get with her. And, although she never said it, I always felt like I was her favorite grandchild.

That day, she took me out to a restaurant. Grandma wore sharp black trousers, a man's crisp white shirt, and a blue and white scarf tied around her neck. The colors of her clothes accentuated her powdered ginger-like complexion.

After we ordered, she sat erect and still, focused on my various observations and questions.

"Grandma, when am I going to get...y'know?" I ran my hand over my chest, hovering over two significant places.

"Oh those? Don't be ashamed, Lindsay. You'll get them when it's time. All in due time. Just like you got Nussia." She winked at me.

Grandma was good at answering questions so I asked her what I should say to reporters because I often sat tongue-tied and close to tears. I usually wound up repeating what I had written in my essay.

"Well, you know what kind of ice cream you like, right?" she said, bunching up a napkin.

"Yep, butter pecan. Chocolate is also right up there, too."

"You can think of a question as asking you what kind of ice cream you like," she said. "Go ahead now and close your eyes." Her face turned serious. "Get comfortable with the question. Take it apart in that mind of yours. Think about how much you like butter pecan.

You know how to describe the taste of the ice cream, right? That's how you can approach any question, really—break it down into something manageable. That's not so hard now, is it?"

I opened my eyes, and, smiling, shook my head. I never have quite figured out what ice cream and questions have in common, or how thinking about butter pecan would help me, but I got better at talking to reporters, anyway.

With all the talk of questions, ice cream and breasts, I forgot to ask Grandma the question that scared me the most: *what if Nussia doesn't like me?*

☙

That night I wandered into my mother's bedroom. My mother and father had kept separate bedrooms since I was six. Hers was the cushy and comfortable one. She once told me they had separate bedrooms because she worked all the time, being a telephone operator and all. Most often her shifts were from twelve at night until nine in the morning, and Dad didn't like to be woken up in the middle of the night.

The vanity table where she sat held all of the magic she used to get her through the evening: a bottle of wine, bath oils, Lindt chocolates, and a variety of perfumes including Enjoli, Charlie, and Chanel No.5. Her eyes looked tired.

"Do you think she'll like me?" I asked. I sat down on the edge of her bed.

"Lindsay, now don't go worrying about that." She pulled a few bobby pins that held her hairpiece, styled like a large French roll, in place.

She added, "You know she won't know any better. You're going to be her first real human contact."

"Mom!"

Giving me a quick glance over her shoulder she said, "Oh, I'm kidding of course. If you like her, she'll like you. You are going to make a big impression on her." She came over and squeezed the top of my shoulder twice. Her squeezes always came in twos—never more, never less—and were always very tight.

I watched her walk back to the vanity table in her slip and stockings; the stockings were too light for her complexion. Silently and deliberately, she pulled the hairpiece off; bobby pins falling everywhere. It was a spider's nest of blackness tumbling to the floor. She winced at the mirror's image and turned away.

Her nightly ritual nearly complete, she poured herself a glass of wine, put her robe on and shooed me off her bed.

"Can I sleep with you tonight?"

"You're too big to be sleeping with me, Lindsay."

She was probably right, but it would be nice to be next to her. I could close my eyes, and the apple-y smell of Enjoli, baby powder, and sweat would carry me off to sleep.

I moped back to the room I shared with Virginia. My sister was on her back staring off into space. Virginia's enthusiasm over Nussia's visit had ground down to nothing. She preferred experimenting with pot and hanging with some of her more rowdy friends who lived in the neighborhood, rather than being excited with me about Nussia's visit. I didn't understand how she could think of anything else or why she would want to. Pot had made her moodier than usual.

"Virginia, do you think we should take Nussia to the movies?"

"I don't know," she said.

"Well, what about the Botanical Garden?"

She rolled on her side. "Whatever."

"Come on. We need to have things planned," I said, whining a bit. "Wouldn't it be cool if we could take her to France to see Grandma's place? We haven't been since we were little."

Virginia sat up and shook her head. "Little sister, did you ever think that she might not want to do any of the stuff we've planned? She's an *alien*." Her lips pressed into a red slash.

"Forget you. I'll plan things on my own," I said, cutting off the light. I lay there thinking about how things would be different when Nussia arrived. Like Christmas every day.

℘

I woke up to the sound of hammering, drilling and a loud beeping sound.

Virginia lifted her head, "What's that?"

I jumped out of bed and opened our door. My grandmother popped her head out of the guest bedroom and looked at me. "What's all this commotion? On a Sunday no less?"

"I don't know." But I did know it was only one month to go, and I was eager to check off another "X."

As I came downstairs, I saw to two large men, carrying a big green box, walking through the living room toward the kitchen. A quick peek out the window revealed the source of the beeping. A large white truck was parked out front.

In the kitchen Mom stood talking to Mean Grits. She didn't look awake; a hasty French braid and wisps of stray hairs framed her face. The clock on the wall said 7 a.m. Too early for breakfast. Sundays weren't guaranteed family time because often both my parents worked during the weekend, but recently they were making an effort to be at home.

"What's going on, Mom?" She ignored me, continuing her rant at the large Secret Serviceman in our kitchen.

"I don't appreciate you smoking in the house. I've told you that before," she said pointing her finger at Mean Grits.

"Sorry, Ma'am." The apology didn't change the coldness of his eyes, though. "We've acquired a house down the block and will be there around the clock for the next several months."

"Great," she said flatly.

With a shake of her head, she finally looked at me and smiled wearily. "Nussia's floatbed is being put together downstairs, hon."

Floatbed! I zoomed down the stairs toward the basement.

The basement was crowded. Boxes leaned against the wall. Mechanical looking parts like dials and levers covered the floor. Three men were moving furniture around.

My father stood in the middle of the chaos. "Christ, this is going to take all day."

"The engineer's late, Mr. Fields. I've already called him twice," one of the Secret Service men said.

"Hi, Dad," I said.

He gave me a curt nod and then moved to open another box.

They covered the main table against the wall in instructions for assembling the floatbed. I looked at the Polaroids that accompanied the written materials. The floatbed was a domed tank, elevated on a short platform. Notes next to the pictures said, "Ideal construction—five feet wide and eight feet long."

"What I don't understand is why this couldn't have been done any other day," my mother said as she walked down the steps. She stood on the last step, arms crossed and her jaw clenched.

No one said anything.

"You couldn't have asked us about our schedule?" my mother said, locking eyes on the nearest Secret Service agent.

"We cleared it with your husband," someone in the room said. I swear, the temperature in the already-cool basement dropped another ten degrees as my mother turned and glared at my dad.

"You neglected to mention that detail, Rodger," she said. I shivered. That was my mom's *you're-in-BIG-trouble-young-lady* voice and I wanted absolutely no part of it.

"Not the right moment, Jesse," my father said in a carefully controlled tone, every syllable clearly pronounced. This was his familiar *I-don't-want-to-fight-in-front-of-company* voice I knew.

I practiced staring at the ground and making myself as inconspicuous as possible. It was easy to fade and disappear. I had a routine from school: first I'd imagine my legs weren't visible, then the middle of my body, then my arms, and finally my head.

"I suppose I should just be glad you're gracing us with your presence. You'll have to make the racetrack wait today, huh?"

I didn't know much about Dad's gambling, except that he liked to do it. Maybe he was doing it more now?

My head snapped up, interrupting my fade out. I saw my father's nostrils flare and how the veins in his neck bulged though he said nothing. Instead, he inspected the box he held and said, "This is what I was looking for earlier."

My petite, easygoing mother sniffed and fixed all the men downstairs with her stare, "For the record, gentlemen, my husband didn't clear it with me. And since I run this house, in the future, I'll thank you all to clear this kind of information with *me*."

I just stood there stuck in place like a barnacle.

As my mother turned, red-faced, she pointed at me, "Lindsay, get upstairs and get dressed like a proper person!"

My mother's anger was rare but powerful and unpredictable, coming and going like a tropical storm.

I slunk off, still secretly excited that Nussia's bed had arrived.

℅

With just two weeks to go and still much to do, none of us were in a good mood by the time the xenobotanist, Alton Cruse, arrived. He was a young white scholar from MIT, and the most knowledgeable man in the world about Fike eating habits. Parading around wearing light blue rubber gloves, he inspected our kitchen while he spoke in terms which included the gastrointestinal rise and fall of the dorba, aka the Fike stomach. He was here to teach us how to cook for Nussia.

It was mandatory that our entire family attend the session with Mr. Cruse. We stood side by side, crammed against the back wall of the kitchen, as he lectured us and paced back and forth. His red hair stuck out in puffs on his head.

He listened and took notes as Mom proudly spoke about the meals she most often fixed for our family.

"Mrs. Fields, this all looks good. Not too much pork—I was worried about the possible pork intake. You haven't mentioned any southern dishes like salt pork, chitterlings, pigtails, and that kind of thing," he intoned gravely.

My grandmother made a grimace. "Mr. Cruse, first of all, our family is not from the South. And, second, what are you trying to imply? My daughter is an excellent cook."

"*Dr.* Cruse," he corrected her, then shrugged, arms opening wide, "I had no idea what I was going to find in your diet."

"It's fine, Ma. Let the man do his job," my mother snapped.

I bit the inside of my cheek. I didn't like it when they fought. I wondered if Virginia had noticed that they were doing it more often. Did the tips of her ears burn like mine? What did Grandma think of their bickering?

"If he's going to teach us something new and help us prepare for Nussia then that's fine, but if he is going to insinuate and speculate about what *we* eat then forget it."

My father, who had been impatiently tapping his fingertips against his leg while *Dr.* Cruise was talking, cleared his throat and moved toward the door. "Look here, it may be the weekend and time off for everyone else in this house, but *I* have to go into the office today."

"Yes, Rodger, we all know that," Mom said. Then, aside, in a low voice, "It's not like *you* ever help out around the house, anyway."

Dad swung back around on his heel; his face contorted with anger. "And what is that supposed to mean, Jesse?"

"Nothing."

I noticed a throbbing vein on the left side of my mother's neck.

"I can call all of this off anytime! Right now if I want to!" he said, bits of salvia spraying my mother's face.

Call it off? I could not have heard that right.

"Dad?" I said.

My stomach hardened, and then it felt like I had to throw up. His words didn't compute and my thoughts were scrambled. It felt like a crater opened in my kitchen and was going to swallow us. Why was he always so upset lately?

"Now, Rodger...that's a bit dramatic. Don't you think?" Grandma said, moving between them.

Dr. Cruse was watching us like he was observing animals in the wild, then cleared his voice and said, "I haven't even got to the part about how the Fike eat."

Dad was still standing close to the door. I looked at him, my eyes pleading with him to stay. He sighed and then waved his hand at the scientist.

"Well, get on with it, man. This is *all* for my Lindsay's future."

Virginia sucked in a deep inhale through her teeth. I elbowed her to be quiet. I was shaking but I forced myself to calm down. I felt like I could laugh or cry without stopping.

I stood very still, squeezing my eyes shut for a moment and then opening them to focus on Dr. Cruse. The worst thing that I could possibly imagine had not come to pass.

Dr. Cruse continued, "The most interesting part of the Fike eating processes is how they digest their food. They cover what they eat with a substance, which is like what oysters in the mollusk family do with bacteria and dirt—"

"I haven't had good oysters since we all went to the Cape," Grandma interrupted.

"Ma, will you let him finish?" my mother said.

"For oysters, the result is a pearl. For Fike...Well, Mr. Fields, about a third of their digested food particles then take on special importance. Hardened food debris is then regurgitated as what's called *monunis*. Fike feel the monunis are part of them, extensions of their Fike spirit, if you will. Fike like to have their monunis where they can see them. They often build community shrines."

He paused and then chuckled. "Now, the young tend not to be quite so reverent, so we'll have to wait and see what Nussia does with her monunis. I'm not an anthropologist, but monuni worshipping is very culturally significant." He pulled out a Polaroid picture and passed it around.

"This picture gives you an idea of what monunis look like," he said.

"My God, Mr. Cruse, you're telling me and my family that they revere their excretions?" Mom said.

"It's not excretions to them. The monunis are still part of them—they just take on a unique form."

"Why didn't anyone say anything about this before? Is there anything contagious about these monnis?" Mom shifted her weight and pulled at the back of her bun.

Virginia and I studied the picture of an adult Fike with slender hands holding up monunis, which looked like hard purplish balls. Cruse didn't mention that each monuni had a stringy curlicue tail of gray matter attached at the end of it. "Ewwww," Virginia said. "That's nasty."

"That is *monunis*, Mrs. Fields, and no, it is not contagious or harmful to humans. I personally have been studying the Fike and their monunis at MIT for the past three years and there has been no discernible dangerous effect on the researchers."

"Mrs. Fields, there is no need to worry about these aliens. There's no possible harm that can come to your family," Mean Grits said with his hands clasped behind his back. He had been so quiet in the kitchen that I had forgotten about him. "Our government wouldn't let anything in your home that wasn't safe." He gave a stern look to Cruse.

"Are we done here? Jesse, you can fill me in tonight," Dad said, rushing out the kitchen door.

Mom rolled her eyes.

"It's vomit. Vomit balls are going to be rolling all around our house!" Virginia shrieked.

"Hush, girl," Grandma said.

I hadn't bargained for monunis either, but I figured I could get used to it—we all could get used to it.

⟡

The most important day of my life finally arrived. Our whole family turned out, and many people from the neighborhood crammed themselves into our house. Mr. Alvarez, the Puerto Rican baker, was there, with a big T-shirt that said, *Welcome Nussia!* The Willacys, our Jamaican next-door neighbors, were present, looking regal in their Caribbean colored clothes of reds, greens and yellows. Mrs. Willacy's hair was done up in a high bun. Kids from school and their parents were there and flashed smiles for the news crew and waved at loved ones watching at home. I thought people only waved and said, "Hi Mom," on television shows, but people were doing that everywhere.

I wanted to be on our doorstep for the greeting, but Mean Grits said no. For security reasons, Nussia would be escorted to the front door.

And, before I knew it, Nussia stood in the middle of my living room.

She looked different from the pictures, and from what I had imagined her to be like. My mother got all weepy when we visited the Grand Canyon many years ago. I remembered she said, "When you're in awe of something you feel deeply." I didn't want to cry, but looking at her made my heart race and feel like it was drumming inside my chest. Like I was as wide-awake as I ever could be. Her eyes took up an enormous amount of space on her face, and they possessed the calming inky darkness of a dream. She didn't have any eyebrows but had deep grooves right where her surricille ended. She was bald and golden all over, except for her palms which were a leathery bell pepper green.

Nussia wore a loose orange and white tunic. Her shoulders were exposed and her family markings, or *acraeturas* as the Fike called them, were visible. The markings told of her family's history for the last three generations. She was large, too, about two of me across—definitely someone Mrs. Willacy would call a "wide gal."

Her surricille was even more luminous in person. I felt transfixed by it, and I imagined it called out to me. I wanted to touch it but restrained myself.

She came toward me like a glowing amber wall of energy and swept me into a hug.

I forgot everything. All the anxiety, the nasty letters, the fights between Mom and Dad. She was here!

Her hug was full and made me feel like everything was going to be alright. She was taller than me, so I fell a little to one side in her grip. She smelled of apples—I wondered if she really smelled that way or if she got that smell while staying at her top-secret location. Did the Fike grow apples?

When the hug finally broke, I bounced back on the balls of my feet, exploding with energy and ideas of things for us to do. Then she spoke.

"Lindsay, I greet you with the highest welcome from me and the Fike."

The sizzle-sound in her voice surprised me. It reminded me of when a hot comb is left too long on a stove and then pulled through hair. An overheated hot comb touching fresh hair almost ignites it—that's how her voice made me feel. I could taste the burn in her voice and, for the first time since her arrival I was a little scared of the alien in front of me.

But then I remembered that this occasion was important, and that she was just as nervous as I was, and I shouldn't fear my new best friend. "Nussia," I said, remembering my rehearsed words, "we are so proud to have you here with us."

As I started speaking, Nussia's large tubular shaped retractable mouth, kind of like an elephant's trunk, puckered outwards. She leaned down slightly, and I felt the briefest kiss land above my eyebrows.

My heart almost froze and then pounded. An undignified squeal escaped my lips. The room swam around me. I pressed my hands to my cheeks. I felt so light for a moment, like I would float away.

That was one distracting kiss. Everyone saw what she did. A new beginning for me. I sucked in my breath and calmed myself down enough so that I could speak.

"I have so much to show you. You will get to know us."

"We will make both Fike and humans proud," she said.

I hugged her again, feeling the warmth of her skin. The apple smell reminded me of Christmas. I smiled up at her and nodded.

But that moment shattered as all the adults crowded in with their cameras and their questions and swept Nussia away from me.

☙

Mom brought out a large bowl of candies to set on the dining table. She tripped over a TV camera cord that had snaked its way into the dining room. The bowl flew out of her hands with candies scattering everywhere. Press people eagerly noted the misstep.

"Damn it, Jesse," my father muttered. He bristled, then bent down quickly, grabbing fistfuls of candy.

"I'm sorry. I'm just a little nervous, I guess," Mom whispered to no one in particular.

Nussia noticed this commotion. She walked into the dining room. She looked at my father on his knees. With her eyes closed she brought her two hands out in front of her. The candies came up from the floor, swirling in the air. They made a colored tornado over to the now floating bowl. The press moved in closer. *Click.*

"We might need you around all the time with Jesse being so clumsy," my father said. He came over and patted Nussia on the back.

"Isn't that sweet?" someone cooed.

"Thank you, Mr. Fields...Dad," Nussia said with only a moment of hesitation, returning his gesture by patting him on the back.

Nussia nodded as if she confirmed something she had been thinking about.

People clapped. Everyone was laughing again, and animated conversation burst out across the rooms. The crush of bodies descended around Nussia once again. This was getting me nowhere. And suddenly I was small and hollow again, like a half-eaten chocolate Easter bunny, discarded for some other treat.

Grandma had yet another reporter cornered between the grandfather clock and the wall.

"What do you think it says about America in this century that your family, a Black family, was chosen to host Nussia?" the reporter asked.

Grandma took a deep breath. "Everyone's harping on the fact that we're Black, from news folk like yourself and others that have been obsessed by this one detail about us—and not in good ways. And to be honest, I am pretty tired of hearing about it."

The reporter's face tightened and puckered like he had sucked on a lemon. He was about to respond but my grandmother continued.

"It is a fact we're Black, but the aliens don't really care now, do they? Why shouldn't we be the first family to host Nussia?"

I had lost Mom in the crowd. I squeezed my way past Mrs. Willacy, who was telling Dr. Cruse that goat meat was just as natural to eat as any other kind of meat.

I went into our kitchen, where Mom stood looking out the window with what looked and smelled like a rum and coke in her hand.

She turned to look at me. "So much going on, baby," she said absentmindedly.

"Yes, Mom. It's okay." I put my hand around her waist. She patted it and then smoothed away a tear from her face. Part of me liked being a help to my mom, being close like this; it wasn't new to me. Another part of me wondered if my friends helped their mothers like this, noticed what they needed.

I was tired by the time everyone left, and where tiredness left off, my frustration caught hold. I couldn't find Nussia anywhere. I hadn't spent more than two minutes alone with her.

I went upstairs. There was giggling coming from our bedroom. Nussia's giggle was like a slap—quick, loud, and sharp.

I pushed open the closed door to find Virginia and Nussia sitting side-by-side. "Hey, you guys disappeared," I said, a little hurt that they were becoming friends without me. Virginia picked nervously at her bracelet.

"We have to get up early, Lindsay. Mom told me she wants you to take your shower," Virginia said quickly.

"Oh."

They were both quiet and sat looking at me.

"Nussia, do you want to sit on the porch for a little while? There's nobody around. You're probably sick of all the fuss," I said.

"No, Lindsay. Virginia and I are talking fine."

"*You're* probably tired. Little sisters do need their sleep," Virginia said, rising. "Nussia, why don't we go outside and let Lindsay get ready for bed? There's a big day tomorrow, too, with the block party and all."

"Every day will be a big day. Big day," Nussia said.

Before I could object, they were making their way out of the room.

As she closed the door, Nussia flicked her tongue out. I remembered reading that the gesture was the equivalent of a human waving good-bye.

I told myself I had the rest of my time with Nussia. What was the first night? Before getting undressed, I fingered the collage on the wall. I wondered if Nussia had noticed her picture there.

☙

Later in the night I awoke and crept downstairs. The whole house was quiet, dark, and asleep. I could hear the stray, sad sounds of Roberta Flack on someone's stereo floating in from our neighbor's house next door. The door to the basement was unlocked when I pushed on it and padded down the wooden stairs.

I hadn't spent much time in the basement since the workmen were there. It was still the same place—though a bit brighter and cleaner than usual. They repainted it in coats of specially formulated gold paint considered soothing to Fike. My mother's homemade curtains of bright red stars against a black background hung in the windows.

The floatbed under the stairwell we had set up for Nussia to sleep in looked sturdy. Dad and the Secret Service men had done a good job installing it. Nussia floated vertically in the little chamber. She slept soundly with her arms folded on her chest. This time I could gaze at her undisturbed. I was so happy that she was here. Now I would have something that I never had before—a best friend. She would be someone to giggle with, play jacks with, talk about boys (Fike and human) with, compare mothers with. Someone to see me.

✆

I woke up the next morning feeling excited all over again. It felt like Christmas. Nussia was in my house! Downstairs, Mom was getting ready to make a batch of eggs.

"I bet you couldn't sleep last night," she smiled at me, seeming more like her usual self without all the reporters and Secret Service men in the house.

"I may never sleep again with Nussia here."

"So dramatic. Go set the table. Use the special dishes." My mother shooed me on.

I did as she wished, running around getting the dishes and silverware in place. I then went and got the special things I wanted to show Nussia.

Then I waited and waited for everyone to get up and join us. It took forever.

Nussia arrived last.

"How'd you sleep, Nussia?" My mother asked.

She paused before speaking, looking to the left and right and then nodding, "Quite comfortably. Is that how you say it?"

I pulled out a chair for her, and she walked over and sat down.

"Yes, very good, Nussia. I'm glad—" my mother began, but I was done waiting on pleasantries.

"Nussia," I interrupted, "I want to show you some things." All around the table, I had assembled small and large boxes covered in gold wrapping paper.

"Presents!" I said.

"Presents?" she looked at me, her dark eyes searching my face.

"Yes, presents!"

I felt time speeding up, just like during Christmas. I pushed one of the bigger boxes next to her.

Her hands touched the outside of the box.

I opened it and pulled out the item.

"I got you a pair of roller skates."

"Let her open them," my mother said. "Lindsay's a bit excited. Nussia, would you like orange juice or cranberry juice?"

"No juice."

"I didn't quite know what size your feet are, so if they don't fit, we can take them back," I babbled.

"Take back?" She looked at my mother and me.

"We can get you another pair," my mother said.

I pushed another box toward her.

"She hasn't eaten yet," Virginia cautioned. I looked at her as if she were crazy.

Mother laid a hand on my shoulder and whispered, "Your sister is right. Nussia might need a bit of time."

I shook my head in disbelief. Who wouldn't have time for *presents*?

Then my grandmother walked in the back door. "Good morning, everyone! Good morning, Miss Nussia. I was just putting the finishing touches out back. Did they tell you that's where your shrine will be?"

"Yes," Nussia nodded.

"Ma, sit down. We're getting ready to eat."

My mother set down a platter of eggs, bacon, sausage, grapefruit (a Fike favorite), pineapple slices, and blueberry muffins.

"And you know besides roller skating, we want to take you to the zoo. Do you have zoos? I think I read you do, but on Fike, you can spend the night in them or something like that. We have a big zoo. The Bronx Zoo." Now that she was here in front of me, I couldn't stop myself from talking.

"It's time to say grace," my mother said, holding up her hands.

We held hands while my father said a rather long-winded grace. Instead of keeping her eyes closed like everyone else, she looked around the table, taking each of us in. When she came to me, she shut them quickly.

I kept staring. I wanted her to look at me. Virginia opened her eyes for a moment and winked. I smiled.

"Nussia, hand me your plate," my father said.

She did so, giving him the first smile of the morning.

I took a breath and buttered a muffin.

Nussia sampled everything and began eating in earnest.

Now that I had stopped talking, Grandma kept the conversation going. I tried not to gawk at Nussia, but I couldn't help being fascinated by her retractable mouth as it extended and nibbled the pineapple slice on her fork.

Although we were all smiling, eating, and Grandma was still talking, I could feel the tension in the room. We really had an alien at our table. I was pretty sure all the humans were wondering when the monunis were going to start.

After a few bites of food, Nussia rose. "I can't eat here," she said. "I have been told it is impolite to create monunis at the eating table. I will go."

The wait was over! I felt a fluttery feeling in my stomach, like the moment you are on a roller coaster ride and are climbing up the first hill.

"We understand about the monunis," my mother said holding her hand out. "It won't bother us."

"No, I will go outside."

Virginia wrinkled her nose, but no one else saw.

"You do whatever you need to," my father said.

Nussia nodded her golden head and walked out to the garden.

"That went well. At least she's not going to make those things at the table," Grandma said as soon as Nussia was out of earshot. "A relief, if you ask me."

"No one asked you," my father said.

Nussia joined us about fifteen minutes later. My mother had brought out her much-loved French toast casserole, and we were digging in.

"Excuse me, family ones. I am tired and will go to rest," Nussia said.

"Of course," Grandma said. "It's been a lot to take in, hasn't it?"

She nodded.

"Going back to bed? Don't you want to open up presents?" I asked.

"No," she said walking to the basement door. She closed it and I heard the new lock clicking into place. For privacy, Nussia could lock the door from the inside. The key hung on a little hook next to the door.

I looked at the unopened presents and ate the rest of my meal in silence.

〇

The neighborhood had planned a massive block party that day to celebrate Nussia's arrival. Folks wanted to show off and show out. On this perfect June day, people milled about. My sister was still upstairs getting ready.

I took Nussia by the arm and tried to talk with her. She sure wasn't acting friendly, even for an alien. Maybe she was shy.

We walked along the length of the cordoned off blocks. I pointed out the street gallery of the block party. Over here were the Dominican and Black men sitting like brown griffins playing dominoes; there in another corner were girls jumping fast in the crisscross ropes. Baby oil glistened on their quick legs. Some lanky teenagers were playing Steal the Old Man's Bacon. There were long tables of food, each platter and main dish sectioned off by pitchers of city champagne—Kool-Aid with ginger ale. I wanted her to see it all. I talked too fast, my words coming out like bullets.

At the other end of the corner a new rap group called the Sugar Hill Gang was setting up speakers and deejay equipment. I was looking forward to hearing them later. Yep, Nussia was going to get a real Bronx welcome.

I pointed out cool people like Peter Newport, my friend from school who always smelled like cocoa butter and had freckles and legendary dimples. He was there with his sixteen-year-old brother Jake. People in school joked about how good-looking they were, calling them the "L&L" brothers, long and light-skinned.

"Peter's going to be my boyfriend one day, I hope."

Nussia barely said a word, politely nodding and declining to eat anything. Not even one nibble from the table. After a while, she looked down at our joined hands. I got the sense that maybe I was holding her too tight, so I let go.

"So, did you like the comic books?"

She stared back at me.

"I sent them to you along with the jacks and…"

"I didn't have time to be instructed on human games," she said, interrupting me.

"Oh."

"What about the letter you sent?" I asked.

"Do you know what I have left back at home?" she burst out. "This is the most beautiful time of year. It's the time when Fike my age get to walk in the forests of Per and practice for when we will be Awakened. And instead, I have this. And you." Nussia flung her arms wide. She rocked her head from side to side.

Her unexpected words and agitation took me off guard. I couldn't speak for a moment. This didn't make any sense at all.

"I'm sorry. I guess I thought…I didn't know how important the Awakening was," I stammered. I quickly added, "I mean I *do* know how important that is." I felt blood rush to my head.

She muttered in her native language; angry sizzling sounds escaped.

I fought back tears. This was going all wrong. She was angry with me, and I didn't know how I could fix it.

"You remind me of my sister, the *minnos a minnos*," she spat out. She pointed to a small spot on her right shoulder that had dense words and symbols on it. The dye surrounding the spot was a deep maroon.

"You have a sister?" I said. What was she talking about? I didn't remember reading anything about a sister!

Virginia came outside and Nussia bolted toward her.

I stood shaking, wanting to chase after her. To call her name.

Nussia. I said her name like a spell that I could use to bring her back to me. A spell that didn't work.

☯

Later that night while we were getting ready for bed, I told Virginia about Nussia's revelation.

"That's strange," she said.

"Shouldn't we tell Mom and Dad?" I said pulling my pajama top over my head.

"If it was that important, they would already know, right?" Virginia said. "Let her keep her secret," she shrugged. "Sometimes older sisters need their secrets."

I looked at her and felt my whole body tense up. I had to make Nussia happy. I couldn't fail at this. I turned away because I didn't want to cry in front of her.

She came over, sat on my bed and gave me a hug, "Stop worrying like it's your hobby."

I leaned on her shoulder. "What do you think of her?" I whispered.

"She's cool. Mysterious."

More like you than me, I thought while soaking up the warmth of her body. She gave me a quick peck on the cheek as I snuggled under the covers. I felt sneaky, competitive with Virginia. It was wrong, I know, to feel jealous of her. But this didn't stop me from happily fantasizing about Virginia being shipped off to a camp for the summer and being unable to hang out with Nussia as I drifted off to sleep.

⟡

A few weeks after Nussia arrived, my mother threw me a surprise birthday party. It wasn't a total surprise. I overheard Mom talking about it on the phone the week before. My mother talked loudly when she drank. On the day of the party, I thought about how different my life was with Nussia around. She came the first few days to school as planned. After that, she was whisked away by the Secret Service men to various places that we didn't know about to get "more instruction on human culture." She spent most of her free time with Virginia. They called me *Elkouri*. It was a name that Nussia made up for me. It sounded like a curse, though I never found out what it meant.

She wasn't even trying to be my friend, let alone a best friend.

I didn't feel like seeing people from school. They all just wanted to see Nussia anyway. Most had made that clear just days after her arrival. They crowded around her when they could, asking her about Fike, questions they could have easily asked me. Often they begged to touch her surricille, and she usually consented.

I walked into the house and smiled as people with colorful party hats on shouted, "Surprise!"

Fourteen. Would it be special, I wondered? I tried to get into the party spirit. Kids packed our house. Someone moved most of the furniture in the living room to create a dance floor. There was even a deejay setting up his equipment. Peter was talking to Virginia. He was looking cute as ever, in his black warm up suit and red sneakers with big fat laces. My attention turned to Mom as she walked out with a huge five-layer ice cream cake, from Carvel's famous store, with little blue roller skates on the top layer. She set it on a long table with my gifts. I went over to admire it.

"Dad sends his love. He's sorry he couldn't make it but promises he'll take you and Nussia both to do something together. Okay, baby?" Mom asked.

I nodded. Typical for my dad. He'd already missed two of my birthdays in a row.

Virginia, looking great in a tight white peasant shirt and her hip designer jeans, pulled out an envelope from the stack of presents and handed it to me. She had gotten me subscriptions to *Tiger Beat* and *Teen*. More photos of Michael Jackson and Shaun Cassidy for my wall. She could be so fucking cool! I gave her a big hug, ashamed that I had wished her to be sent to camp.

My friends clamored for records and the deejay started spinning. This was my cue to retreat to the dining room—I hated dancing. I have two left feet. My sister, of course, didn't—she requested the most popular song of the year, "Le Freak" by Chic and started grooving on the dance floor with the rest of the party.

I sulked quietly in a chair off to the side so that I could watch Peter. Everybody, Peter included, was doing the freak: bending their knees and swaying back and forth.

Peter caught my glance from across the room and ran over to me. "Come on, Lindsay. Didn't Virginia teach you the freak?" Peter said, breathless and all dimples.

He caught me off guard. He had *never* asked me to dance before. "I can't do it," I mumbled, stuffing potato chips in my mouth. My palms were sweaty and greasy—I tried to wipe them off on my jeans.

He leaned over and said in my ear, "I don't want to dance with no one else."

I broke out in goosebumps. Well, how could I refuse that?

I peeked at the dance floor. Everyone *did* look like they were having a great time. Even my mom was showing off in one of the groups. She was doing the Mom thing, staying planted in one place with her arms raised in the air, every once in a while snapping her fingers and shouting, "Woo woo!"

"Come on," he said, pulling me out of my seat.

A crowd cleared out a space for us. This was exactly what I was afraid of—too much attention. I tried to follow Peter and Virginia's lead. I felt sweat sliding down my back, but I think I was blending in okay. I hoped.

Toward the end of the song, Peter danced in front of me. He then improvised on the freak with different arm movements, and it was just...cool. It was ME. Dancing with Peter Newport! Not Virginia, not one of the many girls here, not even Nussia. I didn't want this moment to end.

"Uh, yeah. Go 'head," Virginia said, from another corner.

Nussia moved over to us. I didn't want her to see me with Peter. Something inside me clenched. My scalp prickled. I shouldn't have told her anything about him. I should have kept him a secret. But, why would I want to keep anything from my best friend?

Nussia put her hand on the small of Peter's back. Peter turned, and in an instant the two of them rose at least seven feet off the ground.

"Wow! Mrs. Fields, do you see that?" exclaimed Lila, a Jamaican girl from around the block.

I couldn't believe it. I stared openmouthed. We had seen Fike levitate themselves and humans on television. We'd seen Nussia levitate the candy on that first day. I mean, that's what the Fike did, and I had accepted it. But not like this. Not now. At my party. With Peter.

We stood under them in a circle. Peter looked unsteady as he kept kicking his left foot out like that would balance him. Nussia was above him, and she held him by his forearms. Nussia then let him go, and he bounced on the air. She dipped, and bobbed, almost to the beat of the music. Peter, getting more confident by the moment, strutted in the air.

Everyone was laughing and pointing. Within a few minutes, she had half of my friends off the ground; she didn't need to touch them. I waved to Nussia and kept my hand up. Nussia looked down at me and then away quickly. My arm just stood up in the air, waiting, like a little brown flag with no wind. I pulled it down and lowered my eyes. Maybe no one had noticed.

"You kids are so crazy," Mom said from the dining room. "Nussia, please, please be careful. You be careful with them."

Nussia nodded, still not coming down. The deejay put on another popular record, and soon half of the party was in the air with Nussia.

"Oh, Nussia, this feels so good. You are so cool," Virginia yelled above the music.

As I watched people, I could see that their excitement was about more than the thrill of being up in the air. Something that I had never seen before was happening up there. Some of them had their eyes rolled back in their heads and their bodies alternated between a joyous limpness and then a powerful surge of energy. My airborne classmates had a kind of feverish look about them. It looked like scenes from a documentary on revivals I'd seen on TV. Sometimes, Nussia floated over to them and held their arms, patted their faces, and wiped their sweat onto her face. They looked as if they felt safe and protected with her tending to them. Peter freely stroked her surricille, back and forth; it shimmered. Virginia's eyes were now redder than if she smoked that stuff she wasn't supposed to smoke. It hit me—they were *high*. She was getting them high!

They sure didn't need me. I looked up at Peter, motioned for him to come down. Peter shrugged his shoulders. I guess he couldn't get down unless Nussia allowed it.

Although the Secret Service guys were not in the air, they too were mesmerized and caught up in the drug-like atmosphere. I couldn't stand it any longer. I moved through the crowd, mostly adults that were left on the ground and went to my room. No one stopped me.

Virginia found me later as I finished wiping my tears away.

"Mom asked me to find you. People are still here, you know."

Her eyes were still glassy and her face looked softer. She pulled the chair out from our desk and plopped down on it.

"It wasn't any fun watching everyone else have a good time," I said, my throat raw.

Virginia sighed, leaned back in the chair and looked at her fingernails.

"I can't believe you're in here feeling sorry for yourself," she scolded.

"Nussia just ignored me. You did see it, didn't you?"

Virginia tutted and shook her head. "You're being such a spoiled brat. Nussia was doing all that for *you*! Don't you see that? She made your party! Your party was the best."

I felt slapped. What was Nussia doing to my sister to make her act this way?

My fists clenched. "I'm not going back out there," I said, hitting the bed.

"Suit yourself! Stay in here and rot for all I care. You're acting like you're ten instead of fourteen anyway!" she said, getting up and slamming the door.

❧

After the birthday party, I called Grandma, and she came and got me for the weekend. (When she wasn't staying with us, she visited with old friends in the city.) She assured me that everything would be fine with Nussia, that maybe she was being a tad rebellious and that I should try to get to know her. Try to find common interests, she had said. I thought it good advice.

The day after I returned, while my parents slept, I went out to sit on the porch. Nussia joined me. A bowl full of peaches and nectarines sat in my lap. Nussia took a peach and moved it across her surricille, seeming to enjoy the soft fuzz. Her retractable mouth took small bites from the peach. I tried to ignore her. But I still found her eyes absorbing, and I still wanted her to like me.

"Nice feeling," she said.

I nodded. Our block was quiet. Bits of gray and red firecrackers, pre-Memorial Day celebrations dappled the black tar.

After sitting in silence for a while I blurted out,

"Do Fike girls get a period?"

"We don't have vaginas like human females do," she replied without the barest trace of embarrassment.

I laughed nervously. "You should be thankful for that fact. Periods can be so nasty and sticky. They're a pain. Dad says that Mom gets evil when she has her 'friend.' I think *that's* why they have separate bedrooms."

It was Nussia's turn to laugh. Then she said, "During the Awakening we have what humans would call convulsions. We can wander around ill for days if someone is not there to guide us. The elders must give us our new name. They must help us remove the old surricille, and care for our newly exposed head. My father said that my mother suffered during her Awakening. But the Awakening only happens once in our lives and it's not, as you say, sticky."

"Nussia, what you said before, about your sister and the Awakening..."

"Let's not talk of it. There's a saying on my planet that when one speaks out of turn, the mountains frown." She put her hand over mine, her hand feeling of comforting worn leather. "Tell me more about periods."

She stared at me so I spilled. "Susan, a girl in my class got her period when she wasn't expecting it. The stain got all over her dress. She tried to play it off like she sat in some Pepsi. My period is not real regular yet. I get bad cramps. Grandma says my body hasn't 'settled.'"

"Does Peter know about your periods?"

"No." I squirmed a bit. "Boys and girls don't talk about stuff like that. Earth boys are always saying stupid stuff about periods."

"Oh." Casually examining another peach, she said, "Next time you are with your period and feel bad, I could bring you up in the air. It might make your time go better."

"Oh, really, Nussia? Really?" I got so excited I sprang up and did a little dance around the porch. "I'd be so happy if you would."

In that moment, I forgot everything that came before. Maybe that we could be friends after all. She had just needed time to warm up to me.

❦

Two Fike representatives visited to socialize with Nussia. Mom used it as an excuse to host a formal gathering for friends and local officials. Before they arrived, my mother frantically ran around the house asking if Virginia or I had seen her favorite scarf. "I've looked everywhere!" We hadn't. Then she turned, slapped her forehead and said, "Oh, I bet Ma borrowed it without telling me. She's always doing that." She shook her head and raced off to check on last-minute details. After smiling and faking the answer that Nussia and I were getting along great (I had hopes that things would now improve), I excused myself to get a glass of juice and headed for the kitchen. The door leading to the basement was unlocked. I entered. I was sure I had slipped away unnoticed. Now that I was down here, I decided to do a little exploring. My curiosity and boredom led me underneath the stairwell to the floatbed.

Hearing my mother's constant refrain in my head, "Don't mess anything up," I carefully opened the dome of the floatbed and with some effort climbed in. It was heated and immediately made me feel sleepy. I imagined what it would be like to sleep without pillows, slowly floating up and down the entire night. Fike go into a mini-hibernation each night; they sleep deeply.

I suddenly heard noises from upstairs and panicked. I would get in so much trouble if anyone found me in her bed. They were already coming down the stairs. Who could it be? Mom looking for something from the freezer? No, the meal was catered. Dad? Mean Grits? No, I ruled him and the other Secret Service agents out as they rarely came inside the house anymore.

They stopped at the second set of stairs leading down to the basement.

I crouched, frozen, in the tank.

"Here, here…there are probably no wires here." I recognized Nussia's often grumpy sounding voice. The other belonged to one of the visiting Fike, a high-ranking diplomat.

"Practice English?" Nussia said.

"It is terrible in my ears," another voice, also Fike said.

"I have to hear it every day," Nussia said then paused. "Humans like levitation. Much."

"We know."

"Jerrgil, they like it more than anything else. It makes them feel like a drug… no, like they have been drugged. Better than you thought," Nussia said.

"What else?"

"My monunis give me power here. Different. Not like on home."

There was a pause. "We have no other reports of this power. Continue to monitor. Your father does not need to know. Other Fike representatives do not need to know. Your sacrifice is so great akesshhhh-No more English. I part with practice."

Then all I heard were the sizzle sounds. No one had offered to teach me any of the Fike languages and I regretted that now. They talked for another five minutes and went back upstairs. I stayed perfectly still, wondering more and more about Nussia's intentions.

෴

We were due to be interviewed on *Sixty Minutes* in less than an hour. This was our big exclusive TV debut.

Thank goodness Mom had packed an additional shirt for me as the one I wore now smelled funky and you could see a ring of sweat stains. I could barely concentrate as I was so stressed about being interviewed on TV with no one else there besides Nussia. I kept repeating the words ice cream and butter pecan to myself. They had refused to send the questions to my parents, so my father made us practice the kinds of questions the interviewers might ask us. I soaked my T-shirt on every round.

The makeup woman was dabbing foundation on Nussia and even dusted some powder across her bald head, which made Nussia frown.

The assistant producer, a young white man with strawberry blonde hair, walked in and reminded us we were up in less than an hour. "You both look great!" he said and made the okay symbol with his fingers.

Nussia was more talkative today, and I carried on our conversation that began on our ride over to the studio.

"Does Mean…I mean Mr. Johnson ask you questions?" I almost referred to the head Secret Service agent by my private nickname for him.

"No, he never says anything."

The staff had set up a snack table for us and I got up and grabbed a soda.

"Where do you go?"

"It's what your people call top secret," she said. She paused and smiled, "But it is nothing so fun, Lindsay. I would rather be at home. I am mostly meeting with core diplomats—many are considered elders on Fike."

What she said about wanting to be at our home didn't seem entirely true but I stayed quiet.

Nussia made herself a plate of fruit and cheese.

"Do you tell them about us?"

She smiled, dipped her head. "They let me know what is going on back at Fike."

The alien girl struggled with eating strawberries. In a moment, three fell down her front and left stains on her white and gold tunic.

"Oh no," I said. She responded in kind with an angry sounding unpronounceable Fike word.

"You might be able to get it out quick, if you go to the bathroom and run it under water," I said. She nodded and headed for the bathroom.

"I'll get the wardrobe person," I said.

Before I went to find the wardrobe person, I thought I should check both of our duffle bags for other clothes that Nussia could wear. I ruffled through my bag, reminding myself of what my mother packed. I hastily pulled out a peach ruffled shirt—probably too small for Nussia and also a blue cotton dress that might work. I looked in Nussia's bag, too, and discovered a white skirt and two pairs of sandals. A flash of color caught my eye from one half-zipped inner pocket of the bag. I pulled out my mother's scarf that she had been looking for a few weeks ago.

Nussia entered looking frazzled. The stain hadn't come out and her tunic was wet.

I held up the scarf, "Did Mom give you this to you?"

Nussia looked away and pushed past me, "I need help getting this stain out, Lindsay."

"This is her favorite scarf. What is it doing in your bag?" I could feel the color rising in my cheeks.

Just then, the assistant producer entered, a clip chart in his hand. "Ladies, fifteen minutes," he said. Then taking one glance at Nussia's outfit, he barked, "Christ, we've got to get you into some new clothes. Come with me."

"Yes, thank you," Nussia said.

She left me there holding my mother's scarf. I wasn't thinking about ice cream or the interview anymore.

☟

Despite everything, the interview went well for both of us. Nussia refused to talk about the scarf or anything except the interview during the ride home. When we got home, I caught Virginia, in our bathroom, while she was getting ready for a date. She asked about the interview and I told her about the scarf.

She shrugged. "If Mom didn't give it to her that's wrong. But, we don't know that, do we?"

"I don't think she did," I said.

"But, maybe taking things that don't belong to you is different for Fike. I don't remember reading much about their moral code."

I watched her apply several coats of mascara. She looked great. She wore a black blouse and black pants that were all the rage. The pants looked like exaggerated bell-bottoms and when Virginia stood with her legs together, it looked like she was wearing a long skirt or dress.

"Will you talk to Mom about it?" I asked.

"Sure," she said. "We'll keep an eye out for anything else that goes missing."

"Yes. Glad you have my back."

"Always."

∾

I noticed something was happening between my parents. Sure, they had always had separate bedrooms, ate their meals at different hours, and had different friends. And that *hadn't* changed. But Nussia had somehow inserted herself in the natural rhythms of my father's life: he now ate with her and even talked with her in the monuni shrine. When she first came, Nussia asked my father to expand the shrine in the backyard, which he happily did. They spent much of their time there. Their laughing voices often carried all the way to the front porch. I'm sure he even asked her for gambling tips.

One evening I heard laughter coming from my father's bedroom. I opened the door. My mother sat in a chair holding an almost empty glass of red wine against her face. I looked up and saw Nussia and my father floating up at the very edge of the ceiling in the far-right corner, to the left of the light fixture. They smiled and held on to each other's hands. They were higher in the air than people were at my party. Their positions were also more horizontal than what I had seen at the party; they really looked as if they rested on air.

"Hey, Nussia, take me up. I really want to go flying. I know what you said before, but I can't wait. Now seems like it would be so fun," I said.

"Forget it," Mom said. "She won't bring me up there either, Lindsay."

Her eyes stared straight past me. Nussia and my father ignored both of us.

The way that Nussia was playing with my father suddenly made me very angry. I wanted her to either stop this game or bring my mother and me up into the air. Nussia and my father continued to ignore us. There was a sound coming out of his mouth; it was a sound that I hadn't heard from him in a long while. I realized that it was pure laughter.

My father pointed to a corner.

"Look, here's a big old spider web. It doesn't have a spider in it, though," he said to no one in particular. He laughed again.

"Curl up in a ball, Rodger," Nussia coaxed.

Immediately he pulled his body together tightly. Then just as quick he stretched out of it. He stretched his arms and legs as far out from his center as they would go.

" This...being up on the air. It's like being held by someone who loves you. It's magic."

No, it's a drug, I thought to myself. Nussia had a drug like no other.

My mother held her glass up to them in a mock toast, downed the rest of her wine, and walked out of the room. I followed her, slamming the door.

☙

I went looking for Nussia the next day and I found her tending the shrine of monunis in the backyard. She went out every day after dinner and spent some time with them.

The shrine was decorated with stargazers and purple and pink zinnias. My grandmother had planted her favorite shrub, gardenias, around the borders of the shrine. On closer inspection the monunis were hard yellow and purplish spheres, about the size of kiwis, and were arranged along the back of the lean-to.

I stood away at a distance until I saw that she was finished. I cleared my voice and began, just like I had been practicing for the past few days. This wasn't going to be easy.

"Hi," I said. "I wanted to, uh, talk with you. I haven't been able to see very much of you recently. You and Virginia have just been doing so many things together. Anyway, I'm still very happy that you're here. But," I continued with a nervous laugh, "I feel, Nussia, that something's not right with us."

"My sister wanted to come here, not me," Nussia said quickly, advancing and closing the gap between us.

"What do you mean? Will you please just tell me about your sister?" My words spilled out so fast that I accidentally bit my tongue.

"You really don't *know* about me, Lindsay." She pressed her green palms against my chest, pushing me back forcefully, causing me to fall down flat on my behind.

"Owww! What's wrong with you? Why'd you do that?"

"My parents sent me to Earth," her voice was low and sounded like a growl. "I was told to go. My sister, Lillandra was supposed to be here," she said, pointing to the house.

I got up and brushed the dirt off me. "No one told me anything about your sister, you have to believe me."

She looked away from me, her voice dropping to almost a whisper, "My sister is beautiful, by Fike standards, and is what humans call charming, and we call *meenill*. She became very ill and she could not come here. In her condition, Lillandra would not have survived the trip."

I was stunned by this revelation. No, not only stunned. I didn't want to hear it.

"But you're here now. You're here—that's what matters. We're friends. It will be alright," I said and reached for her hand.

She backed away from me. "You remind me of my sister. She talked endlessly about having a *lulla*, a human friend. But I'm not like her. I'm not like you, either. I've always been different."

"I'm different *too*, not everybody wanted an alien," I said. I could hear the whininess and the desperation in my voice. I felt my neck and ears flush red. I looked at the ground.

"'Humans are not hard to deal with,' my mother said," Nussia mocked. "My father, the *Elkeenier*…the diplomat, pushed and pushed to get me to come, though he could have sent many other Fike my age.

"So now I'm stuck here. Stuck, stuck, stuck. You brought me here, Lindsay! It was your *essay* and your *needs*. I will miss all the preparations and training for the Awakening. I might never be Awakened now, and my parents don't care."

"I don't believe that," I said, shaking my head. I couldn't imagine her parents doing this to her, making her give up everything.

"Please, don't be mad at me, Nussia. I didn't know any of what was going on behind the scenes. I wouldn't have—"

"Tell me, what can I go back to?" Nussia said and stomped her foot. "I'm not one of you. I'm on my own here. Do you understand? I can't be fully Fike anymore. I'm a sacrifice. I don't care about the Awakening now! I hate my parents for sending me. This garden is the only thing I ever want to remind me of home. I have a new family. Virginia and Rodger are the best things about this place."

My brain felt fried trying to understand.

"You've seen how I can do things for them that no one, not even you, can do. My powers through my hands are strong here, and I don't know why. It's special to *me*." She smiled and jutted her chin out, "Even the Elders can't explain it. My mother was right about humans being easy to direct, she just didn't go far enough." After a pause Nussia said, "Humans can be controlled."

She couldn't mean that. A numbness spread from the center of my belly outward. Deep inside, I felt a piece of myself falling away.

I grasped Nussia's hands, looking at her deeply, directly into those dark eyes. "Is there someone else on Fike that might take care of you? I have my Grandma and if anything happened to my parents, I'd stay with her. Do you have someone else besides your parents? Let me help you. Let's try to figure this out together," I said, my voice cracking.

She twisted away from me. "No, and I don't want to see my family again."

"You're still special to me." Though I said the words out loud, they felt hollow inside of me.

"I don't need you to have myself," she said pushing past me.

❧

I left the shrine and Nussia and rummaged through my desk until I found the essay. Why had I even wanted Nussia to stay in this home? I read:

There is something in each of us that makes us special. It is not the obvious things. For my grandmother, it is her sense of adventure. For my mother, it is her cooking. For me, I have a burning desire to connect with something larger than humanity. "Alien" is a relative term. My neighbors are Jamaicans, and some people in my neighborhood think they are aliens. When we can see that what is alien is something that is also in us, then we can live without fear of the word. When the word "alien" can mean friend in all languages, even those yet to be discovered, we will have made something new.

After reading that, I knew what I had to do.

❧

"Absolutely not!" my father shouted. My parents were uncharacteristically enjoying a night together in Mom's bedroom. The television blared a chase scene from *Starsky and Hutch*.

"Send her home, Dad. She is unhappy and doesn't *belong* here. Can't any of you see that? Mom?"

"If Nussia was as unhappy as you think, she'd come to us."

"No, she wouldn't, Mom. She's told me some things."

"Speak up, Lindsay. Now, just what did she tell you?" Dad asked.

I didn't want to say what an awful conversation I had with her. Maybe I wanted to protect her. She clearly hadn't come of her own free will. She felt trapped. I hedged a little.

"Just that…"

"If she leaves now, what will people think of us?" my mother interrupted. "She's just a little homesick. And besides, you and Nussia are scheduled to go to the White House, an event it has taken months to plan for. How would that look if she didn't show up?"

"Do you know what being Lindsay Fields *means* now?" my father asked, rising out of his seat.

I shook my head. Right then I wasn't sure anymore what Lindsay Fields even thought.

He stood up, shaking his finger at me. "It means that the whole world knows you, Lindsay! It means that the whole world is open to you! It means that someday you'll be able to go to any college or university you desire. That includes Virginia too. *Anywhere*. Anywhere at all. It means a goddamn shortcut in a world that doesn't want to give us anything."

"But, Dad, I didn't write the essay for future plans." My parents always talked about college and my future at the most inconvenient times. I was a piece on their special chessboard, in the shadows until there was a move they needed played. They didn't see me either.

"Lindsay, *I* would know if she's unhappy." His words rang with finality.

"Would you, Rodger?" Mom's face hardened.

They excused me from the room. As I walked down the hall, I could hear Mom crying, her voice punctuated by indistinguishable sobs.

∾

It was a broiling, humid August day. I had to go to the store because I had started my period, and I had only two maxi pads left. Mom sent Nussia with me.

"I need some paprika, butter, and some frozen spinach. It would be real sweet if you could pick those up for me while you're out. I've got to run to an early meeting at work soon," she said. "Come right back, you two."

"Yeah, Mom."

She called after us again when we got to the porch. Stuffing more money in my hands, she said, "Get some orange juice, too."

It was going to be a long fifteen-minute walk each way. Nussia and I hadn't talked in days. We walked in silence, with the Secret Service men following in their car behind us. We could have taken a ride with them, but I didn't want to. When we reached the block of stores, I left Nussia outside next to the discount meat market while I went into the supermarket. She stood, fascinated, by the legs of lamb, pig ears, and the fat burgundy cubes of goat meat displayed for sale in the window.

On the way out of the store I saw Peter and his older brother Jake sitting on the hood of Jake's car. Peter wore shorts showing off his freckled legs.

"Hey girl. We just came from playing ball. We saw Nussia and stopped," Peter said.

"Get in." Jake said. "I'll give you a lift home. Can't be walking in this heat."

"That'll be great," I said. My stomach was feeling queasy because of my cramps. I ran over to the Secret Service car and told them I was getting a ride from my friends. Over the last few months, they had worked through our list of family friends and acquaintances, clearing almost all of them. Mean Grits had sunglasses on and gave me a lazy nod.

I walked back over and clutched the grocery bag closer to my chest.

"What'd you get from the store?" Peter asked.

"Just stuff," I said.

"Oh yeah? What kind of stuff?" Peter playfully grabbed at the bag.

"Stuff," Nussia repeated from behind me. Before I knew it, the bag flew out of my hands and rose over my head.

"Don't, Nussia!" I pleaded, but Nussia ignored me and kept them levitating in midair.

"Cool," Jake said. He sat on the hood of his car.

"How long can you keep things up in the air?" he asked.

"For a long time," Nussia replied.

I screamed, "Stop it!"

Most of the contents of the bags dropped to the ground in one heap. The white and blue maxi pad box, however, hovered and then opened. Its contents burst out of the box. The maxi pads fluttered in the air. They twitched and flapped like white mythic birds.

Nussia, Jake, and Peter laughed. Peter laughed so hard he held his stomach and slid off the car's hood.

I ran until I could not hear Nussia's laugh, like a slap across my face, anymore.

☙

From my mother's room, I heard drawers close. I inched closer to the door, which was cracked open. I hadn't come out of my room for almost a day. Finally, my grandmother had arrived.

"Ma, Lindsay has always been a fanciful child. God knows she's the one that brought Nussia here."

"Fanciful my ass, Jesse. She called me hysterical last night—while *you* were at work, of course. Something is just plain wrong about that *thing* living in this house."

How could Mom say that about me? I knew she had been under a lot of stress lately and very busy, but couldn't she see how wrong things were between me and Nussia? And how could Grandma say that about Nussia?

"How would it look to everyone? She's just different. That's what aliens are."

"Everyone? Who the hell is everyone? Your daughter—my grand-daughter—is very upset. I don't care if Walter Cronkite calls us a pack of raving backward ass niggers! That alien needs to go back where she came from. Look at you. You're a mess."

"What do you want me to do? Call it all off? Say that we can't deal with this—that *our* family can't deal? Nussia is not the problem. *Lindsay* is."

"Do you hear yourself, Jesse? When did keeping up appearances become more important than listening to your daughter?"

"You have no right to tell me how to deal with my children."

"Look, I can call a spade a spade. Maybe we were all a bit too hasty about this arrangement," Grandma said.

More drawers slammed.

"Jesse, I'm an old woman and I'm tired. If anything happens to my granddaughter... If I get one more hysterical phone call while I'm over at Maggie's house, I will personally ship that little tyrant back up to her planet my goddamn self."

"Ma, I've got to finish getting ready for work. I'm on an early shift!"

"You think about what I said. I'll take Lindsay with me to France if this mess keeps up. She needs to feel loved. Safe," Grandma said.

I crept down the hall and then back to my room. I heard the basement door close.

Good, I thought. I hoped Nussia heard every word. My grand-mother was no one to mess around with. Ever.

In my bedroom, I tried reading a book, but in a few minutes put it down. I couldn't focus. I couldn't stop replaying Mom's words repeatedly. Did she think I lied to her? That I couldn't tell the difference between what was real and what was "fanciful"? Feeling her words pound in my head made me want to shrink away into nothingness.

℗

After my mother left for work, Grandma called me downstairs for dinner. Virginia and Nussia were nowhere to be found. Virginia was probably out with friends. I tried Nussia's basement door, but it was locked and the key was not on its hook.

"I'm going to talk with Nussia before I leave tomorrow morning."

"Good, Grandma," I said.

"If that doesn't help Nussia get her act together, we'll have to figure out another way. Don't you worry, sweetie."

She got up to get dinner from the kitchen.

Nussia walked into the dining room. I felt her dark eyes sweep over me, but I just looked down at the table. I didn't want to be alone with her. I didn't want *anything* to do with her.

"Now, this isn't my recipe for liver and onions, but it will have—" Grandma began as she came through the kitchen door.

"May I have some dinner?" Nussia interrupted. She sat in the chair next to me.

Grandma rolled her eyes. "Nussia, we called for you." She placed the two dishes on the table.

"I'm sorry. I was outside."

Grandma went into the kitchen and brought out another placemat and plate of food.

"I want to talk with you, now, tonight. We need to talk about you and Lindsay."

I watched out the corner of my eye as Nussia nodded.

"Nussia," she said and began coughing.

She wiped the back of her mouth.

"I want to talk about your conduct regarding my granddaughter. Do you understand me?"

"You want to send me home."

Grandma sat down at the table and shook her head. She took a bite of the liver. After a pause Grandma said, "Nussia, your actions have been unexpl—"

"Yes, unexplainable. Grandma." Nussia dragged the edge of the knife back and forth across the edge of the plate.

"Stop that!" Suddenly my grandmother stopped talking and started coughing hard. I was on the edge of my seat, warily looking back and forth at the two of them. Nussia just stared ahead calmly.

"Grandma?" I got up from the table. "Do you need some water?"

She waved her hand at me. "Not now, child. I'm fine. I've just got some sort of tickle in my throat." Authoritatively she cleared her throat and resumed, "We've all been patient in waiting for you to adjust to this home—*Lindsay's* home."

Abruptly, Grandma started coughing. She placed a hand on her chest and massaged it. I'd never heard explosive hacking coughs like that before. Just as she managed to take a deep breath in, they would start again. The coughing fit turned into sounds of her gagging like she was going to vomit. She pounded the table as if trying to forcefully regain control of her body. The gagging, however, continued. She started shaking, her face becoming blue-tinged and panicked.

"Grandma!"

I jumped from my seat and ran to the kitchen, frantically pouring tap water into a glass. I ran back almost spilling it.

But as soon as I crossed the threshold into the dining room, Nussia's power lifted me up into the air. I screamed. I kicked and fought, tumbling in the air—all I could see was my grandma collapsing on the dining room floor.

The air held me tight and pressed into my back; it burned against my body. Her hold on me gave me the feeling of being smothered in a hot bubble. With all my might, I threw the glass, aiming for Nussia. But, with another wave of her hand she averted it. The glass hit a spider plant on a nearby table before shattering against the wall.

"Stop fighting me, Lindsay," Nussia said, calmly.

A tingling sensation spread through my limbs. It was as if all my limbs had gone to sleep at the same time, but then were being pricked awake. My fears drained out of me, replaced with a sweet warm numbness radiating from my stomach that spread through my body. I watched my grandmother as her tongue lolled out of her mouth, a mottled brownish red. This sweet numbness located itself in my tongue. I could not resist. I sucked that sweetness even as I watched my grandmother's eyes bulge.

I screamed with all my heart, pushing against the numbness, kicking listlessly at the air, but it was no use. The overpowering sweetness intensified across my neck and shoulders making my head loll from side to side. I couldn't resist any longer as the feeling invaded my newly forming breasts, underarms, torso, privates and legs. *Everywhere*. I was defeated.

Grandma coughed one last, horrible rattling breath. With one hand, she grabbed the back of the seat. The other hand pulled off her scarf. Her eyes rolled up in her head and then she stopped moving.

Nussia dropped me hard. I landed on my butt. The sweet numbness died away. My whole body trembled. Silence pervaded the house. Taking advantage of my slowness and fear, Nussia ran to the basement door and locked herself in.

I picked up my grandmother's hand. It felt rubbery and cool. Her ginger-colored complexion was turning a subtle gray. I had to get help. Hysterical, I ran over to Mr. and Mrs. Willacy's house, sobbing, ignoring the lingering tingling feeling in my arms and legs.

ᛒ

"Mommy, you've got to believe me. Nussia did it!" I cried over and over to my parents. There was no real reason for them to understand.

Everyone wanted this whole thing to work. I had wanted it to work more than anyone else. I thought she would save me.

"Girl, you've got to pull yourself together. Do you hear me, champ?" my father said, holding me. "Your grandmother choked on a piece of her food while having a stroke. What you saw was probably awful. However, there's no need to blame Nussia. You've got to be strong for the family."

The bedroom was crowded. My parents were there, Mean Grits, Secret Service agents and a man named Dr. Richards that said he was called in to assist. I didn't know where Virginia was.

"Lindsay, now you know that what you are telling us is preposterous. Don't you?" Mean Grits stood over my bed with a tight face. "Do you really think we would let a violent, unruly alien child stay with you?" He turned to my parents and put his hand on my mother's shoulder.

"I know that this is a time of trauma, but the Fike have never displayed any significantly violent behavior toward humans. Never."

"Where were you?" I screamed. "Why didn't you stop her?"

"She's in shock. Death is a hard experience for anyone to undergo. Kids will look to other things to validate or understand what is happening," the government doctor said casually, preparing a syringe intended for me.

I caught him by surprise as I slapped the needle from his hand.

"You're not the family doctor. Where's Mr. Connelly?" I hollered.

"Lindsay! Have you lost your mind?!" my father said.

Mom said through her tears, "Baby, this is a special doctor just for you."

"We are going to have to hold her down if this behavior keeps up," the doctor said.

"Is that what you want, Lindsay?" my father said.

I couldn't stop myself from crying long enough to get words out. My throat hurt and though there were no burns on my body, my skin felt hot to the touch and as if I had been rubbed with a giant loofah sponge.

"Grandma tried to tell you, Mom," I said, clutching at her hand.

The doctor signaled to one of the other Secret Service men and before I knew what happened, they pinned me, putting the needle in my arm.

Turning to my father, Mom said, "We've got to see what Nussia says. Rodger, do you hear me? Suppose Lindsay…"

"Yes, in the morning, we'll talk to Nussia," a Secret Service man interrupted. "By then Lindsay will remember what happened to her grandmother. She will see things clearly."

My mother rolled her eyes and looked away.

"Being in the air with her, it's not like being held by someone who loves you at all, Dad," I said as he was leaving the room. He did not turn around to answer.

I needed to get up and warn my family, protect them. Nussia's powers were much more developed than anyone knew. She would never be what I had hoped. Maybe it wasn't fair that I had wanted so much from her. Would she kill us all in the middle of the night? My stomach kept cramping like I was having my period, and I felt feverish. I shook in agony and frustration, but then everything went fuzzy and gray and blank. A different kind of numbness settled over me.

༄

I woke up in the middle of the night disoriented. Then, I remembered what had happened to my grandma. My body was wobbly, but my heart was clear. I tried to run through everything that had happened on this horrible afternoon in my head. Where were the security people when Nussia was killing Grandma? They must have been at their headquarters, or taking a food break. Maybe Nussia had done something to them and that's why they weren't around earlier, I thought soberly.

I knew what I had to try. Quietly, I slipped from my room and gathered the things that I needed for my task from around the house in the darkness. I crept downstairs and tried the doorknob to the basement, grateful when it opened without protest. I made as little sound as I could pulling the door open. I paused once on the other side and then gently locked the basement door behind me.

"All in due time" are the words that I heard when I stood next to Nussia's floatbed. Nussia was perfectly still, asleep. Her body levitated a few inches from the bottom of the floatbed. Every few seconds the top of her surricille gently bumped the top of the tank, and then she'd float down again. I quietly opened the top.

I waited until she floated back to the top of the tank. When she reached me, I carefully caught her right hand and put one of my mother's gardening gloves on. Touching her made me cringe and fight a wave of nausea. While I had her hand, I took the strips of masking tape that I had pulled off and left at the end of the tank and wound them around her gloved hand. I held her right shoulder and reached across to get the other glove on her hand and repeated the taping. I released her and she floated to the bottom of the tank. I was thankful for the depth of her sleep. I knew she would hover for at least a minute before floating up again. The next part was going to be much harder. My father had long ago stopped working out at home. He had abandoned the cast-iron plates, at my feet, to the back of a closet in the living room. I could not lift his 25-pound plates, so I settled for carrying two 10-pound plates. I reached down and lifted one of the plates. Breathing heavily, I put the first plate on her forearm. Her body tilted sideways. I got the other weight into place on her other side, pinning her how I wanted, so that when she woke up, she wouldn't be able to use her hands—at least for a few seconds.

Next came the shears. I stabbed at her surricille, sloppily making two large gashes. Nussia's eyes flew open and her tubular mouth stiffened. Then I used my hands, tearing pieces of it back—it was soft under my fingers, and gave way easier than I expected. I had never touched or rubbed Nussia's surricille before. I didn't know if this would work. Although the sight of her and what she did made me want to hurt her, that wasn't my intention. She was screaming now, writhing on the bottom of her floatbed in pain. Her screams weren't at all like the sizzle of her normal voice—this was a jumble of ancient alien sounds merged into an overpowering eruption of emotion.

The sedative had made me weak; weaker than I should have been for a task like this. She twisted violently and when my hold was broken, Nussia shot up through the floatbed with the force of three people and physically threw me back against the basement wall.

Dazed and hurting all over, I tried to get up but the room was spinning and all I managed to do was lay on my side. I touched the back of my head and my fingers came back slick with blood.

"What have you done?" she shrieked.

"Your Awakening," I said, heaving. "Everything is different for you on Earth. Maybe it can still happen and then you can leave."

"I'm not going back! This family is mine! Not even the Elders can make me stop." Blood flowed from the angry-looking wound and streamed down her lips and chin. She stood upright in the now levitated tank.

"No! You'll never be a part of *this* family. You're a murderer!" Even with all of their problems, they were still mine.

"They need me. Your father needs me. All humans need me, they *want* me." Her retractable mouth snapped open and closed over and over.

"You're drugging them or doing something. But soon they will figure it out or it will wear off or something," I shot back.

"Will they?" Nussia said, as her eyes crinkled, and a hideous smile crept across her face. "The sight of you is sickening," Nussia said. She bit at one of her restraints.

"You made choices, too, Nussia. You've done terrible things." I wanted her to stay focused on me and not the bag that I needed to get to.

"No one knows what I want. The Elders think they can control me," she shook her head from side to side. "They can't. They want me to spy and report to them, but here I will do what I want. They wanted me to be an experiment—well, I will be one that no one ever forgets!"

In the distance I heard a ferocious banging on the door. Dad and Virginia's voices.

Her dark eyes pierced me. The strips of blue tape floated down from one of the gloves.

With my breathing coming in shallow gulps and my back aching, I got up and used my last bit of strength to reach the bag laying on the float bed's platform. I dumped the monunis on the floor and stomped on them. Many of them cracked easily under my feet.

"No more ways to hurt us!"

Nussia was pulling off the gloves.

Nussia gaped at me in shock and horror, throwing her power at the monunis that weren't crushed, levitating them into the air. I snatched at them but they were already above my head.

"You stupid human child," she spat.

"I don't need you. Not now. Not ever," I said.

"I know."

These were the last words I remember before I choked and entered darkness.

℗

Nussia. I said her name like mine. It is a nightmare that has come to pass.

The doctors say that I suffer from debilitating paranoia and extreme depression. The room I'm in is large, with a TV and paintings of bright yellow flowers. It has a desk and a small couch. The door is always locked except when I get to go outside, which is twice a day. Most days I don't want to walk but stare out of the window. The doctors say I'm in a special kind of hospital, but as far as I can tell, I'm the only one on this part of the floor. When I recovered from the concussion, my father decided I needed some time away from the family. He told me that even if everything that

I claimed about Nussia were true, it was still not a good enough reason to hurt her. I told him I was trying to awaken her. He didn't believe me and said I should have come to them. I can see how it looked different to others and even how shaky my plan had been. On TV, I saw him telling the press that there had been an "adolescent disagreement" between Nussia and me. I haven't seen my family in a long time and have been given no way to contact them.

No one knows where Nussia is. The night of our altercation, she ran out of the house before my father could restrain her. Mean Grits and his team slipped up on their job. From the TV I learn that the Fike are upset and the President says diplomatic relations are strained. The National Guard had been called in to New York City to try to find her. Lynne, my private nurse, updates me. She's a slender, red-headed Black woman. She thinks I have set back civil rights by 100 years and tells me so daily.

Everyone thinks that I fucked up. That I'm the ugly, unpredictably violent American from the Bronx. *Click.* They don't know Nussia like I do. Anchormen say that I am a maladjusted and jealous young girl. When the camera zooms in on the average person on the street and a news reporter asks for an opinion, they say things like, "What do you expect? That's the way they are. They can't control their own, let alone an alien. Choosing that family was a mistake."

When I try to sleep, I hear Nussia's sizzle-sounding laugh and wake up screaming.

☾

Lynne brings my breakfast in and says with a triumphant smile, "They've found her."

"Alive?" I said, surprised at how much I was hoping for the opposite.

"Yes, and you're the luckier for it," she adds.

She turns on the TV. She keeps the remote with her and when I don't take my medicine, she takes it away. Watching TV is the only way I have to keep track of the days.

"She's such a trouper. Twelve-hour surgery with intergalactic communication from the Fike. A miracle," Lynne chirps while handing me orange juice.

I drink my juice and say nothing as I watch Nussia on the screen. The news clip shows Nussia looking peaceful with her head bandaged.

"...extensive surgery on her surricille. But the real question is whether Nussia, our brave visitor from another planet will be allowed to return to the Fields's home," an anchorman declares.

The next news clip shows how, in the wake of all these problems, three families are fighting to host Nussia. None of the children or the families had entered the original contest. The families describe themselves as "concerned citizens." One little white girl named Susan Raffety from New Hampshire says in a cultivated voice, "I've always wanted my own alien." Her father, a slim gray-haired man adds, "Yes, Nussia could ride horses here, swim...they do swim, don't they?" He questions his daughter. She nods affirmatively. "Yes, Nussia could enjoy the fresh country air." Aiming right for the camera and America's heart, Mr. Raffety says, "Should we let this family have another chance given the unusual circumstances that have surrounded Nussia?"

Lynne boos at this.

Then it cuts to Dad. My throat tightens.

Standing erect and with lips tight, he stands on the front porch of our house pointing his finger declaring, "I will fight any family that tries to take Nussia away from this family. I will fight them all the way to the Supreme Court!" Men in black suits that the anchorperson identify as his legal team stand next to him. Mom and Virginia stand behind my father. Virginia looks tired, dark rings border her eyes. Her hair has lost its sheen and her face looks older. I wonder if she misses me, or if Nussia's effect on her (and my father) is still strong. Is it chemical? Does it work long distance? My mother is stiff with glazed-over eyes. Is she so deeply ashamed of the way things worked out that she drinks herself to sleep? I miss her the most. Sometimes I dream I lie in bed next to her and that she smells of Charlie perfume and peaches.

"There is no reason why we can't provide a loving home for the rest of the time that Nussia remains on Earth," Dad drones on. "We need to keep Nussia with people that she knows, at least until she recovers. Anything else will be traumatic for her. Our daughter Lindsay has been under a lot of stress from the death of her grandmother. We've only recently learned how unstable and ill she actually is. She's being treated by the best doctors available and will return to us as soon as she has made a full recovery."

The news segment jumps quickly back to Nussia, who says she wants to stay with my family when she leaves the hospital.

I turn my face as I don't want Lynne to see how empty this makes me feel. Sucking in my breath, I go back to the television.

I watch her carefully. Her dark eyes are just that to me now, alien and dangerous, yet familiar. Trapped in this hospital and discarded, I flinch as I consider Nussia's past and my future.

"This opportunity for myself and my people I will never let go," Nussia says.

Nussia makes me see that my essay should have read, "When we can see that what is human is also sometimes what is alien, then we can begin to understand ourselves and them. All the good and the bad."

Lindsay. I say my own name for myself.

URBAN WENDY

MARISOL PULLS ANOTHER STRAND OF RED HAIR FROM A perfectly glazed Dunkin' donut, holds it up and looks at the stray bits of delicate pink icing clinging to the hair. Marisol reminds herself that none of her other team members working this shift have red hair, nor do any of the other employees. Wendy is here.

☙

When Marisol announced she was leaving Wendy's to work at Dunkin' Donuts two weeks ago, her co-workers warned her.

"Expect a visit from Wendy," they said. Marisol looked at the goofy-looking freckled girl on the napkins she had handed out so many times to snot-nosed kids, harried mothers, and dope addicts.

"She doesn't like it when we leave without warning," one of them whispered.

"You gotta be kidding me. I'll tell her a thing or two," Marisol said. She filed their concerns of Wendy the phantom stalker under "another urban legend," said goodbye to the drab brown uniform and the never-ending work of keeping the salad bar clean and organized, and sought her fortune among coffee and donuts.

Marisol's first week away from Wendy's had been peaceful at Dunkin' Donuts. No dreams, no nightmares, no prognostications from any cartoon characters with red hair. By the second week though, Marisol fielded daily complaints about bad donut batches, curdled creamer, and mixed up orders.

❦

Now the hair. She twirls her fake emerald stud earring while she thinks. She needs this job until her jewelry business turns a profit. She sighs and pushes her thumbs into the small of her aching back. She arches, but there is no satisfying crack of vertebrae. Too many nights, she thinks, hunched over her small table littered with clusters of garnet, peridot, and citrine, checking internet orders, hoping for a big sale. Not much luck so far.

"This isn't what I ordered." A man plops down a box of donuts.

Marisol peers in. "What's wrong?" she asks, straining under her customer service smile.

"I ordered vanilla glazed. These are hot as hell." He rests his beach ball sized stomach onto the counter. She plucks a small red candy off a donut, smells it and puts it into her mouth. It burns.

Her fingers rush over the register. "I'm so sorry; I'll get that corrected right away."

By the end of the day, she's fielded twenty-six wrong orders. Yawning, Marisol makes her way from the Dunkin' Donuts kiosk through the long subway tunnel to the station, dodging the many sleeping men and some women, packs of young men, and users of one kind or another. She keeps her head up and a watchful eye as she walks the badly lit corridor. She knows that 1986 has been a cruel year so far with the highest number ever of reported rapes, muggings, and stabbings in subway stations. She hugs her purse and wipes powdered sugar from the front of her jacket.

A tug at her elbow makes her look down at the small girl walking beside her. The girl's face is a spray of pimples and freckles.

Her red pigtails are lopsided and when the girl smiles, her mouth seems to open and lengthen like a tiny alligator's. Marisol pulls away. This is not happening. The girl says nothing but follows. Marisol weaves through the crowd, trying to mix in with the crush of people and catch her breath. The train is coming and Marisol picks up the pace. She boards, and a quick glance back through the smudged and graffiti covered train window confirms that she has lost whatever that was.

☺

Marisol does not believe in spirits, but her family does. She knows at least one thing to try. Later that night, she grabs a white 7-day candle from her mother's stash under the sink and lights it. She runs a bath, dumps in rosewater and sea salt to ward off whatever Wendy is. She slips her dark body into the bath and tries not to think of hamburgers, donuts, or little red-haired girls.

☺

Marisol feels calm the next day. Everything's going okay.

"Smoke break?" her co-worker with blonde bouncy curls says.

"Sure," Marisol says and nods. "I'll cover." They're in the slowest part of the day—12 to 2. No kids going to school or coming home and no one yet needs an afternoon sugar lift. She watches as her co-worker leaves the kiosk.

"Marisol," she hears her name whispered. She looks over the counter and then behind her. The voice gets louder. Is someone behind the condiment stand? Marisol comes around the counter and looks into the pack of straws, near the soda machine. The straws are covered in their white coats except for one. She pulls the fiery red one out. It glows in her hand. Holding the straw close, she sees the tiny plastic face of the freckled girl smirking.

"Stop following me," Marisol says. "You're going to get me fired."

"I didn't want you to leave. It's not your time to move on yet. I know about more than burgers," Wendy says.

Marisol's face reddens. "You ever try working a salad bar after church congregations come in? I hated telling people to stop picking at the olives if they hadn't paid for the salad. Wore me down."

"I'll get you a different station," Wendy says.

"I need better pay," Marisol says.

"If you come back, I could work on that. I miss you." Marisol sees Wendy's lips thin out and upturn briefly, but her small imprinted face looks uneven.

Marisol considers. How many more pieces of malachite could she buy with a raise?

"Is that all you want? Better pay?" Wendy says.

She shakes her head at such a stupid question. In the palm of her hand Marisol feels heat from the straw. She shuffles the straw to her other hand. She feels the warmth from the straw penetrate her hand and travel up through her arm.

"What are you?" Marisol says.

"Total quality control," Wendy says as the straw dissolves in Marisol's hand.

Marisol wonders if she's had too many vanilla frosted donuts.

☙

Late that night, exhausted, Marisol walks through the subway tunnel, noticing it is more deserted than usual for this time of night. She feels weighed down by the two boxes of day old donuts she carries. She rounds her usual corner. She feels someone walking too close, but when she turns around he's already there covering her mouth and pulling her to him. The boxes fly from her hands, open as they hit the ground and spill their colorfully frosted contents. The man smells like sweat and onions. From memory, she executes the only move that she remembers from a high school self-defense class. She lifts her right foot and stomps on what she prays is the top of the man's foot. He registers no pain but responds by slamming her into the wall. Pinning her, he leans in and bites the top of her eyebrow.

When a scream finally erupts from Marisol it carries with it a cry for help, for it to not end like this. Between the pain and body-shaking fear, a sliver of regret pierces her. She thinks of all the attention she pays to cuts of amber, tourmaline, emerald, and sapphire rather than to the feel of the sun kissing her face, her mother's gap-toothed smile, or the simple pleasure of bouncing her niece on a knee. Ashamed, her mind stretches into the night, discharging energy like a thin finger of lightning.

Another guttural scream mixes in with Marisol's, and in a moment she feels the man's hands drop away. Marisol turns and sees a man in ragged clothes looking stunned. Blood trickles from his ears. People are coming toward her asking if she is alright. Hands with tissues dab at her scraped and bleeding face. She pants, a metallic taste rising on her tongue. She overhears someone say, "Wasn't a little girl with her just a moment ago?" Marisol looks past the crowd into the tunnel, but just sees strangers.

"A little red-haired girl?" Marisol asks with a croak, her voice dry. No answer back.

Tonight she'll light a fat red candle, one her mother uses to invite an emissary in. She'll wait and listen. Tomorrow she will go back to burgers and fries. Donuts aren't for her after all.

ETTA, ZORA, AND THE FIRST SERPENT

ETTA KNEW THAT NO ONE SHOULD TALK OPENLY ABOUT SPIRITS.
As she listened to the writer Zora Neale Hurston spin a tale to the
room of guests, she also knew that this charismatic, six-foot-tall,
big-boned woman with a dimpled face was trouble, plain and simple.

While other party goers danced at the front of the apartment
to the tunes of Cab Calloway and Louis Armstrong, many were
crammed in this back room hanging on Zora's every word. She'd
been holding court for the last half-hour. Etta sat at a small round
table, on a hard chair, squashed between two large men. She flexed
and pointed her foot as was her dancer's habit. She gathered that
most of the people here were like Zora: writers, actors, spiritualists.
Strange people. She didn't belong.

Etta knew about spirits, though—haints and night shift-
ers—from her grandmother and her own eyes. Her family grew
up with a house spirit. A mean, frightening thing. Loved to make
blood stains appear on her mother's clean laundry. Spirits weren't
nothing to play with, and you damn sure didn't goad them.

Her roommate had invited her to this party and then had the bad manners to leave early. She should have followed, but she couldn't take her eyes off Zora. No one could.

"I believe the devil is nothing but a clot of misguided spirits. Like a hive mind. One is called the First Serpent. That's who I want to find," Zora said.

Etta chilled, as if someone had raked his or her fingers across her arm.

"Zora, you're going to make all the ladies faint," said a man sitting next to Etta. He was dressed in gray slacks, a handsome double-breasted black sweater, and black and white oxfords.

"I've been known to make a lady or two swoon," Zora said with a smile and a wink.

Even after living in Harlem for a year, Etta could never get used to the ways of city folks. At seventeen, she knew she had seen more than all the people in her hometown combined.

"Trying to catch something so evil…Your soul could just burn up," a woman said, sounding slightly breathless.

"If my soul is that flimsy, then it must not be any good," Zora replied, her big face taking on a mischievous grin.

The crowd erupted with laughter.

"Scandalous," whispered one of the men sitting next to Etta. He fiddled with the brim of his bowler laying in his lap.

She was a good performer; Etta would give her that.

Lila, the host, a woman with wispy hair and a slight face, walked in and said, "No one has touched the chiffon pie. Zora, let my guests get some slices and dancing into them!"

Zora bowed. "I would never keep anyone from your pies, Lila. To be continued."

As people stretched and went in search of dessert, Etta stood, determined to make her exit.

Zora, a cigarette in her mouth, held out an arm, touched Etta.

"You're not buying what I'm selling?" she asked.

Swallowing hard and feeling put on the spot, Etta mumbled, "Nothing against you, but taunting spirits is dangerous."

"How would you know?" Zora asked.

Etta looked down.

"The spirits ain't nothing to be scared of. I've studied a few and they are in many ways just like us: petty, vain, bold, misunderstood, and sometimes glorious," Zora said.

Mustering up her courage, Etta asked, "Why do you want to talk to the First Serpent?"

Zora leaned close. "Because he can give me something I want very badly."

Etta could see the desire in Zora's eyes, like a child on Christmas morning.

"Ms. Hurston," Etta began.

"Zora, please," the woman said, lighting another cigarette.

"Spirits have a way of coming at us. They're smarter, older. I know that you've studied lots and traveled, but—"

"I hear you're from Florida," Zora said, turning a little to make way for folks entering the room, plates piled high with pie.

Etta's mouth opened and a tiny yelp escaped. So the rumors about Zora knowing people's business were true. She closed her mouth and nodded. "Yes, from Little Hill."

"That sounds more country than Eatonville."

Someone from my home state! Etta perked up. "It is! You blink and you'd miss our main street and the General Store."

The cigarette smoke made a halo around Zora's head. "Working at the Cotton Club," Zora said, stubbing out the butt in a nearby ash tray.

Etta took a step back. "You keeping tabs on me?"

Zora wiggled her eyebrows. "Nothing stays secret in Harlem for long, Etta. What's it like?"

"They put all the light girls up front," Etta said, her hands springing up to cover her mouth. She looked around to see if anyone else had heard, a flush creeping across her cheeks. "Never mind."

Zora's expression changed and her face took on a hungry, wolfish look. "Now, that's not fair at all," Zora said with a shake of her head.

Etta knew she had said too much. *But it's true and there's no one else to talk to about it.*

One of the men who had sat next to Etta approached. "Zora, you gonna pick up where you left off?"

"In a minute," she said without taking her eyes off Etta.

"Sounds like you got something that weighs on you. Maybe the spirits can help. You come find me."

Etta stood there for a long moment, thinking on Zora's words.

❧

Etta massaged her ankle and tried to hold her tongue.

"You gonna fall like that every time, Etta?" snarled Albert from the front row. "You're off cue."

Albert was a thin, weaselly brown-faced nothing of a man, but a nothing of a man in charge of the twenty dancers at the Cotton Club.

You just hopping around, puffing yourself up because one of the owners is here. Etta had gotten a good look at the new investor when she walked on stage. Mr. Stitt. A pink, walrus-looking man stuffed into a chair a few tables back. With his reddish hair curled around his face, he nursed a drink, saying little. The way his eyes followed the girls gave Etta chills. She had heard rumors that, when he visited, he didn't just like to see the rehearsals; he liked to meet the girls.

The day had started out bad. She arrived at work with little sleep from bad dreams to find the dancers practicing the "savage island" number again. At Albert's insistence, long-legged and almost-white Laney—who took forever to learn the steps—was up front. *She's a terrible dancer. She can shake her body, which ain't dancing in my book.*

Laney missed her cue again, wrecking the timing for all the other dancers. But, of course, no one was going to point that out.

Laney looked at Etta and sniggered.

Etta cut her eyes at the woman. "Laney, your timing was off." Maybe it was the conversation with Zora last night that had loosened her tongue. She wouldn't have said anything to Laney before, just swallowed her anger. Being in Zora's presence for just a few minutes had emboldened her.

Albert's face contorted as he came storming up on the stage. Towering over Etta, he bellowed, "When I ask you what went wrong, then you get to speak!"

All the other dancers except Laney stiffened.

"That's right," Laney said. "Correcting me, humph," she added with a tap of her foot.

"Perhaps they need a break," the pink walrus said.

Etta saw a familiar change come over Albert's face. It was the look he had when he wanted to blow up at someone—usually another Black man—but couldn't because the man had some sort of advantage over him. Either the other man was bigger and meaner or he was a musician that Albert needed in the band. He wouldn't dare shout and rage at this powerful white man. That much Etta knew for sure.

Albert pulled his lips in, plastered on a fake smile, and nodded. "Excellent idea, Mr. Stitt. Everyone take fifteen."

He leaned down and whispered between clenched teeth into Etta's ear, "No more fucking lip from you."

Etta turned away from his sour breath, stomach churning, and continued tending to her ankle.

"Etta?" a girl's voice said.

She looked up. The twins, Big Georgie and Little Georgie, had their hands extended.

She smiled. "I'm alright girls, thanks." *They're always looking out for others.*

They waited for her to get up and the three of them walked to the dressing room.

"You doing okay?" she asked.

They nodded. Out of all the girls here, they were Etta's favorites. They said they were eighteen, but she suspected that was a bold lie that they got away with because of their talent, and like Laney, the hue of their skin was what some Negroes would call "bright." Both possessed a curtain of hair that nearly reached their bottoms. They, like Etta, had no kinfolk in the city.

When the door closed behind them, the dressing room erupted in conversation. Some dancers reached for cigarettes, others hairbrushes, and some just flopped down on their seats. Etta noticed that the light-skinned girls sat together, as did the girls who had café au lait coloring, as did the darker girls, like herself. *Like a beautiful zoo, but a zoo all the same.*

"Country girl got a voice, eh?" someone said.

"Albert will come and slap you down. Don't sass him in front of the white man," another dancer admonished.

Laney walked into the middle of the room. "She's so country, she barely knows how to put on her drawers the right way, let alone how to talk to anyone."

Amber-skinned Delilah, one of the oldest dancers at the Cotton Club, who usually kept to herself, rose from her chair. "Knock it off, Laney. She was right, you *were* late."

Laney sniffed and shook her head. "Y'all bitches just jealous of me because you know my jelly rolls are the best. The men come to see me." She patted down the curves of her body and shook out her wavy hair.

"Why it got to be about me or any of us being jealous?" Etta said, feeling heat rise in her throat.

Laney walked over to Etta and said in a tight voice, "You wouldn't want me to say something bad about you to Albert or Mr. Stitt?"

Looking up into Laney's eyes, Etta smelled her perfumed breath and saw the little pink tongue wiggle. She thought of the good money she sent home to her family disappearing. Etta shuddered when she thought about working at the shady knock-off clubs in Harlem. Etta choked down her anger and said, "No."

The door popped open and Albert walked in with no warning knock. He looked around the room and snapped his fingers. "Laney and twins come with me. Drinks at the bar with Stitt."

"Great," Laney said and grabbed a shawl.

Etta and the twins looked at each other.

Albert stomped his foot. "Now, not yesterday. Move it!"

"Why he want them?" Etta said.

Pointing his finger at her, he said, "He don't want *you*, so mind your business."

Laney strutted, saying over her shoulder, "You girls just follow my lead. Keep your mouths shut."

Etta's heart spasmed as she watched the twins leave. She didn't trust Laney and she definitely didn't trust the likes of the pink walrus.

ᧁ

Etta stood on the stoop of her building and looked up at her dark apartment window. She began climbing the stairs but turned when she heard her name.

"No one's home," Zora said with a smile, pointing toward the apartment. "Your roommate is out for the night."

Etta looked down at Zora who stood at the foot of the stoop. "How—?"

"This is the time most dancers finish for the night. My best time to write. I'm done and needed a walk."

Etta sighed. She wasn't sure if she should go upstairs or keep talking with Zora. She kept thinking about Little Georgie, who had been asked to go for a ride with the pink walrus, and the worry on Big Georgie's face.

"Come," Zora said, waving her hand.

Etta followed, frustration and curiosity mixing together in her heart. They walked a few blocks in silence. Then they talked of their towns and the downhome meals that they missed so far away from loved ones. They walked to a late-night diner, one Etta had passed many times.

The waitress greeted Zora. "Anywhere you like."

Zora nodded and chose the farthest booth.

After getting settled, she gave her order to the waitress. "Two egg creams, please, and two grilled cheese sandwiches."

Etta's eyes widened then narrowed in suspicion. "How did you know I like egg creams?" Egg creams were a delight. Frothy, cooling, and sweet. She would do just about anything for an egg cream.

"Just a guess," Zora said with a shrug. "Most folk new to the city do."

Watch yourself, Etta. Zora's a charmer and spinner of tales.

Zora folded her hands on the table. "I'm looking for a dancer, Etta. A very good dancer."

"A dancer? To do what?"

"In the archives at Columbia, I stumbled upon some interesting ideas about the First Serpent, something no one knows anything about," she said, her eyes brightening with each word.

Zora compelled her attention, so although "archives" sounded foreign to Etta, she nodded.

"The First Serpent has Egyptian roots. Egyptian as in African," Zora said. "There's an order to things and, just like ants, bees, and wolves, beings like to live in groups. So do spirits. I want our people's stories—the foremothers and the slaves, those who are gone. I want those secrets. I want stories that no one else can write. I need the First Serpent to put me in touch with those spirits."

Etta shook her head. "That's crazy."

"No crazier than anything else."

Etta looked around to see if anyone was overhearing their conversation.

Zora waved her hand. "People aren't listening to us."

"Why me?"

"I like you," Zora said.

Etta blushed and shrugged, "You know lots of people in Harlem."

Zora leaned in, "I sure do, but sometimes I get a read on people, a feeling about them and what they can do. And, besides we're country girls, right? Making our way in this city—that takes some doing."

The waitress placed their orders on the table. Etta's face registered how good her egg cream was.

Zora took a bite of her sandwich then said, "You help me and I'll help you."

"What? I don't need your help," Etta said, turning her head to look out the window. She turned back to find Zora watching her.

Zora stroked her chin for a long time before speaking.

"At the Cotton Club," Zora said, leaning back in the booth. "Your job. There are people that you don't like there. They don't see you, Etta."

Etta sat up, "Do you have spies everywhere?"

"No spies. It's just an old story," Zora replied.

"My grandmother taught me to believe in Jesus," Etta blurted.

"Well, that's good. I believe in him, too. But not *just* him."

"Spirits should be left alone," Etta said, folding her arms.

"Suppose you could be the best dancer, not just at the Cotton Club, but wherever you wanted?" A slow smile crossed Zora's face.

Etta stared open-mouthed and shook her head. Zora was mad. Isn't that what her roommate had said? That Zora was a bit touched? Still, Zora's magnetic personality and unusual ideas drew her in, and *that smile*? Almost irresistible. She wore a long colorful scarf that hung over each of her breasts. As she talked, it was as if she were dancing with the scarf moving from hand to hand. Zora kept talking. "You understand the arts. You understand what it means to strive for something, to love it."

Etta slurped the last of her egg cream and fiddled in her purse for money.

Zora reached over and grabbed her hand. "It struck me recently that I need to do something bold. Something that will speed things up. Us country girls have to take things into our own hands. You think the world is ever going to treat us fairly, Etta?"

Etta leaned back and considered. From what she'd seen so far, Etta had to admit that the world probably wasn't going to treat either of them fairly. She had held such high hopes for New York but the big city had yet to deliver on her dreams. Although there was nothing like the Cotton Club in all of Florida, what good was it doing her being there if, like Zora said, no one saw her talent?

"You love to dance, right?" Zora asked.

"More than anything else," Etta said. The twins' faces flashed in her mind. Out of all the other girls, she sensed they loved the work as much as her.

With a nod and chuckle, Zora said, "Thought so. You'll find, I'm not usually wrong. That's all you have to do when the time comes. The First Serpent is very fond of dance. That's where you come in. Dance for the love of dance. Do you think you can do that?"

"I'll think on it."

"Don't keep me waiting," Zora said, placing money on the table.

✦

Tonight, Etta wore a skimpy two-piece outfit: a halter top and shorts with a feather headdress. Normally, she'd be cold in such a flimsy outfit, but now her anger kept her warm. She had never danced with such heat flushing through her chest.

The club was full, and the band's horns and drums created an atmosphere of intrigue and excitement. The "savage" number was in full swing. She swirled and dipped in time with a line of five dancers. Etta should have been thinking about the music, the choreography, how her muscles responded to the power of the dance. Instead, her mind kept flashing back to Little Georgie's bruised arms, swollen eye, and sad face in the rehearsal room before the show. How Big Georgie had argued with Albert and the slap she'd received. How Laney's churlish laugh sounded in her ears, and Laney's words to Little Georgie. "Everybody got to grow up sometime. I was nine when it was done to me. And he didn't give me no money, either."

Albert had chimed in, "Didn't you get some money, girl?"

Little Georgie sat on the chair, head down, hugging herself.

Laney smirked, walked over, and grabbed the girl's hair like she was nothing but a rag doll. "Stitt *did* give you some money, right nitwit? You knew to make sure he gave you some money, I hope."

At that, Etta had thrown a perfume bottle at Laney so fast it clipped the side of the pretty woman's head, stunning her. The room flared into a knot of knees and fists with Albert yelling that they would all be fired if they didn't get their asses ready to dance.

Drums thudded, and she saw Laney's dolled up face, the sweat-soaked leering face of the pink walrus, and Albert's smugness. She imagined them as balls in front of her, so when she kicked in time with the music, it was with an extra, bitter force.

But she couldn't kick away the memory of Little Georgie's tears and the numbed, stony look of her twin. No one was looking out for them. The twins, like her, were alone in the city and they were so young. *I should have stopped Laney. We all should have.* She decided then, in the middle of a leap, that she would help Zora and also ask for a favor from the First Serpent. For the twins.

Zora finished casting a six-foot-wide circle of what she said was baking soda and salt around them. In the middle of the circle she created a smaller circle from heavy rope, she said to, "properly bind the spirit." They sat in Zora's living room, both dressed in white. "Whatever happens, don't stop dancing. You understand? And don't ask for a favor until I tell you. This is a powerful spirit."

Etta nodded.

"You're distracting it, calming it while I talk," Zora continued.

"Yes," Etta said.

"If you break the circle, spirits can escape."

After Zora issued several exotic incantations, Etta swayed from side to side, finding her inner rhythm. She danced, slowly at first and then concentrated on making every breath a joyful exploration of how she could move, forgetting herself, letting go. She hadn't been able to dance with this much freedom in months, maybe since she'd moved to New York.

Zora periodically whispered, "More." And, "Faster."

After a while, Etta felt the air in the room swell, and then in another moment, a breeze whipped up her skirt and tickled the length of her spine. Her feet registered the degree or so change of temperature in the circle. Sweat dripped from her face and neck as she strutted, kicked, and leapt in the salt circle.

"That's it," Zora cried.

Etta gyrated her hips and contorted her limbs. She jutted her right elbow to the side while her left arm made wide arcs in space. She dipped down and jumped high. Dancing in the presence of the unknown was nothing at all like regular performing. Her fingertips vibrated, feeling more alive than ever before. Her heart hammered in her chest, her mouth felt as if she had swallowed sand, and the hair on the back of her neck and arms stood on end.

She opened her eyes and saw Zora on her hands and knees bowing, greeting something. Etta moved as close to the rope circle as she dared.

"Great one," Zora shrieked. "I am your humble servant. Your loves, beauty and dance, are present."

Her stomach clenched as she saw a gigantic gray cloud rise from the floor into the smaller circle. Etta blinked rapidly and stared. *Zora's plan is really working!*

The gray cloud grew into a figure. Its scaly head was reptilian, its neck extended in the characteristic hood of a king cobra. The rest of the spirit's body remained shadowy, human-like.

"So many have forgotten me," the First Serpent grunted.

"I venerate you," Zora said.

The First Serpent turned its head toward Etta. "Very beautiful."

Etta's knees shook, and she could barely focus on keeping her body upright. The spirit's voice was deep and penetrating. *Just keep dancing!*

A rip in the very air around her popped her ears, and before Zora could say another word, the spirit had coiled itself around the writer.

Etta screamed and jumped toward the struggling Zora.

"Keep dancing!" Zora shouted.

Etta continued as the First Serpent's gaze locked onto her. She hopped on one foot and then the other, fear making her movements jerky and uncoordinated.

"Dancer!" it called.

"First Serpent, great one, she has not called—" Zora began and then stopped, as the air rushed out of her. She closed her eyes, still struggling feebly, a wheezing noise coming from her open mouth. Then all motion ceased. The spirit released Zora's limp body.

"A strong vessel she is, Dancer," the First Serpent said, flicking its tongue at Etta.

"Zora!" Etta called.

"I remember when humans danced for me all the time. You remind me of one of my favorite dancers from eons ago."

Zora's eyes were still closed, and Etta wasn't sure if she should talk to the spirit.

"Gr...Great Serpent," she began, her tongue trembling. "Great First Serpent, I am nothing. Zora knows everything." *Shut up, Etta!*

The First Serpent gurgled a noise that sounded to Etta like a laugh.

"What troubles you, Dancer?"

Her mind ran through every dance step she knew or had invented. Her body responded, she arched and whirled as never before.

The circle felt stifling, and no matter where she moved, it was as if invisible flames licked at the bottoms of her feet.

"Dancer, I have been long away from humanity. What troubles you?"

"I...I..."

"Answer!" the First Serpent bellowed.

Etta trembled, but unable to resist the power of the spirit, she began talking about the Cotton Club, about Laney, about the pink walrus, about Albert. About her life in great detail. More words rushed out of her as she talked about how she worried for the twins, how much they meant to her. The First Serpent seemed to sop up her anger, her indignation, and her dissatisfaction. The more she talked, the freer she felt.

The First Serpent said little as she talked and hopped around, breathless.

"Etta, stop talking!" Zora was awake and unsteadily rising to a sitting position, a look of panic on her face. She got to her feet. "I banish you! I send you back to your dead place."

"Zora?" Etta started.

"Quiet!" Zora said, holding out her palm, her face taut, eyes focused, jaws gritted under the attractive high cheekbones.

The entire room shook, and Etta almost lost her footing.

"Doors once opened, Conjurer, do not close so easily," the spirit said.

Zora locked eyes with the First Serpent and shouted a flurry of commands in a strange guttural language, rapidly opening and closing her hands, shaping her fingers into gestures and at such angles that Etta had never seen before and not thought physically possible. That looks like it hurts, she thought.

The First Serpent's chest expanded to twice its size, and the creature hissed. The sound started low but grew to an ear-splitting shriek causing Etta to cover her ears. Zora's concentration remained unbroken though her body shook.

After a tug of wills, the First Serpent's presence slowly dissipated.

Etta realized she was still dancing and abruptly stopped.

Zora picked up a white handkerchief and wiped the sweat from Etta's face. With her knees cracking on the way down, she lay on the floor, and motioned for Etta to sit.

"What happened to you?" Etta asked.

Zora looked at the ceiling and let out a long sigh. "The spirit was too strong for me. I fainted or maybe was in a trance. That's never happened before."

"Well, great," Etta snapped. "I didn't know what was going on with you, so I talked to it."

"How long were you talking to it? How long before I came to?" Zora said, rising onto her elbows.

"I don't know," Etta shrugged. "It was hard to stop. Maybe I was in a trance, too?"

"You just needed to dance."

"Oh, don't be angry with me," Etta said, fighting tears.

"Did it ask you questions?" Zora said.

Etta nodded and told her everything. Zora shook her head. She stood and said, "I need to open the circle. Stay put."

Etta hugged her knees to her chest.

Zora said a prayer, and boomed, "We ask for the protection of our ancestors and for any invited spirits to return to their realm. Thank you elements of Fire, Water, Air and Earth."

Etta rose and they stepped over the circle.

Zora hushed Etta as she rushed to grab a green leather diary on a nearby table. She scribbled nonstop for a few minutes.

When finished, Zora said, "You know what I thought as I came to?"

Etta shook her head.

"That it was probably the wrong spirit to contact."

Now you tell me!

"Okay, here's what we are going to do, I'm going to give you some things to protect yourself." She opened a cabinet and started pulling down small bottles of liquids and pouches of herbs.

"Protect myself?"

"The First Serpent showed interest in you. Way too much interest."

"What does that mean?" Etta said, sitting down on a chair. She put her hands on her face. She thought she would have felt accomplished in helping Zora. Instead, she felt a deep coldness spreading inside her, she had let Zora down. And, she couldn't even remember if she had asked the spirit for a favor for the twins.

"I want you to take these things and use them as I say, and I want you to cover any mirrors in your apartment." Zora dug out some sheets of paper and began writing.

"All I did was dance and a little bit of talking. I didn't even ask for a favor."

Zora sighed. "It's okay. It's my fault. The spirits are tricky, and I thought I researched that one quite well."

"You were wrong about it," Etta said, her nerves so frayed she felt as if she couldn't stop shaking.

"I know, I know, Etta. I'm sorry." Zora opened a sugar canister and pulled out some money. "It's not much, but this is for you," she said, tucking several ten-dollar bills in one of the herb-filled pouches.

"What about your storytelling? What about getting what you wanted?" Etta asked, taking the items Zora offered.

Zora shook her head and pointed to a small desk where a typewriter sat. "I'll find another path to get at my stories."

A flush of anger raced through Etta. "You tricked me!"

Zora's eyes flashed. "You're upset. It's a lot to see a spirit summoned."

Etta felt as if her life were folding up around her. *Why did I ever trust Zora?* "You got something for yourself, though, didn't you? You so smart, you figured out something, something I didn't see! What did you write down?"

Zora folded her arms. "Stop talking nonsense, girl."

Shaking her head, Etta didn't know what to believe. "City folk all alike, everyone got an angle."

Zora's eyebrows gathered together, and she sighed. "That's not true of me. I got ahead of myself, is all."

"Liar. You were never planning on helping me with dance or anything else, right?" Etta said, unable to hold her tongue. Zora's pained expression gave Etta a momentary pang of satisfaction as she made her way toward the door.

Etta walked home, feeling the weight of Zora's items in her pockets, looking over her shoulder at each sound, flinching at each shadow. She couldn't help feeling that Zora was hiding something from her. But why would she do that? She should never have listened to Zora. She should never have ignored the little voice in her head, the wisdom of her youth: *you don't mess with spirits.*

✆

After the visitation, Etta's week dragged on. The memory of the encounter became increasingly dreamlike. Life had not changed for the better, and Etta felt silly ever thinking that it would. What troubled her most and made her heart hurt was that the twins had stopped showing up to work. No one knew where they lived, and within a few days, they were replaced by two new dancers. It seemed like she was the only one who missed them. Who remembered them? It made Etta shudder to think that the cold city had swallowed up the twins and spat them out somewhere else.

In a few days, Etta's anger at Zora had cooled. She missed seeing her and feeling some connection to home and another life. On several nights, she walked over to the diner to try and catch Zora there. Each time, the waitress said that Zora hadn't been there. The waitress noted how unusual it was for Zora to be away so long. She added, "I hope she puts me in one of her stories someday. Wouldn't that be something?"

Etta nodded politely.

With an hour to spare before work, she made her way to Zora's apartment. She knocked several times, but Zora did not answer.

Pressing her ear to the door, Etta could hear Zora's typewriter, a steady sound of clacking.

"Zora, please let me in."

The quiet hall closed in around Etta. Worry pricked at her. Her clammy hands grabbed the doorknob and she gave it a strong turn. It opened.

She entered with care, surprised that Zora would leave the door unlocked. She walked through the long foyer and past the empty dining room.

The typewriter's continued clacking caught her attention. Etta's nose wrinkled as she registered a vinegary smell permeating the apartment.

"Zora?" she called.

A moan came from around the corner and Etta followed. Everything in the living room looked rearranged from her last visit. Zora's table with her typewriter and pile of books was in the middle of the room. Zora sat with her back to Etta, her hands moving rapidly. Her usually carefully styled hair hung limp and looked like she hadn't attended to it in days.

"Zora!" Etta exclaimed, as she reached the other woman. She placed a hand on Zora's shoulder and all but reeled at Zora's musky smell. "I need to talk to you."

Zora didn't move or respond to Etta's touch. Etta came around the table, and her throat tightened. Her heart raced.

Zora's eyes stared straight ahead, her lips pulled in a thin line, rigid. It was a shell of a face, a mask. The only trace of softness was the shimmer of tears in her big brown eyes.

Etta watched, as Zora's hands flew over them. They struck the keys with an unnatural ferocity. She hit the carriage repeatedly. As soon as she came to the end of a sheet, she loaded a fresh sheet, her movements mechanical, automatic, and began again. Only Zora was typing, but the clacking sound bounced everywhere, making it seem as if there were ten typists in the room. It was maddening.

"What's wrong with you?" Etta said, gritting her teeth and grabbing the woman's shoulders again. She shook Zora, but Zora continued typing. She grabbed Zora's hands and received a stinging shock.

Etta cried out, releasing Zora, almost losing her balance. Despite everything, Zora had meant something to her and she hated to see her in this state.

Etta stood there not knowing what to do.

Zora's eyes focused on Etta and she muttered, "Not what I wanted. I was arrogant…Foolish. So sorry, Etta. Can't stop."

Tears formed in Etta's eyes. "What can I do?" she whispered.

Zora said, "It found a way—"

"Dancer," a voice said from behind her.

Etta spun around and flinched, her insides reeling.

The First Serpent stood in front of her, more man now than spirit. Average height, the man-spirit wore a heavy black coat. Etta noticed the olive hue of his skin and how his nose had developed from a slit to a short bridge with flattened nostrils. The iridescent sheen of snakeskin covered his bald head.

Backing away from him, she knocked into a sharp edge of Zora's table.

"Do not cry for her," he gestured with long tapered fingers. "She is getting her wish. She will now know so many tales that she'll never run out of things to write."

"She's not her," Etta choked out.

"No, not anymore," the First Serpent replied. With a slight nod, he continued. "She will always be my subject, but…" He paused. "She may return to herself after a time."

Etta turned and bolted.

∽

Heart thudding and out of breath, Etta said nothing to anyone when she arrived at the club. Gulping down a glass of water, she ruminated. Zora hadn't known what she was getting them into. Etta could see that now. She had put her faith in city people, and they were just people after all. She would call her grandmother tomorrow and confess. Maybe there was some way to help Zora. Yes, that was what she would do.

During the first show, she felt like the First Serpent was lurking unseen somewhere in the audience, watching her with unnatural desire, approving of her. Etta danced through the first number in a nervous daze. She fumbled through the second, almost missing her cue.

Backstage after the set, Delilah placed a hand on Etta's shoulder. "What's gotten into you? You've been jumpy all night," the older dancer said.

"Nothing," Etta murmured.

Between sets, the dancers massaged their legs, stretched, and talked. Etta stayed out of Laney's way, although tonight, Laney seemed to be in too good of a mood to bother anyone. She hummed a popular tune while brushing out her hair.

Delilah glanced over at Laney. "What's got you so happy?"

Laney smiled and put the brush down. "After the show, Stitt and me are going away for the weekend to his place in Connecticut." She pointed to a small brown bag sitting under her vanity table. "It's in the country and everything."

Delilah scrunched up her nose. "I can't believe that you are still messing with him."

Neither can I, Etta thought. A chill ran through her.

"He's come to his senses and has stopped toying around with little girls," she turned and shot Etta an icy look.

"You're a fool to believe that, Laney," Delilah said, shaking her head.

Disgusted, Etta looked down at her costume. She tugged on the buttons in the front of her sailor's outfit to make sure they were secure.

A knock on the door signaled that their break was over.

As Etta filed out with the other dancers, she heard a faint hissing sound. She froze, her mind going blank. Laney bumped into her and cursed. Laney's subsequent shove jolted Etta into the present.

Later that night and accompanied by a group of other dancers, Etta walked down Lenox Avenue, away from the Cotton Club. She saw Laney, wearing a tailored red coat that complemented her ample bust and showed off her tiny waist, get into a cab with the pink walrus. The cab, driven by a slender figure in a black coat, pulled away from the curb and into traffic.

As it passed, the cab driver glanced at her. Etta sucked in a half breath when the streetlight illuminated the driver's face. *No.* She couldn't have seen that: a face cloaked in unnatural shadow, a slit of a nose.

"Where are you going?" Delilah asked, as Etta quickened her pace then broke into a run.

"I need to see about something," she called over her shoulder.

The cab slowed, and she weaved through traffic to catch up to it, her ribs aching from the evening's demanding routines and this fresh exertion. Reaching the cab, she saw that someone had rolled the front window down. She peered inside.

"Good evening, Dancer," the First Serpent said.

Oh, no! "What are you doing?" she cried.

"Doing you a favor, for sure."

No, no, no! As icy terror scraped her insides, she ran to the back passenger door and attempted to yank it open. When it didn't budge, she pounded on the window.

Laney, rolled it down. "What do you want?" she demanded.

"Get out of the car. You have to get out of the car, now!" Etta said.

The pink walrus leaned toward Laney. "What's the meaning of this? Is she drunk?"

Car horns blared at her; she was holding up traffic. "Laney, look, I know we haven't gotten along, but get out of the car. Please, I didn't mean for—"

"She's always trying to take away my good. She's jealous." Recoiling from Etta, she turned to the pink walrus. "Will you fire her?"

"Right now?" the pink walrus asked.

"Yes," Laney hissed.

"Done," he said with a wave of his fat fingers. "I'll tell Albert on Monday. Roll up the window. Drive, cabbie."

Etta was still trying to open the passenger door when the cab sped away, almost taking her with it. Releasing the door handle, she tumbled to the street, and cars swerved by her.

"Etta!" Delilah called.

Etta stood, watching helplessly as the car raced through a red light. She turned away but heard the terrible pitch of the cab's screeching tires, the sound of shattering glass, and the metal scraping of two vehicles colliding.

Etta heard a cacophony of screams. Night goers and shopkeepers came out to look.

Her coat flying open, she rushed to the scene of the crash. A truck had hit the cab head-on. The driver's side of the car was crushed. Laney had burst through the windshield and was sprawled face-down on the hood. The cab's winged female hood ornament had pierced Laney's head. Blood streamed from her torn, once-beautiful body.

A long, mournful sound came from the other side of the cab. Etta's stomach twisted, and she dashed around the cab. The pink walrus lay on his back, halfway between the car and the ground, blood pouring from his nose. Etta reached him as his enormous body convulsed. His arms jerked up, as if to grab her, then his body sagged, and the light left his eyes.

Etta saw no one in what was once the front of the cab, but spied a long brown and beige discarded snake skin on the ground.

Turning away, she hugged herself as people rushed past her. Gulping big breaths, Etta, saw the image of Laney's punctured head, couldn't shake it.

Struggling to keep down her bile, she looked up and cried out as she saw the First Serpent approaching.

"Is this the way to greet your master, Dancer? Do you not appreciate my finesse in dispatching those loathsome humans? Should I receive nothing for my part in their demise?"

"I didn't want that!" Etta screamed, stumbling backward. She cowered as he neared. But when she felt his touch on her face, it was lighter than expected. Tender almost. The hand on her face moved lower, to her neck, and then rested lightly on her collarbone, his palm hot over her pounding heart. Her mind loathed his nearness, but her body, obeying his silent command, relaxed, and she leaned into his touch. As the First Serpent stepped back, she stumbled toward him, warmth spreading in her feet. They moved, tapping right and then left of their own volition.

Behind her, she heard Delilah calling her name. The sound of Delilah's voice grew faint as the First Serpent kept his small, tawny colored eyes fixed upon Etta.

A tingle meandered through her, an oily, silky feeling that began at the top of her head and slithered down her spine. In the night's haze, Etta's body jerked, crouched, and leapt. She couldn't control it. No matter how she tried to make her limbs obey her thoughts, they refused. Her body spun. It contorted in a manner that she knew it shouldn't. As she moved about, a feeling of perfection flooded her awareness, quelling her despair, connecting her to a thrill that she could only call divine. A leap and a twirl. She was on the best stage—a stage between worlds.

"And, now Dancer, you shall dance for me."

As her life's energy seeped from her body, each of her movements felt less artful and more puppet-like. Her conscious thoughts sank into a dark bog; she understood just how right her grandmother had been—spirits were nothing to fool with.

FAMILY LINE

YOU BARELY NOTICE YOUR MOTHER'S TEARS AND YOUR FATHER'S
solemn hug on the Amtrak platform as they release you into the
muggy night. You're the oldest cousin and they say it's time for
you to make this special trip. You overhear your mother say to your
father, "Maybe, it's been long enough now and everyone's forgotten,"
but you don't pay it any attention. You're looking good in black
jeans, wearing a gold belt that spells Nate. You're eager to get out
of here as you've had one too many close calls with guys much
tougher than you, even though your younger cousins Violetta, Corey,
and Little Tate are as interesting as a drawer of socks. You've only
met them once at a family reunion, their drawl and talk of porch
sitting made little impression on you. You will call them "Bamas"
as a matter of course. You're a sixteen-year-old Bronx boy about to
visit your backwards cousins in North Carolina for the first time.
A familiar twitchy feeling of restlessness runs through you like a
racehorse that's been held at the gate too long.

⚭

You arrive and they love your wavy hair, your swagger, and your
tales about spraying graffiti all over the city. By two weeks later,

you've kissed all the hotties, rumbled with two guys, and seen all the snakes, raccoons, and trees that you can take. Just when you think you'll die of boredom, sitting on their grand wraparound porch, Little Tate taps you on the shoulder and says, "We got a book—a special book." A year younger than you, but much taller and meatier—linebacker ready, there's nothing little about him.

"This book is how Edward, one of our ancestors, got his freedom," Violetta chimes in with a dimpled smile. You peg her for slow because of her lisp and, although twelve, she's babyish, wearing her hair in a one-sided ponytail.

"Never heard of—" you begin to say.

"Yeah, he stole *Beasts and Spells from the Savage Lands* from his master's library and learned its secrets," Corey, Violetta's twin brother, interrupts, as he has been doing during your entire visit. A contrast to the steady mountain of Little Tate, Corey's jumpy, impatient, picking at scabs on his legs and arms when he's not running his mouth.

"Shut up, Corey," Violetta says.

"Edward was an OG, original gangster," Little Tate says, laughing.

You lean back in the chair and any lingering doubt about how stupid your cousins are vanishes. "Don't they teach you anything down here? Will you believe every dumb story you hear? Nobody ever earned their freedom with a book."

"Nate'd be afraid to see the book," Corey goads.

He's in your face now and you want to slap him. He's a bully even without Little Tate's girth and confidence.

"Cousin probably ain't never even been in the woods at night. That and the book make you run for the next train to New York," Corey says.

"Me, scared of a book?" You howl with laughter and the pink Kool-Aid that you've been drinking snorts out your nose. "You crazy? Hell, I tag trains in the middle of the night. What's some old book to me? At home, I've got men who'll shoot me as soon as look at me." For a moment, you remember the train yards, the petty fights, and the effort it takes to stay out of trouble.

Your cousins nod in unison and Little Tate looks satisfied, as if he just scored a field goal.

౦

With the challenge in the air, you and the pack of cousins trudge through their woods to see the slave shack where this book lives. You've never been to a slave shack, or any shack. Although it's getting dark and pinpricks rise along the back of your neck, you say nothing. You're tough. And besides, they're just fucking with you, right?

The walk is short and soon you spy a building roughly framed and fashioned of uneven logs chinked with mud, roofed with tarred clapboards.

"Edward's shack was closest to the big house because he tended to the master," Little Tate says.

"Big house burned down a long time ago," Violetta adds as she opens the door.

Your eyes adjust as she lights two blue candles. Pitiful place. Not even the size of the smallest bathroom in your house. No furniture, just a mud floor, one window and musty rags moldering in crevices in the wall closest to you.

In the middle of the room an encyclopedia-sized, gilded, blue book sits open on a rotted log.

You're not surprised that a book is here, but you are impressed with its size. "So you put this book here? Just for me, huh? Probably got this from some used bookstore before I got here," you say.

"This is where the book stays," Corey says, leaning down and brushing his fingertips across it.

"It's been in the family *forever*," Violetta says and she also bends down to touch the book. Her fingers glide across the width of it. Smoothing her skirt with care, she makes a place for herself on the log.

"Never heard about it…besides, slaves down here weren't taught to read," you say.

"Edward's master collected rare books and some slaves here could read and our Edward could read some," Corey answers you and gives a nod to his brother.

"Ever think about what you might do if you were a slave?" Little Tate asks.

Of course you've thought about this before, had conversations with friends. It felt different then, in school with lots of people around and tall buildings everywhere. Here in this smelly old shack, their questions claw into your stomach. You know you're in the heart of something terrible that went down, book or no book. For a moment, you finger your name belt and imagine everything about you stripped away and extinguished. A momentary panic shoots through you like when you're running on the train tracks and it's dark and you have to make sure not to touch the third rail. One touch of the rail and you'd be gone. "I'd run, escape." That's what a racehorse would do, you think.

"Please," Little Tate says, holding up a hand. "We all like to think we would've run. Some people did run, some people stayed—"

"Edward didn't do any of those things!" Corey shouts. He is standing so close that some of his spit lands on your arm.

Violetta looks to the book and back to you as if she is waiting for something. You think what a good actress she is because her mouth trembles some and she looks frightened.

Everybody pauses.

"Tell him," she says.

"Edward called a beast up and it did his bidding," Little Tate says.

"Oh brother," you mutter. These Bamas are so dramatic, you think.

Still, you lean in closer to the book trying to imagine your ancestor moving his mouth slowly over the words on the pages that looked like "Ye Olde English" —*betimes, shew, drync*. It reminds you of a recent class on Shakespeare and Chaucer. A class you liked. How did he do it, you wonder? How did he steal the book and when did he read it? Despite how ridiculous your cousins are being, a tiny bit of admiration for Edward snakes up inside you.

"At first the beast did," Violetta says, a nervous giggle and a belch escaping from her lips.

"What happened?" you ask. "Edward start getting greedy? Like the beast was some kind of genie?"

"No, he asked for small stuff—more cornmeal, a blanket, bowls," Little Tate says. Little Tate now bends down, just like his siblings did, and lingers on the pages of the book, turning some over. "He did *everything* Edward asked."

"Then Edward tried his hand at bigger things, like asking for the overseer to get sick," Corey adds. You notice Corey's chest puffs out with pride as he talks.

Swirling blue mist rises from the pages of the book. For real. You squat down and place your hand on the stump. Feels real. You squint, looking around for the gizmos, wires, cables, or machines that could produce this special effect. You were sweating when you walked in and now the air feels cool in the shack. They are better at this hoodoo trick than you thought.

"It promised him things," Violetta says.

You flinch when Corey roars, "The beast said it would kill the master!"

"But, he wanted something in return," Violetta continues.

"A sacrifice," Little Tate says rising.

"Poor Edward had a son, Nate. He was sixteen, too," Violetta whispers. She gets up and stands next to Corey, clasps his hand. She no longer seems so young. Corey and Violetta look united, purposeful. You wonder how long they have rehearsed this moment.

"I get it…This is where you're trying to scare the city kid!"

"No, that beast wanted the son. Edward gave him his son for us…so that we could be free. Edward started over again, a new man, with money and land. He did it for us," Corey says. Violetta reaches for his hand and he takes it and gives it a little shake.

They all point at you—eyes big and wide.

"You're the special one. The beast waits for one boy in every generation," Little Tate says. "One sacrifice."

A faint shape forms in the mist. Familiar...from field trips to museums. Dogs of Egypt. Anubis? Book of the Dead. Hermanubis. Half-man, half-jackal. It's the head of a large jackal, its muzzle a yellow and dull gray. Soon its white torso appears. Its presence fills the room. You stare at its pointed salmon-colored tongue, drooling saliva. What you see forming in the mist makes you doubt everything you know.

Violetta is the first to weep and shuts her eyes. She leans into Corey for a moment, "They never told us it was so big."

"Shut up!" Corey says through clenched teeth.

You rush headlong for the door and smack into the bulk of Little Tate.

With studied ease he turns you, holding you firmly under the neck and arm in a lock. Part of you wonders how many times he might have rehearsed this move. How long had he been preparing?

Straining, you push off the ground as to tip over your cousin, but it's like Little Tate has anticipated all possible moves. Your free arm reaches out, trying to grab any part of him. Little Tate's quick jab to your jaw makes you see stars.

"You're going do this right, Nate. We have to do this, just like our parents did."

"And those before them," Corey says.

And now you remember your mother's last embrace, holding on so tight like she was losing you forever. You remember the quiet stories at family gatherings of distant uncles and cousins, all dying young, drownings, car accidents, fires and disappearances—always in North Carolina.

"But...but, we've been free...are free," your dry mouth mumbles.

"Beast don't care," Corey says now with a self-assured laugh.

"Hey, hey…you can make a different choice," you say, straining against your cousin's grip, hearing the pleading in every word you utter.

"Who knows what'll happen if we don't offer someone up. What we'll lose?" Corey says with a shrug.

Little Tate's lips brush against your ear, "He's family; just like you," he whispers.

In the struggle, you start to wonder—what had you done with all that freedom you had, gathering up around you like champion racehorses in a pen?

Little Tate releases you back to the center of the room. As Corey's knife rams into the soft spot above your collarbone and you fall, you see no doubt in your cousin's eyes. You see a beast's shadow and the madness in your family's eyes.

The wound is deep and although your fingers grip the long knife and pull it out, you know it is over. You've seen this before on the streets, too many times.

Violetta yells, "We've got to get some of his blood, or they'll be mad. It's leaking out so fast."

"I know, I know," Corey says.

Little Tate bends down next to you and with trembling hands tries to unscrew the top of a small mason jar. The disc-shaped lid rolls away from him and next to you.

"Stupid!" Violetta calls out.

You turn your head away from your cousin's fumbling. You thought you might die along train tracks running from the police, or shot for your sneakers, or beaten by men who have nothing better to do. Lots of people die for stupid reasons. For less than this, you think. For less wisdom, for less freedom, for less than Edward's sacrifice. Your blood finds its way down your chest, to your stomach, and drips into the belt buckle. You clutch it. I am Nate. I am free now and will die free.

DOLL SEED

She stood in a brass doll stand on the window shelf in Mrs. Lovey's Irresistible Toys and Candy Store looking out on Eighth Avenue and 72nd Street. The casual passerby would have easily missed the momentary gleam in the doll's eyes. She awoke that day and named herself Chevella because that was the only word she could remember from the old language of the doll world. She didn't remember much of her life before; all she had now was the rubbery plastic odor of her, the mahogany sheen of her doll skin, and the intense yearning for love that yokes all doll forms to the human world.

A sharp voice pinched into her newly awakened mind.

"The new one's here. Finally. Your body's been sitting around *forever*. Didn't think anyone would come." The voice continued, "I'm Missy Ann No. 13. Little girls always come in and touch me. One time a *Negro* girl even tried."

Chevella could not yet fully use her new doll eyes, so she could only dimly see the other doll nearby. Standing twenty-two inches tall next to Chevella was Missy Ann No. 13. A cream-colored doll with cascading brown hair tied in ponytails held by thick red, white, and blue satin ribbons. Dressed for a picnic she was, with a crisp white shirt, navy skirt, and a straw hat clutched in her hand. A dainty picnic basket graced her side.

Missy Ann No. 13 added coyly, "I won't be here long, but stuck in *that* body, I bet *you* will."

"Be nice, *mon cheri*, or later I'll come and pull on your ponytails," another voice inside Chevella's head countered. "Welcome friend. I am Marie," Marie continued. Her voice had a light, musical quality.

"I am...Chevella," she said, testing out her dollmind voice.

"Yes. we shall talk now, and later you'll be introduced to the toys. They can't speak dollmind to dollmind like us."

And then she heard the voices of the other dolls in the toy store clamoring, raking across her awareness like a flock of hungry seagulls on a vast beach. They chattered about the card games they would play in the evening, how much they appealed to little girls, and how stupid the toys were.

As a thin ribbon of night enveloped the city block, a fluttery feeling in her stomach snapped her mind to attention. The forced stillness of her limbs faded away. Her scalp tingled and heat flushed her body. Now she awoke as a person would from a long nap. Her eyes took in everything. She stretched her fingers slowly and circled her wrists. Gaining confidence, she rolled from her feet onto her toes, holding onto the doll stand, feeling the exquisite coolness of the windowsill underneath her. Wrapping her arms around herself, she breathed into the hug, luxuriating in newly felt senses. Not only could she hear, smell, and see like during the day, but now she could taste, speak aloud, and move. Looking down, she ran her hand across the soft gingham dress (complete with a white handkerchief in a side pocket), white lace frilly socks, and black shoes. Her hands reached and felt for her straight ebony hair that hung down past her shoulders and complemented her well-formed head, dimpled cheeks, and wide-set eyes. When humans looked into Chevella's eyes, they would unconsciously register an alertness and curiosity that set her apart from other dolls.

Awake and alive. She had made it over from the doll world to the human one.

℃

The other dolls and toys gathered in the middle of the store as they did every night, enjoying their nightly rebirth as much as Chevella was enjoying hers. The Original Enchantment that binds the tongue and movement of all toys and dolls during the day fades away at night. And, away from human eyes, toys and dolls took on all the physical sensations of life. Lucienda, a white yarn doll with slate-colored buttons for eyes and pig-tailed golden yarn hair, waved her knotted hands at Chevella.

"Come down and join us, Chevella," she said.

Chevella turned, watching and listening, wanting to understand her new world. Her nerves pressed down into her stomach like tightly coiled springs ready to burst. Unsure of how to proceed, she fiddled with her handkerchief and took in the scene. The shelves on the far side of the store held large jars of candy: butterscotch, jellybeans, gumdrops, and lollipops. The smell of saltwater taffy, licorice, peanut brittle, and chocolate tickled her nose. A small fire engine truck's siren screech jarred her. She saw many toys gathered in the center, including stuffed giraffes, Jack-in-the-Boxes, plastic guns, and rubber balls. Nearby, Missy Ann No. 13 played with marbles.

She noticed several other Missy Anns dressed alike. In fact, she counted thirty-six Missy Anns! Missy Anns Nos. 1-15 were dressed as picnic goers, Nos. 16-25 were dressed in nightgowns and each possessed a pillow, and Missy Anns Nos. 26-36 were dressed as elaborate princesses with a chicory blue bodice, billowy white taffeta dress, white satin gloves, and matching blue slippers. Marie, an elegantly dressed doll with tight brunette curls (who also waved to her), and Lucienda stood out in the sea of giant Missy Anns.

Marie and Lucienda stacked lunch pails to help Chevella climb down from the window shelf. The fire engine drove up below her, startling her with his scratchy, yet strong voice. "Hey, Chevella, let us get to know you. I'm Sammy," the Fire Truck said. His enthusiastic greeting matched his outrageous candy-red color.

The chatter died down and soon all the dolls and toys focused on Chevella. During the introductions Missy Ann No. 28 said, "How is she going to *choose* a human?"

Missy Ann No. 36 nodded. "Yeah, I don't see how she is going to choose somebody. As dolls we *have* to choose humans with our doll seed—that is the law."

Chevella shrank back from the group and tried to gather her voice. Before she could respond, Missy Ann No.15 addressed the group:

"Does she even have a doll seed? Why did she come through here—to this store?" Missy Ann No. 15's head shook so hard while asking these questions, one pigtail ribbon slipped off.

Caruthers, a mint-colored unicorn, walked into the center of the circle, cleared his throat, and paused. By far the largest toy in the room, everyone drew back and the Missy Anns quieted. They clumped together, their soft red lips holding a collective girlish pout, yet Chevella noticed the flat coolness of their eyes.

"Leave our newest one be," Caruthers said. "We all come for a reason. She still might be able to choose somebody." Turning toward her, Chevella felt the reach of his wise golden-brown eyes all the way down to her toes. She stood straighter.

"Can you feel your doll seed?" he asked kindly.

"What is that?" Chevella asked.

"Only your most important thing," Missy Ann No.15 huffed.

"It's the one thing that keeps us from being a toy," Missy Ann No. 36 said, coming to lean against Missy Ann No. 15, adjusting her friend's ribbons.

Caruthers swung his head to look at the cluster of Missy Anns to the left of him, snorted and stamped his left foreleg before turning back to Chevella. "There are those among us who sow divisions as their pastime. The Wind Mother and Father of Offerings who sent us to tend to humans care for us all. They created us from the same elements that make up humans—air, earth, water, ether, and fire. Dolls have just a tiny bit more fire and ether than toys. Toys have more earth in them. Such small differences."

"We don't have to listen to a giant ass," Missy Ann No. 13 said. She turned, snapped her fingers, and most of the Missy Anns retreated to the other side of the room behind the counter.

"Good riddance," Sammy the Fire Truck said.

Chevella wanted to lean against Caruthers' sturdy frame and collapse. "I am a little weary," she said, feeling very stupid. She gripped the cloth in her pocket for comfort.

Marie moved to the center, dressed in the high couture of the eighteenth century: a pastel pink silk Josephine dress with a high waist and low bodice that fell to ankle length. Three small red feathers poked out of the bun in her hair. A perfectly round mole dotted the left side of her face and she held a small parasol. With a firm, gloved grip, she turned Chevella and guided her out of the circle.

"She just got here from the other side," Marie said in a stern, but kind voice. "Leave her be. Don't any of you remember what it was like?"

Chevella felt the stares of the remaining Missy Anns burning into her back, but the group's conversation sped on to discuss the day's radio shows. *I have no answer for them,* she thought. It was all still so new—the toys, doll-speaking, doll seeds, the smell of candy, the freedom of movement.

"Rest now," Marie said, gathering up her dress. She took one of Chevella's hands and they climbed the lunch pail stairway. With care, she eased Chevella back into her doll stand. "All will become clear later."

The next night Missy Ann No.13 pointed a finger at Chevella and said to the group, "She's not doing her choosing. We have to choose. Can't she feel her doll seed?" She looked around at the assembled group, dolls mostly in the front and toys in the back.

"I don't understand," Chevella said, her stomach lurching. During the day, hadn't she stared at many people? Didn't her hopes rise when a girl of about five with carrot-colored hair, clutching her mother's hand, came to the window gazing at her? But then the moment passed, and the mother tugged on the little girl and the crowd swallowed them. All day, near misses.

I should appeal to humans, Chevella thought. *I'm here, ready to choose and be chosen; ready to love.*

"Oh, how can she choose when she's a doll who looks like a Negro?" Missy Ann No.13 said throwing up her hands.

"She probably doesn't even have a doll seed," Missy Ann No. 22 said, lying on her stomach, absently doodling with a discarded crayon on a sheet of yellow construction paper. Under her breath she added, "She'll never get bought because she'll never be able to choose."

The princess Missy Anns halted their several games of checkers. They sat up, alert, nodding in unison with their fellow dolls.

"Take it back," Lucienda said, rocking from side to side and clenching her yarn hands.

"I'm only saying what I see," Missy Ann No. 22 said.

Sammy the Fire Truck's sharp bell (one of his many sounds), snapped like a whip as he rode around the circuit of the room.

Chevella closed her eyes for a moment and rubbed her head.

"Now wait a minute. How would either of you busybodies know?" Sammy the Fire Truck said, flashing his headlights on Missy Ann No. 22 and No. 13. "Chevella hasn't even *tried* yet..." he turned to face Chevella. "...have you?"

Before Chevella could answer, the Missy Anns rose like a well-ordered flock; they clapped their hands over their ears and chanted, "Horrible toy!"

"Stop it!" Marie said. She rushed to the center of the circle, pointing at Chevella with her parasol. "Listen to me. Dolls are special. We become the form and the shape given to us. We understand humans because we are like them, in looks and temperament. By night, we see, hear, taste, touch just like humans. We feel on the inside, too. We have doll seeds, that's our essence—that's why we can choose humans. We understand who they are and who they can become."

Lucienda added, "We can sometimes see their thoughts, too."

Marie nodded. "Yes, it's the extra ether, or star space, in us."

Questions raced through Chevella's mind. "Where's your doll seed?" she asked Marie.

"For every doll it is different. I feel mine on the inside of my cheek," Marie said.

"It could be anywhere in you, you just have to feel for it," Lucienda offered, her lively button eyes looking back at Chevella with tenderness.

As if holding court, Marie sermonized to the others, "See, I am French...that is what I know...croissants, the history of the..."

"...more like a common tart," one of the Missy Anns sniggered.

"...I have come to know everything French. Think about what you know, and what you feel deeply, Chevella. You will know things about humans, all humans."

"What do *they* know?" Chevella said in a whisper pointing to several of the Missy Anns who were off to the side of the circle having a spirited conversation about how they might feel when their paint flaked off, and their hair fell out.

"They know how to be silly little girls," Marie said, louder than Chevella's whisper.

Putting her crayon down, Missy Ann No. 22 drew up to her full height. "*We* are the most popular dolls of our day. Aren't we Missy Ann No. 5?"

"Personally, I'd like to run every one of—" Sammy the Fire Truck said.

"Don't," Marie said pointing her parasol at him. "They love it when they can divide us."

"Maybe Chevella can go home with Mrs. Lovey," Missy Ann No. 23 called out. She reclined on a chaise lounge supported by a pile of pillows taken from one of the giant dollhouses.

"She's got some strange ideas."

"They know what some little girls dream of," Lucienda said with a sad wistfulness. Chevella sensed Lucienda's yearning and the feeling of it settled into her heart.

"We can feel that we're *wanted*. We sell all the time," Missy Ann No. 23 jeered.

It's true. Chevella couldn't count how often Mrs. Lovey fussed with them. Or, how disappointed a girl would sound after her mother found out the cost of a Missy Ann and announced she just couldn't afford one of them. The sharp and penetrating cries of the girls' regret knotted up her stomach for hours.

"Negroes don't have any money to buy dolls or toys. Mr. Lovey says that all the time," Missy Ann No. 5 interjected and cocked her head to one side.

"He also said that Japan was going to win the Great War," Sammy the Fire Truck said.

"Shut up, toy," Missy Ann No. 13 snapped. "Why do you think you know what's best for dolls? No toy can choose a human like a doll can."

"Oh yeah? Dolls are so damn special cause of your dumb extra part. Toys have our own special connection with humans. We're not *that* different from you."

Chevella sucked in her breath as Sammy the Fire Truck backed up, revved his engine and careened toward Missy Ann No. 13. Her blue eyes widened, but she stood perfectly still with her big pale foot raised ready to crush him. He drove up, then used his brakes, stopping less than a quarter-inch away.

"Enough!" Marie shouted.

Missy Ann No. 13 nodded to the other dolls, lowered her foot, and walked away.

Defiant and proud, Chevella thought. *Not shrinking like me.* Looking around, she saw in the smugness of the Missy Anns' creamy faces how they wore their sense of being wanted like a knight's armor; strong, resistant, and durable.

After glaring at Sammy the Fire Truck, Marie resumed, "Your doll seed is what is given to you for the new world. It will develop sure and true. And, when it does, you will be able to choose. The doll seed draws us into perfect correspondence with humans. It's why we were created. We can choose many humans, many times, again and again."

"What happens if I don't have one? Or, if I can't choose?" Chevella asked, looking around the circle.

Shaking her head, Marie said, "No, *cheri*, that is impossible. You *must* have one."

"It is not impossible, Marie," Missy Ann No. 16 said, giving her a sidelong glance. She skipped up to the group. "Remember Miranda?" A sour, thin-lipped smile spread across her face. The accusatory question hung in the air, quieting the entire store.

Chevella shuddered. For a moment she considered crawling under Caruthers, who was snoring in the corner. Instead, she composed herself and asked, "Who's Miranda?"

"It is a sad story." Lucienda shook her head. "She—"

"She JUMPED DOLL," Missy Ann No. 31 said, laying a gloved hand over her heart.

"If you do not use the doll seed then you can't live. It is too painful for a doll to not find love and be loved. Miranda did not ever use her doll seed. She never chose. She jumped doll." Marie said.

"And went back to the old world?" Chevella asked.

Lucienda shrugged, "When dolls jump, who knows *where* they go."

"If a doll jumps, it's because no one wanted her and she couldn't make it on this side," Missy Ann No. 16 sneered. "Food for thought, eh, Chevella?"

"We don't know what made her jump doll," Marie said, sitting down on a nearby cushion. "But I think when we can't or won't choose, a void gets created on this side and we can tune into it. I've heard that when humans drive over a tall bridge, they sometimes wonder about what it might feel like to put one leg over the railing. What it might feel like to fall into the open sky. What it might feel like to surrender. We can feel like that, too, but because we are part of the Original Enchantment and connected to humans the feeling opens something else up from the other side."

"None of the Missy Anns have ever jumped doll. Never needed to," Missy Ann No. 16 said, folding her arms.

Just then a high neigh broke through the conversation. "Jumping doll is just that, Chevella—talk and legend." Caruthers stood and shook his white mane. "You concentrate on finding your doll seed and you'll please The Wind Mother and Father of Offerings."

"We've been talking of nothing but somber business tonight," Marie said, squeezing Chevella's hand. "Mrs. Lovey keeps the radio on during the day. If you listen to it, you'll learn the ways of humans and that will help trigger your doll seed."

❧

Chevella stood in the toy store for three months, morning through sunset, waiting and trying to push herself into the minds of humans. Marie and Lucienda gave her daily pointers up to the day they were bought. Marie chose a doll collector: an older woman in a tailored gray suit who was visiting her niece in the city. A gangly girl with black wavy hair and protruding teeth bought Lucienda. Lucienda chose her with ease. Chevella's sadness snaked through her whole body when she saw the child outside the store throw Lucienda up into the air and catch her, then snuggle her friend close.

She waited and tried to do as many of the Missy Anns had done, call humans (mothers, fathers, sons or daughters—it did not matter to her) to her being—choose them. Lucienda's parting words, in dollmind were, "You plant an image of yourself in them and your doll seed moves around, makes itself known…and you have someone. It's not hard. Just have patience, Chevella."

She spent hours searching for it. She scanned every part of her body, probing for the very essence of her like a surgeon looking for a tumor, listening for something to whisper back to her. Was it in her ear? In her tummy? Behind her nose? Her attempts to enter a human's mind were momentary tadpole-like extensions, barely breaking the surface of their thoughts. She floated about in the jittery flotsam of the person's conscious ideas with no real direction, unable to sink deeper.

Learning about humans went easier. She kept listening to Mrs. Lovey's radio. And she did learn of the times. The Korean War, the Mau Mau rebellion, and the kids who died a quiet polio death all fascinated her. She learned of human imagination and dreams, how they cheered when Rocky Marciano became world heavyweight champion after knocking out Jersey Joe Walcott, how Mrs. Lovey and her husband loved the hit song "Singin' in the Rain," how people couldn't tell if Elvis was a sinner or saint. Listening to the radio drowned out the taunts and mental static the Missy Anns emitted, a buzzing, malignant frequency.

One afternoon she noticed she had one white gentleman all to herself. He looked at her and she could feel him wanting to come in. She sensed he was thinking about a doll for his six-year-old polio-stricken daughter, a wheelchair user.

Yes, I can do this. I can choose him. Straining with the mental effort, she squeezed her insides and telescoped her mind outward, reaching for his.

Missy Ann No. 15 on the window shelf (she had replaced Missy Ann No.13) shouted in dollmind, "She's trying to get this man!" nearly breaking Chevella's concentration. Other Missy Anns whooped and collectively surged forward with group determination, reaching for him like an eagle hunting prey.

Don't! She pleaded. This was the fifth time they'd done this to her! She was pleasant to them and laughed at their inane jokes, but nothing helped since her other friends had left. Hurry, she told herself. She entered his mind, placing her doll image there. But shortly, as if she rested on a glass surface, her image faded. Some unconscious part of this human with watery blue eyes laughed at her, mocked her. She could feel his desire for a different doll. A doll of fairy tales, fantasy, and soft pink lips. A line of dolls that looked like his family.

She drifted. Tried to pull free from his mind, but how? Ugh, hadn't she asked Marie and Lucienda about this? She bumped through gray tunnels full of long yellowish tubs, the baths of his imagination and memories. But she tired quickly and soon his mind's eye began moving her again. She needed to get herself back.

Then she lay on her stomach, deposited by force, into one of these tubs. A see-through version of the man stood over her, in a silver-colored suit, peeing on her. A wave of human urine splattered onto her doll image. It felt as real as she did at night. The steady stream hit her back and she felt the weight of it soaking through her clothes. Straining, she drew her energy into her center to fight his mental vise. Pulling away from his thoughts with a final tug, she left his mind.

"She didn't get him," Missy Ann No. 15 announced.

"Maybe one day, Chevella," Missy Ann No. 11 said with the merest hint of sympathy.

Chevella, too stunned from the encounter, couldn't reply. Had they seen or felt what she felt? No, she realized, or they would be cackling right now. Would someone want to pee on any of the Missy Anns? she wondered. She drew into herself, tucking away the shame and confusion like a handkerchief into her being. She would never tell anyone what she had experienced.

Later that day, Mrs. Lovey worked on rearranging the items on Chevella's shelf. As usual, she talked while she worked.

"When is a nice Negro girl going to come in and get you? You're occupying some of my best shelf space." Mrs. Lovey shook her head and fiddled with the hem of Chevella's dress. "I'm going to have to sell you to my maid. Her niece would like you," The shopkeeper sighed, "But she'd never be able to afford you. Maybe I was wrong about this…about you."

Chevella simultaneously heard the disappointment in the woman's voice and the collective snickers of the Missy Anns.

Later, Chevella tried to let Sammy the Fire Truck's words comfort her.

"Do not cry too hard. *I* have been here a long time, too. My price is so high I will need a wealthy housewife to buy me," he said, punctuating his thoughts with a cheerful ring of his bell.

They sat behind one of the large dollhouses. She bent down and gave the truck a gentle pat. He did his best to console her after hearing her story and she appreciated him for it.

"Yes, Sammy," she said, not believing him at all.

⟲

On a bleak, gray winter afternoon, a Negro man approached the window and looked at Chevella. He pressed up close to the window, his breath catching in the December air and fanning out over the glass. Chevella took in his face: a generous mouth with a full lower lip, a sharp chin with a cleft, a flared nose, and a thin, perfectly groomed mustache. Below his prominent forehead were inviting, deep-set, brown eyes that reminded Chevella of a sunflower's soft furry center.

It was his eyes that made her heart leap. At first Chevella read his face as human-attractive, yet also sad and all wound up with hope for events of the future. But upon a closer look, she could feel, rather than see, a breeziness of personality that could burn the sadness off. Chevella then felt a sharp stabbing pain in the back of her left knee. It spread across the entire back of her knee, pulsating with a current of doll life. *My doll seed!* The throbbing created a rhythm in her body and the steadiness of it made it effortless to slip into his mind and peek at his thoughts.

"I have it! I have a doll seed! How do I use it?" she blurted out to the other dolls. "He's mine!" Chevella shouted, hearing the sharpness of her urgency.

"Go ahead, he's Negro," Missy Ann No. 15 said, then almost as an afterthought, muttered, "Like I would want him."

The comment pierced her, stripping away her momentary joy. Chevella hesitated, then lost her concentration and the man walked on into the cold city air. He receded into the throng of people. The pain in her knee quickly subsided.

She sat, not knowing what to make of Missy Ann No. 15's statement. It reminded her of the feeling of being peed on, a casual, primal act. She waited and wanted to ask someone, but who could she ask? Wasn't she supposed to try for Negroes, too? Is that what she knew? Did she know anything at all?

∾

After losing the man, Chevella became a sentinel, more determined than ever to find her potential human again. She wanted him to come back. Over several nights, she kept by Sammy the Fire Truck's side and under the protective and calming flank of Caruthers. She tucked away her anger and regrets and made quiet company.

One day, an hour before dawn, Chevella awoke to a hissing sound in her mind. Slowly the hissing subsided only to be replaced by an insistent humming of juuuu, juuuuum, juuuuuu jummmm. She saw that Missy Ann No. 15 wasn't in her stand.

"Chevella! Chevella! Chevella!" Their voices called out to her. The humming continued. "Juuuuuuu Jmmmm Juuuuuuuuum. Chevella."

"Missy Anns?" she called out.

She got down from her stand and watched for a moment. Most of the toys were preparing to settle back in their places for the morning. Some nodded to her as she passed by, others gave her a quizzical look.

She walked over to the farthest end of the store, kicking a loose butterscotch. The door to the basement was ajar. It led downstairs to the storeroom, a place that she had seen once months ago.

"Who's there? Missy Anns, are you down there?"

The only reply she got was the voices calling out to her.

"Stop it!" she said in her dollmind voice. She turned around to go back to the window, but their voices bugled inside her head. She pushed at the door. Chevella went down the large stairs slowly. She'd come to the edge of a stair, sit down, and then edge herself over it, jumping down to the next step. She tired by the fifth step. And still the humming persisted, growing stronger and stronger; she stopped and held on to a plank of wood between the railings. Determination urged her on, for a moment overriding the fear pooling inside her.

At the bottom of the stairs Chevella looked around, her breath labored. One the two overhead bulbs provided a dull light. In the middle of the storeroom, boxes of unopened toys, wooden pieces of an unassembled rocking horse, and newspaper stuffing surrounded her. Wads of twine resembling snakes lay along the floor, and a broom stood in the farthest end of the corner. A small heap covered with a bright peach colored cloth toward the back of the room caught her attention. The cloth had crooked letters in black paint spelling out her name. It covered...something. The something was talking.

"JUMMMMM," the collective voice said.

Slowly she approached the cloth, squeezing her handkerchief. A ring of mouse feces surrounded what was under the cloth.

"I know you're down here, Missy Anns!" she said, suddenly afraid of what sat under the cloth.

Chevella pulled back the cloth and felt her stomach clench from fear at the nightmarish sight before her. She stood transfixed by the figure of a large doll three times as large as the Missy Anns. The doll's head drooped to one side like overripe fruit, and what was left of its blonde hair looked like clumps of cooked spaghetti left to rot. Chevella forced herself to take in its face, which was smeared with black paint and had deep grooves under its eyes. The doll wore a faded dress the color of applesauce. Her dirty stockings were dotted with holes, and the big toe of the left shoeless foot poked obscenely through the stocking.

To be so near a doll, yet everything about it abandoned and gone caused Chevella to crouch and cover her face. Was this Miranda? For a moment, Chevella felt as if, like this poor doll, all her love would leak out of her, never used, never known.

Suddenly, bright light flooded the room, and then came the Missy Anns, running from every direction, forming a ring about her and shouting:

"JUMP DOLLLL JUMMMP DOLL JUMMP DOL JUMMMMMPPPPPPPPPP DOLLLL!"

The Missy Anns pecked at her, pinched her, pushed her, and bounced her around the circle.

"As a doll you are worthless!" Missy Ann No. 33 shouted.

"You don't belong here..." another voice said.

"Please, please, stop," Chevella cried. "Help! Help me!"

They chanted and whooped around her. They pushed! The doll crashed into her, causing her to fall on the wooden floor with a thud. The dead thing pinned her. Chevella writhed and screamed trying to get from under it.

Her dollmind grasped for the wild, sweet face of the man who came to the window. *If I get out, I will choose him. He will come and take me away.*

From what felt like far away, she heard Caruthers demand, "What is this madness?"

His voice boomed from the top of the steps, calling on the Missy Anns to stop. A moment later Chevella felt a soft mouth carefully hold her leg and pull her from under the dead doll.

One of the Giraffes nuzzled her face. Caruthers continued to scold the Missy Anns. Chevella held the face of a Giraffe close, holding on to the furry knobs on either side of his head, feeling herself shake uncontrollably. The Missy Anns retreated like muttering vultures, cheated of their feast.

༝

Daybreak approached as all scrambled to get back to their proper places. The toys did a good job of cleaning Chevella up, though a speck of paint remained on her right palm that they could not remove. The Missy Anns stayed quiet, but their silence radiated an oily, palpable displeasure, making the air feel thick and sticky.

They knew they outnumbered the toys by three to one. As the Original Enchantment crept over her limbs, Chevella could still smell the places where the mouse feces touched her skin. Chevella vowed to turn her outrage into fresh determination. She would leave the store! The man would save her, she knew it.

When the Negro man came again later that afternoon her heart jumped. She locked him into her gaze; he would not escape this time. The doll seed popped twice behind her knee. She wished she could reach down and rub it, but she concentrated all the harder on him. Putting her in his mind, she saw him surrounded by different children—his present, she assumed. This picture stroked anticipation and a feeling new to Chevella—giddiness—washed over her.

After a moment, he came in, sauntering through the glass doors. He waited patiently in front of the store.

After finishing with a female customer, Mrs. Lovey looked up and said, "Yes, may I help you?"

"Yes Ma'am," the man said with warmth, "Mighty fine store you have here."

"Thank you, we've been here for many years."

"Uh-huh, my wife has passed by here several times. She loves your displays," he replied. "I'd like the doll up in the window...the Negro doll, please."

Good riddance! Missy Ann No. 15 shrieked.

Chevella ignored her. Nothing any of the Missy Anns could do was going to spoil her moment. In fact, giddiness bubbled up as she realized she would never see the Missy Anns again.

When Chevella heard the register ching ching and Mrs. Lovey wrapped her in tissue paper, she was sure that some adorable girl like the man, all sad smiles and breeziness, awaited her.

As they approached the black car, the man chatted with Chevella. The sun came through the clouds and Chevella felt as if it smiled for her.

"Oh now, honey, what's your name? The lady in the store never told me. Well, sit back, and enjoy the ride," he said, sliding her in the back seat, removing the paper, and bending her so that she could sit up. "There you go."

He opened the driver's door, slipped in, and, looking in the rearview mirror, said, "I'm Benny. You sure are one very *lucky* lady. We're going to meet Mr. Kenneth Clarke. You have got to play your part. We all play our parts. Yes, indeed."

Chevella listened but her attention was drawn to the bustling life on the streets. So many people!

"—I'm just a peon, a graduate student that is, but one day I'm going to do what Dr. Clarke is doing." Benny looked back at her in the rearview mirror again, laughing.

"Yes, in just a few more years, things are going to be real different. Change is blowing strong through all of us. Indeed."

Small piles of letters, journals, and magazines addressed to a Benny Harwood at the New York University, Department of Psychology, lay on the seat beside her. *Benny. My Benny.*

His car smelled of cigars and hibiscus and jasmine, the kinds of flowers Mrs. Lovey sometimes kept in the store. The smooth ride gave her mind the freedom to wander back to the incident of the previous night. It doesn't matter, she told herself. *I can choose.*

Yes, and oh yes, how she would be the envy of all in that little store. She would soon be held in the arms of children with their love, kindness, lollipops, and playground wisdom. Chevella daydreamed on. She rode with Benny, the man who bought her, who saved her, whom she chose. She rode along ready to start her new life; the only regret that stood on her heart was not being able to say a proper goodbye to Sammy the Fire Truck and Caruthers.

Later that night when Chevella could move, she slid herself carefully from the hotel nightstand where Benny had sat her and made her way over to his bed. She had waited for so long for this moment, heard so much about it from other dolls, and here it was. The snuggle time! Close-up, she sat next to Benny and looked at him. Her Benny. She put her ear close to his heart and relaxed into the rhythm of his life. She curled herself around his arm. It would be hard to tear herself away at dawn.

ᦏ

1953

The little Negro girl standing in front of Chevella had two thick braids on each side of her head and wore a stained green jumper. She stared at Chevella for a moment and then went over to Emma and pointed at her. Without hesitation, the girl pointed to Emma and said in her clear, six-year-old voice, "That's who I want, Dr. Clarke. This doll."

"Very good," Dr. Clarke said from across the room in his throaty rich voice. Dr. Clarke was a well-groomed Negro man of about forty with an even complexion and a smattering of various sized dark moles scattered across his face. He made a mark on the thick sheets of paper stuffed into his clipboard.

Again, Chevella thought, spirals of rage rippling through her. It had happened again. How many times, she wondered, would this scene repeat? She sat in the makeshift "laboratory" of Dr. Kenneth Clarke and Benny—his graduate assistant. This "laboratory" was really a hot schoolhouse in Charleston, South Carolina.

For the last year she had sat with Emma, a mostly silent doll with dull, tawny colored hair and a milky complexion, and watched as little Black and white girls and boys tried to answer a set of questions developed and delivered by Benny and Dr. Clarke: Which doll is prettier? Which doll looks cleaner? Which doll would you want to take home with you if you could?

Interested at first in what Benny, her chosen, wanted, she went along with the psychology experiment—whatever that was, giving it her best. She thought that if she complied, she'd be free. She did not want to choose again, she wanted to please Benny. She kept trying to choose the Black child, thinking that would make him happy, but that exercise yielded no special attention or tenderness from Benny. So, with effort, she began to block the Black children and try not to choose them and that seemed to make Benny and Dr. Clarke happy. Then she aimed for the white children.

One day it occurred to her that Benny seemed happy if she could choose no one and if no one chose her! Her doll seed ached from trying to choose and he had no idea about her pain.

Frustration ran through her as she let the memories flood in. Anytime a Black child did pick her, which was rare, Benny and Dr. Clarke would make a pained face and shake their heads, scratching their marks down with care. She was fixing Benny now, wasn't she? She had stopped choosing anyone. On strike now, she refused to probe the kids' minds one bit. Not even one bit! She sat and watched them all pass by her. It had meant day after day of blankness, the moments running into days, days running into weeks; all her joy and love shriveling up. And she always felt so tired. Too tired to try to snuggle with Benny, impossible most nights because she was usually with Emma in the car's trunk.

She looked at Benny as he escorted the child out of the class-room. *Traitor.*

꩜

Benny sat on the edge of an old school desk, shuffling through papers. Dr. Clarke poured himself a cup of coffee from his thermos.

"Kids are hard work, Dr. Clarke."

"I know," the older man said, nodding. "You have been doing a fine job. How's Carolyn holding up?"

"Oh, the traveling has been hard on her, but thank goodness we're staying with some of her folks here in town."

"Glad she could come and visit with you, on this leg of the trip, and that she's got family here," Dr. Clarke said, taking a sip of his coffee.

"But they don't understand what I'm doing with you," Benny said, excitement strumming his voice higher. Chevella noticed how after a long day with kids or traveling and setting up, Benny liked to "stretch his thoughts" with Dr. Clarke. Dr. Clarke struck her as a good listener and most reflective at the end of the day.

Bored, she reached out to Emma in dollmind.

Emma. Want to talk?

Emma stayed silent. She was hardly a companion these days.

"Her people think we're just trying to stir up trouble. They think because we're trying to show how detrimental racism is, we're saying that whites are somehow better. That we want to be white—that white schools are better. Dinner time's different now. Oh, we argue about it all the time. Older folks can be," Benny hesitated. "Sorry sir...no disrespect."

"None taken, son," Dr. Clarke waved him on, Chevella thought, encouraging his ideas.

"I try to tell them what a free and open society might look like. The fact that children consistently choose that white doll," he said, pointing to Emma. "Means something."

Dr. Clarke took his glasses off and rubbed his eyes.

Nothing to say. Emma finally answered. *Dumb men.*

I don't think they're dumb. Chevella's thoughts drifted to the differences between humans and dolls that her travels gave her time to think on.

It's the small lick of fire in us that makes us so like them, Emma. We are like them at night. We feel and move, but our bodies don't bleed or get hurt in the same way. The fire element in their bodies pumps their blood and gives them passion. But when things aren't right among them, we feel that, too. Benny's reaching for something better—

And it ain't you. Dumb men with too much fire.

Chevella sighed and wished for the company of her old friends from Mrs. Lovey's store.

"Old ideas will never get this country out of the mess we're in, Benny," Dr. Clarke said.

"That's true, sir."

Dr. Clark cocked his head and nodded as if he was ready to move on to another subject.

He paused then said, "Well, Benny, I've been holding out on you. I have some great news. It should make you feel a whole lot better. This morning I had a conversation with Thurgood."

"Yes," Benny said, raising his eyebrows.

Why do you think we're tired all the time? Dumb men. Emma said. *They have their reasons.*

Trying to make us choose over and over again. It's wrong.

"I didn't want to tell you until we were finished for the day." Dr. Clarke leaned over and grabbed Benny's shoulders. "Thurgood and his men want to use our work with the set of desegregation cases coming up before the Supreme Court."

Benny's mouth quivered. He let out a shout, then self-consciously looked around the empty schoolhouse. "I don't believe it. Your work will be famous."

"If they win son, and there's no guarantee in that," Dr. Clarke said. "But I would like to buy you a drink before we each go our separate ways tonight. A friend from Howard told me about a place not far from here."

"You're on. I can call and let Carolyn know I'll be late."

They talked on about the implications of this development as they packed up the dolls, stray papers, and books in a big suitcase. Their voices raised and lowered, and they laughed, too. They locked the suitcase with the dolls in Dr. Clarke's car and left to celebrate.

Emma and Chevella listened as the men's voices trailed off into the sticky South Carolina air.

"All this going to be over soon, better enjoy it while you can," Emma said.

"Maybe it's a good thing. Supreme Court. What does that mean?" Chevella asked.

"Doubt it. Dumb men," Emma said with a grunt.

Chevella trusted that Emma knew of what she spoke—Emma had been the second white replacement doll for this experiment. Chevella wondered what this change meant for her. *Benny is mine.* She knew Benny's smile and his moods. She knew Benny liked to eat his grits with ham, buttered rolls, and applesauce, if a diner had it on hand and if the diner served Negroes, which wasn't often in the South. She knew Benny talked a lot about the Klan, and how careful a driver he had become on Southern roads. She knew Benny loved his wife, even though she was barren. She knew how he tapped his feet when trying to decide on something important and how he sometimes held his breath when the children were choosing between her and Emma. And she came to know Georgia, North Carolina, South Carolina, Virginia, New York, and Washington, D.C. How could she not? And she came to know the schools of the South, the often dirty, rickety facilities with leaky roofs.

And, she also knew Benny never bothered anymore with her hair; her plain white dress was smudged from motor oil that he had forgotten to wipe off his hands somewhere between Ohio and Virginia, just like Emma's. Her hair was beginning to mat, just like Emma's. Chevella wished she could move and stamp about and shout. *How can I choose a good human when he wants me not to?* She still didn't understand the strange world of humans. She wished Marie or Lucienda were around to guide her.

When she looked at Benny's face, she no longer saw breeziness. Instead, she saw ambition, progress, and the eager desire to make his mark on history. Fire, fire, fire! Did he or Dr. Clarke really look at the children anymore? she wondered. They hadn't noticed the troublesome little white boy, with kind eyes, who had rubbed snot on her. He had picked her up, inspecting her. Up close, she heard his stomach growling. Had they heard? Did they care? She wanted to ask them, when this *case* (she thought that was the right word) goes to court and all is said and done, then will she and Emma be loved? Would she snuggle with him more? She loved Benny, but she longed to be with a child. Where was her child? Instead of a child companion, she had gotten speeches, theories, and the cold calculations of adult men.

ᘓ

1958

Chevella sat in Minnie's Resale Shop on an oak-lined street in a small town in West Virginia. No fancy doll stands or candy smells here. The patrons that came were down on their luck. How she missed Marie, Lucienda, and Sammy from the toy store, and even the occasional hesitant touches of the children in the experiment. Minnie, the proprietor, was friendly enough, but she didn't know a thing about how to make toys and dolls look good. Chevella was crammed in a small box of used toys, between a Jack-in-the-Box with a faulty spring, a small hand-built log cabin house with two logs missing, a stuffed rabbit, and a collection of battered toy soldiers. The toys were all friendly enough, but they were toys and she was a doll; she tried to keep her attention focused on her future, but her memories drew her back.

Benny, my Benny! I miss him. Since Benny's death in a suspicious car wreck in Missouri, Dr. Clarke abandoned her and Emma to a thrift store and left to continue his research up North. She had made up her mind: she would not make the same mistake again. She was not going to be betrayed again. She would choose differently and better this time. She would choose a child.

Today, several families milled about. There was a white woman of about thirty-five, squeezed into a long polka dot dress and black buttoned-down shirt, with her meaty feet forced into too-small shoes. At her side was Katherine Ann, her dark-haired eleven-year-old daughter. The mother and daughter pair strolled around the perimeter of the resale shop; the mother clasping her daughter's hand tightly. Katherine Ann's mother released her hand upon seeing a chenille bedspread, and Katherine Ann headed toward the toys.

At the same time, Denice, a Black girl of about nine with a bottom tooth missing and a smell of peaches, spotted Chevella. She picked her up and was about to run to her grandmother when she paused.

Chevella's doll seed popped and she momentarily reveled in the forgotten sensation, but with all her will she ignored the tug toward Denice and fixed her attention instead on the white girl coming toward her. She tossed and turned in Katherine Ann's mind, finally feeling the freedom of a child's imagination; here was wonder and possibility. Yet part of Chevella's attention was drawn back to the Black girl's kind eyes. Pulling away from the other girl for a moment, she zoomed into Denice's inner space, feeling deep pools of gentleness—this girl talked to flowers and made daisy bracelets for her friends.

No, she thought, she wasn't going to make the same mistake again. She was not going to be betrayed again. Negroes have problems. *I don't want you, go away*, Chevella thought. *Too much trouble you'll be.* She pushed out of the girl's mind. For a moment, Denice looked befuddled, and shook her head, but Chevella continued focusing all her effort on Katherine Ann.

It felt different. Benny was gone. Maybe her doll seed was broken. It always ached and it hadn't worked right since.

For a moment more Denice absently played with Chevella's hair, then dropped her back into the box, as if given an electric shock.

Katherine Ann arrived at the box of toys and reached for Chevella. Katherine Ann brought Chevella close. They carefully studied each other.

"Katherine Ann? I'm ready to go," her mother called.

"Over here, Mama," the girl replied.

Pride washed over Chevella; she would not be alone for long. *I have chosen.*

"Mama, I want this doll," Katherine Ann said matter-of-factly.

At first a look of disbelief, then displeasure, flared over the plump woman's face.

"No. Put that thing down," she said in a tight, clipped voice.

"Mama, I *want* her. I think she's pretty. Please. You said I could have whatever I wanted from the sale bin. Remember?"

"Don't be simple, Katherine Ann," she hissed, snatching Chevella from her daughter. "She's colored."

"I know," the girl said, rolling her eyes. "But, she's the only doll here. I looked."

"Kids are hard to argue with," Minnie said, approaching the feuding mother and daughter.

The mother blushed as Katherine Ann promptly took the doll back.

"What if I make you a deal?" Minnie asked.

The mother glanced around and lowered her voice before asking, "What kind of deal?"

"Eleven dollars for the doll and the bedspread. If you're taking that bedspread, that is. How's that?" Minnie asked amiably, slightly rocking on her heels.

"Mama, please. You promised." Katherine Ann said and squeezed Chevella.

Chevella heard the wheezing ching of the register and a hand stuffed her in between the folds of the chenille bed spread. She felt safe.

✑

Cuddling with Katherine Ann the night before had Chevella in a good mood. Katherine Ann sauntered to school the next day with Chevella tucked in her bag. At recess, Katherine Ann and her friends gathered in the play yard and headed toward the only shade available and their usual spot—a bench under an old mulberry tree.

Sue, a blonde girl with buck teeth said, "My dad gave my brother and me our first allowance. I'm gonna save mine up for something I really want."

The girls began setting up their playthings: paper dolls, toys and tea sets. Chevella imagined they did this every day.

Katherine Ann casually pulled Chevella out of her bag and sat her up on the bench.

"Ewwwww…*What* is that?" Glenda, a red-haired girl cried, pointing.

Screwing up her face, Katherine Ann said, "It's a doll, stupid. Mama got it for me at the resale shop."

"It's ugly," Glenda replied, sticking out her tongue. Sue nodded.

"Don't say that," Katherine Ann said, blushing.

"Why your Mama got you a darkie doll?" Sue asked.

"Ewww," Glenda repeated.

Without waiting for a response, Sue shrieked: "She's got a darkie doll! Katherine Ann's got a darkie doll!"

"Does your mom like a house full of darkies?" Glenda said, and within a few moments her ranting solicited the attention of girls at the other end of the yard.

"Katherine Ann's got a darkie doll!" Glenda continued, varying her pitch, sometimes cooing, sometimes raising her voice.

"Stop being such a jerk. She looks better than anything else around here," Katherine Ann shouted.

Chevella agreed. Most of the toys, she noticed, looked down on their luck. Just like the kids.

Several of Katherine Ann's friends snickered and stared. Other girls joined in with Glenda's taunting and soon the whole schoolyard surrounded the little bench. Katherine Ann seemed not at all prepared to face a set of screaming kids, and while they shouted at her she bowed her head and traced her foot around a small hole her shoe dug in the ground.

Sue grabbed Chevella and threw her up in the air. While aloft Chevella remembered when she saw Lucienda thrown in the air by a child. *This has gone all wrong,* she thought.

"Give her to me!" Katherine Ann said. In a flash, Katherine Ann took hold of Sue's shoulders and began shaking her.

A pinch-faced woman, her hair held in a low bun with a pencil, broke up the group of shouting girls and confused boys.

"What's going on here?" she demanded as she got between the girls. "Are you all a bunch of ruffians? Little ladies don't scream and they surely don't pull on one another."

Sticking her chest out, Sue said, "Mrs. Richardson, Katherine Ann's got a darkie doll." Holding Chevella by her feet, as if handling a dirty diaper, Sue handed her to the teacher.

The teacher blinked, then looked at Katherine Ann and back down to Chevella. She pulled in her lips several times and shook her head.

"Is this your doll?" Mrs. Richardson asked in a tone that reminded Chevella of the Missy Anns.

"Yes," Katherine Ann said in a voice so low, Chevella could barely hear her.

"I see. Katherine Ann, start packing up your things. Your recess is suspended. Glenda, Sue, and Katherine Ann, you have detention today."

Glenda called out. "Why we got to get blamed?"

Mrs. Richardson just looked at her. "Miss Taggert, are you up to questioning my authority today?"

"No Ma'am," Glenda said.

"Good, because for a moment I thought you were. This nonsense has already interrupted my lunch break, did you know that?"

"No, Ma'am," Glenda pouted. Chevella could hear some of the girl's bravado draining away.

"And that's enough for everyone," Mrs. Richardson said, addressing the group of staring children. "Go back to playing."

The girls packed up their things. Glenda and Sue headed to the school. Katherine Ann lagged behind. Mrs. Richardson stopped Katherine Ann. Holding Chevella at arms distance, she said, "This is not a doll you need, or one you should have."

"But, I..." Katherine Ann stammered.

The teacher's green eyes, which Chevella had initially thought looked warm and kind, flashed coolly when she added, "I'm sending a note home with you to your mother. A disturbance like this will go on your record." As Mrs. Richardson huffed off, she threw Chevella to the ground.

As the kids walked past her without making eye contact, Katherine Ann tentatively picked Chevella up out of a puddle of ice cream, lollipop wrappers, and leaves. The leaves were still green, but with a hint of yellow and orange brown, foretelling of the coming fall.

 ⑤

1968

Darkness enclosed Chevella. They had been working off and on in Katherine Ann's bedroom, she guessed, for the better part of an hour.

"I just don't know what I'm going to do. She was all I had," Chevella heard Katherine Ann's mother say.

"We are going to get you through this...step by step, Suze. And God will help too," said Justine, a friend of the family.

"Can you do her clothes today, you think?" Justine asked.

"Yes, I'll try. Everything else we can tell the superintendent to get rid of."

"I'll go downstairs and get the rest of the boxes for Goodwill." Katherine Ann's mother approached the closet where Chevella sat in the corner of a shelf on top of a pile of clothes. She heard Suze's sobbing, but focused on her own trough of grief. Katherine Ann's overdose six days ago in this cramped, run-down flat on the Lower East Side of Manhattan, did not surprise Chevella. She thought about how the apartment contained the remnants of the two Katherine Anns: the creative, imaginative child and the rebellious woman. Half-finished sketches, oil paints, and used brushes sat against a wall in the living room, and whimsical fish were drawn on bedroom walls in blues and oranges. Remnants of the recent Katherine Ann were there, too: stolen cameras, silverware, and radios waiting to be traded for drugs, piles of smelly clothes, puke in the bathroom, and needles in every room.

After the school incident, Katherine Ann hid Chevella from her mother. After Katherine Ann moved to New York, she occasionally took Chevella out from the closet and talked to her about her art and dreams. Chevella used all that time to think.

I didn't choose right that day, Chevella thought. *I chose out of fear and ignored the goodness that had been in front of me—acting more like a human than a doll.* It was never a perfect fit between her and Katherine Ann, yet the girl had always showed kindness to Chevella. And Chevella felt grateful to have known a child—a troubled child, yes—but a child all the same.

Katherine Ann's mother muttered and squinted. She had been separating shoes and now, with effort, tried to match them up. It was a meaningless task, something to give her hands to do. Chevella understood.

"You take care of her, hear Lord? She was a good child, strange but good. She should have never come to this disgusting city." She rose, ready to tackle the top shelf of the closet. Chevella saw Suze's hand reach up and touch her leg. Grunting, she brought Chevella down along with some winter sweaters.

Seeing Chevella, she yelled, "You! How could she keep you?"

She threw the doll across the room.

Please, I loved your daughter. I chose her, probably for the wrong reasons then, but I still loved her.

"You ugly thing. Mess all started from the damn day I ever helped bring you home for her." Suze walked over to where Chevella lay crumpled, her dirty white dress up over her bruised body. With a howl, Suze picked up Chevella by her legs and smashed her against the wall.

Katherine Ann's mother clawed at Chevella, ripping the old, faded, stained white dress with ease. She pulled Chevella's arms off, threw them across the room.

"What is it? Suze, what are you doing?" Justine ran over and grabbed her friend's shoulders.

Shaking, the woman slumped incoherently to the floor. She pushed the doll in Justine's lap and said, "Get it out. Get it out."

Justine looked back and forth between Chevella and her friend. She grabbed a bag of trash, went outside around the back of the building, and threw both the bag and Chevella in a dumpster.

∽

It was finally dark. She had been in and out of waking for some time. She heard the rats first; they squealed and squeaked on their nightly prowl. It took her a moment to sit up and assess the damage. Both arms were gone, like her clothes, and she still had a sizeable hole above her thigh from a careless cigarette burn inflicted by one of Katherine Ann's roommates, years ago. She jerked her legs and examined her feet. They were eroding into nubs of rubber, most of the toes gone years ago.

Moving from under a bit of rotting cantaloupe, she listened. In the distance she heard voices talking. After a few falls, Chevella slid her way down from the heap of trash into the night air and slowly shuffled toward the voices.

Rounding a small bend of rubbish with tires piled high, she stopped. This close up, she heard the voices with clarity.

"Hello, up there. Who's there?" she boomed in the loudest voice she could muster.

"Be quiet, someone's here," a voice said.

She squinted in the night and waited.

"A doll, a doll. Hello, you up there. Are you a doll or a toy?" Chevella said.

"Toys and dolls, if you must know."

"More dolls than toys," another voice said.

"I'm coming up," Chevella said, pleased with the prospect of company. Without arms, however, she could not easily climb her way up through the debris. She fell on the same bent blender blade four times. After a slow attempt with little progress made over an hour, she resigned herself to shouting, "Hey can you come down? I can't get up there."

The long silence made her think that they had left.

"Later," a female voice said.

As the inky blackness of night thinned and gave way to dawn, she settled herself and waited. The next night she called to them again. She kicked over a rotting book and sat on the edge of it, waiting for the voices to come down.

"This better be worth the trip," she heard one voice say.

"Shut up and move your arm up some," another voice said.

Two figures descended the mountain. A baby boy doll carried a blue rubber ball, bigger than a tennis ball, but not by much. She saw that he was a well-constructed doll, with eyes that blinked.

Chevella gasped when she saw that his companion was a Missy Ann No. 17, though worn and without her pillow. Half of her face, a hideous storm of charred blacks and purples, revealed an empty eye socket and a gaping mouth. Her blue nightgown was cut, now functioning as a top that stopped at her stomach. In her arms she carried the head of another Missy Ann—Chevella couldn't tell which one. The Missy Ann's white, almost-bald head reflected the little light the sliver of moon offered.

"Well, look who it is!" Missy Ann No. 17 said. Her voice sounded deeper than Chevella remembered.

"Chevella," the head said.

Chevella could see that the years hadn't been kind to either of the Missy Anns. Etched into the face of the Missy Ann head without a body were deep black grooves over what were once delicately painted flaxen eyebrows.

Chevella's hopes for good company sank.

The baby boy doll put the ball down and it rolled to her.

"Hello. How did you come here?" the ball asked.

"Someone threw you in the trash, didn't they?" Missy Ann No. 17 said.

"It's not true," she started and then stopped herself. It was true. Turning her attention to the baby boy doll and the ball she said, "I'm Chevella. What's your name?"

"I'm Edward and he's Star," the baby boy doll said.

Overcome by the absurd situation, she laughed. "We're the same now, toys and dolls, aren't we? There is no one to choose. Not now. Not here. We're all in the big human trash heap."

Pointing her finger, Missy Ann No. 17 stepped forward and said, "No! We were in a fire in a girl's house. Isn't that right Missy Ann No. 2?"

The bodiless doll cocked her head to the side, "Someone will always want us. We can be cleaned up and restored. No one will ever want you. You're even uglier than before. Much uglier."

Star the Ball rolled back to them. "How unkind."

"Shut up, toy," the Missy Ann head said.

"Yes, you wait and see. Sometimes humans come by this dump to scavenge," Missy Ann No. 2 continued.

Star bounced himself up and into Edward's arms. Edward said, "We're going to watch the pigeons near the gutted pickup truck. Do you want to come?"

DOLL SEED ∾ MICHELE TRACY BERGER

"No," Chevella said. Sitting down, a heavy weariness came over her. She knew they were right in a way. What chance did a dirty dark doll in a garbage dump have? What was left for her? For any of them? But if a doll seed can choose humans in life, she wondered, can dolls follow humans in their death? The vacant face of Miranda flashed in her mind. No, she wasn't like Miranda. Miranda had only known pain and coped as best she could for any doll. Chevella had loved. She had given her heart. And, she had been loved too, albeit briefly. Couldn't she know something? Neither Benny nor Katherine Ann died normal deaths, she thought. She ruminated on all that Marie had taught her about dolls and humans. Sitting there an idea hit her as if it floated to her on the wind.

She got up and shuffled. "Hey, Missy Anns!"

"What is it?" one called back.

"I want you to help me JUMP DOLL."

"What?" cried Missy Ann No. 2.

"She's lost what little sense she once possessed," Missy Ann No. 17 smirked.

Chevella, with her unsteady gait, approached them. "Can you do it?"

"I don't know…Why?" Missy Ann No. 2.

"Why do you care?" Chevella said.

"Of course we can," Missy Ann No. 17 interrupted. "We'll be glad to get rid of you."

Star rolled from around the heap toward the dolls, but Missy Ann No. 2 screamed. "Get out of here, toy!"

The Missy Anns' weak voices started the chant. Jummmmmm Jummmm Jump doll. JUMMMMM. At first all she could feel in the rhythm of the chant was a choking anger, heavy and python-like. Chevella struggled for breath. She let their sounds guide her down past the hurts, slights, and memories of mistreatment she held deep inside her.

"JUMMMMMMPPPPPPP JUMMMMP…"

Now the chanting felt different, as if each breath took her closer to what she believed could be true. She felt their every syllable swell in her like ripe fruit, filling her with potential.

Maybe she could follow humans from one place to the other. Maybe, somehow, dolls and humans were connected in the doll world? Humans called death the final resting place, but if they were chosen by a doll and loved, where did they really go? *What were dolls without humans? What were humans without dolls?* Maybe the Missy Anns were the ones afraid this time, she thought. Yes, in the vise-like dollmind frequency, she could feel their frenzy, their suffering from holding onto a place that was misery and pain even for them. Their world had shifted right under them. Did they know they couldn't cross over because of their fear, because they could not let go?

"JUMMMMPPPPPPPPPPPPPPPP!!!!!"

It started as if a fly landed on her arm. Then her body felt as if many flies were landing on her, walking and probing her body. She felt something gently pushing down on her remaining limbs. The noise of the dolls began to fade away. Her skin prickled up as she felt the darkness drawn to her, sticking to her, exploring her. Her skin drank in the pleasant sensations. The earth trembled; she lost her balance and fell onto her face. She rolled in the dirt and debris as the ground opened, as if being ripped apart by unseen hands. She slid eel-like down into the rip. In her last thought, she laughed: the Missy Anns were wrong, as usual. This moment felt like a homecoming.

She awoke on a riverbank and knew herself as Chevella. Her form was different now, less human-looking. She gazed at her gray spindly body and was reminded of giant mushrooms. Her mind latched on to Benny and Katherine Ann, the names she could remember from the human world. Other gray forms sat on the bank or stood near it. Rising, she saw the river was deep with memories—millions of memories bursting to the surface and retreating again. Every single moment of her life on the other side bubbled up. She doubled over and shuddered as déjà vu swept through her.

After some time, she turned away and looked around. *Others here must be seeing their lives, too.*

A form like her, but taller and even less human-looking approached. The white mycelial-like buds on its head extended and touched her face. "A jumper. Rare here."

Its face (a generous term in Chevella's opinion) was perfectly round, lineless and with an opening ringed by short tentacles.

"Where is here?" Chevella asked.

"The dream place of The Wind Mother and Father of Offerings."

"Do human souls pass through here?" she asked. She could feel the odd sensation of her "head" swelling as she spoke.

The slender stalks that were caressing her face retracted.

"No," it replied.

Chevella's body sagged to the ground. The ground felt damp and comforting.

"But," it continued, "Humans are made with the five elements."

"Yes," she said. Looking up at it, she blurted what she remembered, "Fire, ether, air, water, and earth."

"In this place, the Elements themselves can be called upon and asked to yoke together what once formed a human soul. When made, if it wants, the soul can stay here for a time." The form bobbed its head, "It is a weighty task."

"Show me," Chevella said.

And, the form did.

THE CURL OF EMMA JEAN

Jessa

Jessa knows that she is one signature away from freedom. She takes comfort in the fact that she will never have to tell her sister, Chelsea, the truth about her three-year-old daughter, Emma Jean. Hoping her sister will get to the point soon and talk about her inheritance, Jessa sits perched on the edge of the white wicker sectional, fidgeting and tapping the backs of her flip-flops against her heels. She sees none of the official papers she needs to sign. No lunch either, just some almonds in a red ceramic bowl. Her stomach gurgles. Where is Mr. Cartusciello, the family lawyer? Her intuition tells her something is amiss, but she squashes her concern. Wasn't it better to do this business sitting on her sister's patio than meeting in his office?

While she waits, Jessa mentally ticks off all the ways she's been good. No denying her at this annual "fitness" meeting, the last one she's obligated to attend by their father's will. Clean for three and a half years. Check. Gainfully employed. Check. Money saved (well, a teeny amount). Check. Community volunteer. You bet!

She does some deep breathing, feeling her ribs expand, belly going soft, and tries to read her sister's energy.

❦

Chelsea

Chelsea shakes her head and reaches a manicured hand for her wine spritzer. She knows that, despite everything, Jessa, her younger sister, seems to have enormous luck on her side. Jessa is taller and shapelier than her. Giving birth to Emma Jean in her mid-twenties has not done noticeable damage to Jessa's body. The only thing Jessa has ever produced that seemed truly perfect was Emma Jean. But now she knows the truth about her, too.

"It's too late to play games, can't you see that? You think you can keep cutting Emma Jean's hair and hide what she *is*," Chelsea says.

"Is? You're making her sound like a Martian. She's got a hair condition, that's what her pediatrician says, and I trust him. Kids her age get all sorts of things. When are we going to sign the papers?" Jessa says, fingering the strap of her blue and white, over-stuffed, cloth shoulder bag that sits in her lap, crammed with toys, children's books, and herbal tinctures.

Chelsea watches as her younger sister's round face cinches taut, a pinkish hint of discomfort growing across the milky complexion, reminding her of a radish. Jessa takes her index finger and taps the edge of her mouth. A flash of Jessa's tongue peeks through and then disappears. *Jessa tells a lie the same way, all the time with a tight smile and bulging eyes, just like when we were girls.*

Chelsea's been waiting for this moment, gathering evidence, biding her time. She's enjoying how disoriented Jessa appears to be. Jessa's unsteady gaze flicks up at the sky and then across to her daughter, Emma Jean, anywhere but at Chelsea.

Chelsea drinks in the mess that is Jessa, the worn green flip-flops, the tacky, pewter, cubic zirconia, oversized fairy earrings, the flouncy green skirt that hits mid-thigh, the lemon V-neck tank, and the multiple necklaces with small nodes of quartz, amethyst, and citrine hanging at their ends. Jessa told her she wears the necklaces for protection. She needs them since she's an energy healer now. From addict to energy healer, all in just a few years. *Right.*

⟲

Jessa

Her mind spins on how she will spend the money. The first thing she would do, of course, would be to move from her crappy apartment and as far away from Chelsea as possible. No more food stamps, that funny-colored money. No more squeezing out soap from public restrooms in little baggies. And she'd move her boat, The Explorer, sitting unused at the club for so long! She'd go sailing again and show Emma Jean so much.

Poor big sister, she thinks, looking at Chelsea. The early thirties weren't being kind to her at all; already squint lines and wrinkly eyelids covered by toad-skin-like bumps were noticeable. And the first signs of gray peeking out at the temples. And why does she always get so dressed up for their meetings? The pearls again. The predictable white and green sweater set, beige khakis, and green ballet flats with a golden buckle. So matchy-matchy! Jessa fakes a smile and tries to muster some compassion. After all, she knows that Chelsea's got a hole in her spirit. Yup, a shotgun leak in her heart chakra. Instead of energetically radiating what should look like pink streamers from the midpoint of her chest, Chelsea's center squeezes out meager squiggly lines, the color of chalk.

One of Jessa's spirit guides helped her see this deficiency in her sister after getting clean. Nothing could be done about it. "Free will," the spirit guide said.

She breathes again, feeling her sandals in contact with the earth. She shouldn't be thinking about Dad's money, exactly five million dollars. She knows she needs more spiritual work in this area. Her teachers (physical and nonphysical) have told her that. The guru she met through Marcus, her boss, said that one should feel neutral about money. For example, if a tree falls on your car and destroys it, you should have no disturbance in your energy field. But she knows her energy field is disturbed right now. Very disturbed. She has plans! She wanted to scream at that guru and throw her bag of veggie chips at him. Jumpy Mind had wanted to hurt that man. Jumpy Mind was one of her two voices, kind of like friends who never left you alone. Jumpy Mind had said, "Maybe where he was from—a hut in Thailand—money was nothing. NO THING. Maybe he had never shopped in Berlin or at Le Bon Marche." But she remembers her life before the addiction. She feels her face flushing, looks down, and tries to busy herself by adjusting Emma Jean's jumper, picking at nonexistent lint.

Peace Mind, her other voice, now reminds her that the rush of money and the rush of drugs feel similar.

It would be easier if I never had the taste of wonderful things, but I have, she thinks.

ᗡ

Chelsea

Opening move made, Chelsea savors the way her sister looks—vulnerable. The color of Jessa's top reminds her of a baby chick. Chelsea wants to squeeze the baby sister-chick as Jessa's chest slowly moves up and down. She runs through a partial list of the many stupid and embarrassing things her younger sister has done over the years—sleeping with Nestor, the sleazy El Salvadorian study abroad student; totaling every car their father gave her; developing a coke habit during high school and keeping it after; attending several colleges and leaving all without a degree. Having Emma Jean with no husband in sight. And ever since Jessa's recovery, her keeping company with people who swoon over colonics, raw juice diets, and "energy beings." *Jessa is always running into trash and letting it cling to her. I've been a pillar, holding her up, protecting her. No more.*

Emma Jean, on the opposite end of the sectional, makes a noise and sucks on her index finger. The sisters both turn to look at her, taking in her thin frame and enormous eyes, the color of ash mixed with a drop of turquoise. As usual, her head is a patchwork of barrettes holding down a dense thicket of hair the color of discarded twine, covering the many bald spots. *Emma Jean is always getting anything and everything stuck in that mass—leaves, twigs, staples, gum. It looks more like a midden with each passing day. Pitiful.*

In the distance a flock of geese flies by, their honks punctuating the late summer day. As if attuned to the natural way of things, Emma Jeans opens a hand and points her fingers toward them. "Birdies!"

"Yes, little mama, look at the birdies. All done with your puzzle?" Jessa says.

"No," Emma Jean says.

"I should have figured it out before. I should have seen this coming," Chelsea says moving forward, sitting beauty-queen straight. "How selfish you are."

⌀

Jessa

She fights to keep her composure. Jumpy Mind tells her to ignore the jab and reminds her how close she is to the MONEY. Peace Mind says to ignore the comment because Chelsea is clearly looking for a fight.

Jessa looks at her daughter and, for a moment, her heart thumps in her chest and tightens. She shouldn't have brought her. Chelsea has been looking at her like something foreign, strange, and expendable. She'd grown colder to her niece over the last year. Jessa hates that she doesn't even make enough to hire a decent sitter when she needs one.

She thinks about the secrets she's kept, and a shudder runs through her. No amount of crystals or energy training prepared her.

She knows she can't say that she wasn't warned. She was. *I knew what I wanted; I just didn't know the price.* When the doctors told her she was having trouble getting pregnant, she didn't want to take drugs or get fertility shots. She didn't want triplets or octuplets. She just wanted one healthy baby, to feel something growing inside her. After the addiction, she had wanted to make something beautiful, whole, and hers.

The doctors could find nothing wrong with her. Nothing. No blocked tubes, no hormonal problems, everything should have worked fine.

She decided to try what women have always tried—the old way. To get help from the other side. She knew that all Fairies, although interested in human cycles, especially birth, are fickle. Most spirits are. Her teachers, Marcus and especially Emily, stressed that to her over and over.

She began with the ones called *Keshalyi* who are associated with the Roma and are known for being awash in fertility. She saved her money and laid her table with tall glasses of milk, fruit brandies, and sweet sugar cookies. To a sincere petitioner, they are supposed to appear, sparkly and shimmery—like Tinkerbell. She petitioned them again and again. She could have rotted at the table waiting for them. Nothing.

Emily said, "Let it rest, you're only 23. Why rush into having kids anyway?"

But Jessa knew it wasn't in her nature to stop, which is why she loved coke. You could fly long and hard on it. You never had to stop.

When she asked Emily about *Faunus*, Emily scrunched her heart-shaped, pockmarked face and shook her head.

"No one knows his playbook. Ancient, unpredictable, and understudied."

"But known for fertility," Jessa said.

"Forget about him. It's said that he brings nightmares and whips women with tree branches. He's like untamed forest growth."

"That wasn't in the book I read, but it sounds like he has a bit of kink to him."

Emily gave her one of her teacherly looks, drawing in her lips and chin, and did not laugh.

Jessa tried a different tack. "He's like Pan."

"He's not like Pan at all, though there are images of him that people have confused with Pan. Pan is playful."

Looking up from the box of coconut juices she was unpacking, Emily asked, "What happens when you take a cup to a waterfall to gather water?"

"If I only had a cup, I'd get water from the base of the waterfall."

"That's not what I asked," Emily said, frowning. "The cup gets obliterated, that's what. No one knows anything about Faunus because he's a primordial spirit. He's not mean; he just doesn't know anything about romance."

"He's something," Jessa said.

Jessa has always yearned to go from Nothing to Something.

~

Chelsea

"Why didn't you tell me about Emma Jean earlier? Did you even think about what she would do to our name, our reputation?" Chelsea says. "No, you probably didn't. You never have thought about the family and what it needs."

Emma Jean looks up from her dog chasing the cat puzzle, "Auntie Chel-chel?"

Chelsea ignores the open and innocent way Emma Jean looks at her. She's got Jessa on the run now and she feels her pulse quicken with the delicious rush of adrenaline.

~

Jessa

Jessa's stomach growls again, louder this time. Peace Mind wants to get back into the act. Jumpy Mind is about to shout. When they both talk, she gets a migraine. She cocks her head to the side and listens to her breath again. She draws in the breath, holds it for a moment, and lets it release slowly. She rummages in her bag for the homeopathic anxiety tincture. Jessa tries to refocus the conversation. *I'm just a signature away from my freedom. No more questions about Emma Jean.* And, with the money in hand she could leave and figure things out away from Chelsea, family, the community.

She ignores the way Chelsea is looking at her while she lets the dropper almost touch her tongue and squeezes the amber liquid on it. She likes the slight taste of the alcohol.

"Dad wouldn't have wanted us to fight," Jessa says as soft as she can. "He was smart to have you watch over me in the way that you have. I know it's been work for you, being responsible for me, the executor and all. I've been lighting a candle for you every day even though you don't believe in—"

Jessa notes that the mention of their father makes Chelsea suck in her breath and her face flush.

Chelsea interrupts and holds up a hand, "Don't bring our father into it. He's probably turning over in his grave at the mess you've made."

Jessa, for a moment, can almost feel Chelsea's anger swelling, overheating her from her feet to her head. The white squiggles coming from Chelsea's heart zoom around and go up, down, wrapping around her sister's frame now like webbing. Jessa's never seen anything quite like it before.

"I never knew people really said that phrase—turning over in one's grave," Jessa says, hoping to diffuse the tension with a humorous aside.

"You think you're so clever…saying that Emma Jean has a hair condition. What was it two months ago? A staph infection? Before that—inflamed hair follicles?" Chelsea scoffs.

Jessa squirms and licks her lips.

"So many things don't add up," Chelsea says.

"Mama, I gotta go potty," Emma Jean says rocking from side to side.

"Sure sweetie, let's go," Jessa jumps up, delighted to have a distraction.

"It's not like back in high school. Some things can't be covered up," Chelsea says as Jessa and Emma Jean walk down the hall.

In the bathroom, Jessa helps her daughter with her jumper and, after she's settled, squats down and rests her head and arms on the cool sink. Emma Jean bats at the toilet paper.

"Don't do that."

"Mama?" Emma Jean says.

Jessa can hear the sound of a river rushing over rocks in her daughter's voice. She feels a throbbing in her hands. A sense of dread creeps over her. She has to go somewhere where she can think and can get help. Someone who would know what Emma Jean is. *God, I have fucked everything up.*

"Get out there and get your money," Jumpy Mind shouts.

Jessa makes sure to wash Emma Jean's hands. Before she opens the door, she studies the plush beige towels on the towel rack. She used to know towels like these. Funny, the things you miss, she thinks. She carefully lifts one off the rack and rubs it against her face. She savors the softness of it. Jumpy Mind says she can have a soft life if she can get back out there soon.

She opens the door and sees Chelsea against the opposite wall with her arms crossed.

"If we can just get to the papers, Chelsea, we'll be out of your hair. Where's Cartusciello? Is he going to be late?"

Chelsea's eyes harden and she leans in close, "Don't you know what you've done? You're just lucky Emma Jean didn't come out any darker," she says through clenched teeth.

"Dark, dark, darrrrrk, Chel-Chel," Emma Jean squeals.

Jessa stops mid-step, she feels cartoon-like; her fairy earrings keep shaking as if about to take flight.

"Marcus, at the co-op," Chelsea snaps. "One of your teachers?" Chelsea asks the question, but knowingly rocks back on her heels. "All you could talk about three years ago was Marcus. He did this and that. How he had studied energy healing with the Hawaiian kahunas. Or was it the Aboriginals? It doesn't make any difference anyway."

Jessa tries to follow her sister's words. Marcus was the co-op owner, yes. Did she talk about him from time to time? Sure she did.

"He has those dreadlocks. Long ones down his back. And now Emma Jean's hair becomes easily matted, doesn't it? It took me some time, but I put it together."

Jessa lets out a yelp, "You think Emma Jean is *Black*? That Marcus is her father? You're fucking crazier than I thought!" Jessa covers her mouth with both hands, eyes growing big. She looks at Emma Jean and shakes her head. Jessa whispers, "Emma Jean, Mama said a bad word...you just forget that."

Emma Jean looks up for a moment, shakes her head, and then skips ahead of them back down the hall to the patio.

"Denial is always the first strategy for addicts, isn't it? Oh, I'll give it to you," Chelsea says as she follows Jessa back to the patio. "You've made a valiant effort—best in all your life. But only in your make-believe world do your lies make sense. Maybe you're even sleeping with the pediatrician who writes those prescriptions, but it still doesn't change anything."

Jessa turns and stares at the woman she has known all her life. Her stomach cramps. She wants to focus on just one thing—the money—but she's so confused about what her sister is saying. She backs against a wall and tries to steady herself. The room begins to spin and she holds on to her necklaces for comfort. Her sister's energetic webbing continues to grow more and more elaborate around her body; it is tightest around Chelsea's middle and throat.

❧

Chelsea

Rage shoots through her. *For once, Jessa, tell the truth.*

〇

Jessa

Everything Emily had told her made her want to conjure Faunus up and receive a boon. She got on a Faunus kick, which felt like a new addiction. She never needed a reason for a new addiction. She told herself that this one was safe. She bought toy stuffed goats (online specialty, not too many people sell stuffed goats) and toy wolves—his totem animals. She read everything she could about him. She offered spring water and just a little touch of scotch. She prayed to him as she showered, as she worked, as she lay down to sleep. She took more energy courses, learned how to call light into her fingertips, and read about other Fairy spirits. She persisted and showed her dedication, her readiness. Nothing.

Applying herself kept her from thinking about the coke. Her sister never understood anything about her recovery. She couldn't stop, even when globs of her sinus fell out, and it burned through most of her nose hair. Even when her parents cut her off. It wasn't until she found herself trying to score in the back of a Target parking lot and had just finished giving her third blowjob that she saw a spirit. A man with flaming blue hair, hovered in front of her and said, "You know how seeds are the hottest part of a pepper?"

She nodded.

"Kid, you're all seed."

She backed against the wall of the store and shook her head from side to side.

"You real?"

He reached over and touched her wrist and drew on it, a raised blue circle, using one fingertip.

It stung and she winced. "Ouch."

"As of yesterday, your guardian angels quit you. You're now in my district. I think you still might want some help."

He stayed and counseled her. He told her to learn about energy and spirits and how with practice she could solicit their help for herself and others.

"You've got some natural talent," he said.

She went into rehab that evening.

After she got out, her life started getting better.

He, however, never gave her the rundown about what spirits to call on and which ones to avoid.

ꕥ

Chelsea

Jessa sinks down onto the sectional, her skirt poofs out around her, deflating like a party balloon. Her face slackens and she closes her eyes. She laughs (from somewhere deep inside). Chelsea is glad that, in her sister's nervous laughter, everything is dropping away, all pretenses. But then Jessa shakes, holds herself and the laughter turns into a coughing fit. Each laugh-cough seems to strip something away from Jessa. Chelsea doesn't want her sister to disappear, just to come clean and pay for her mistakes.

"I was warned," Jessa says finally. In her hysteria, both fairy earrings slip off.

"Emily tried to warn me," Jessa says in a raspy voice. Her eyes roll back in her head for a moment.

"Emily?" Chelsea says. Chelsea searches her mind to call up a face. Emily, that ditzy looking woman with the fat, pimply chin? Another person from the co-op? What was Jessa talking about? Chelsea screws up her face.

"He kept coming to me. Night after night. I bled so much."

Jessa's face is drawn. Chelsea has never seen her sister so shaken, so pale.

"Are you saying Marcus raped you?"

Chelsea's mind works overtime. More work for her. This would be so much more difficult; with Jessa's past, there was no way a rape trial could move forward. What would their friends think of her younger sister? No, she couldn't have that scrutiny on the family. She would talk with Cartusciello. She could buy Marcus out. Force him out. Make him go away.

"We can make this right. No one needs to know. You just let me handle the details," Chelsea says nodding.

℗

Jessa

Once it began, she did not know how to stop it. He came to her regularly in her dreams. She thought she could bear his visits. Faunus appeared as a giant man with the lower body of a goat. Her dream body was always outstretched, her arms comically long. He would jump on one of her outstretched arms, and with his forelegs stomp on it repeatedly. The pain was unbearable.

He whipped her body with branches, a storm of leaves, and with other animals' body parts. After calling animals to him and stroking them until they shuddered, he'd douse her in goat and wolf semen, although he never entered her in the dreams. She'd wake up sweaty, her fingernails piercing the sheets, often in the midst of a hip-rocking, swelling orgasm, the taste of bliss falling from her lips.

She should have told Emily about the visits, but she didn't want her teacher to be worried. Or disappointed. She wanted to be a good petitioner, a good manipulator of energy. Wasn't she chosen to work with spirits?

When she missed her period a month later, she knew that she had been given a boon. It worked, it worked!

Only after Emma Jean arrived did she worry. As her daughter grew, she could see that she was different. Emma Jean's gurgles sounded like a rushing river. Before her eyes, she had seen her daughter's hair form locks, but they were small, and she could pluck them off easily. They smelled like wet earth, dead leaves, and river rocks, like him. She told herself that they were harmless things. After Chelsea had asked her about a long, matted lock of Emma Jean's that seemed to spring up overnight, she really knew. She didn't want to know.

Chelsea's question that day had driven her back to her book about spirits. On a closer look at the entry about Faunus, her breath caught. She had originally failed to notice where it said, "Various spirits indicate their spiritual children by causing hair to spontaneously form "locks." Clutching her stomach, she read the words over and over, comprehension sinking in. Faunus had answered her petition, just not in the way she had expected.

Jessa covered her tracks through one of her old drug contacts. She found a doctor who provided a false diagnosis for Emma Jean of an ongoing hair condition and wrote prescriptions for various salves and creams. It meant bad sex, three times a year, but she paid that price dutifully.

ᗡ

Jessa

Jessa shakes her head, her left hand working the top knuckle of the right. "Her hair, it keeps curling. The coils are constantly sprouting up. I sometimes have to cut her hair ten times in a month," Jessa says, her eyes red from crying. She feels as if someone has unscrewed the valve of her life, and she is losing pressure like a tire. Everything is coming through. Peace Mind says it is good for her. She thinks her crying sounds like a low horn. She trembles. Jumpy Mind berates her.

"Who knows what happens in those genes," Chelsea says.

Jessa lets out a sigh. "I wasn't strong enough."

ᗡ

Chelsea

Chelsea feels like she is conducting this conversation under water. *Jessa has become delusional.*

"You've never been strong. *I've* been the strong one," Chelsea agrees while patting her sister's shoulders.

Chelsea looks at her niece and curls her lip in disgust. It was worse than Chelsea thought. Her sister really needed her. *Keeping this from me has driven her over the edge.*

"This all needs to be orchestrated with care, and I'm willing to do it. You know that she can't stay with you much longer. You're barely making a living. It's time to give up the charade. We're going to get her in a prep school far away from here."

"What?" Jessa says and looks at her with those buttery soft hazel eyes.

"I've already looked into it. Come," she says invitingly, "...the papers are in the study."

〇

Jessa

Jessa jolts forward and reaches into her bag for a tissue to wipe her nose. The papers! Jumpy Mind is excited and tells her to run. She ignores the command.

"Get your dolly, little mama. We're moving," she says to Emma Jean.

With care, she gathers up her daughter who has just let out the biggest fart. Emma Jean squeals with delight and claps her hands. Close to her body, she buries her head in the girl's neck and smells the baby powder she sprinkled on hours ago. Under that gentle smell though, she can smell the wild smell, too. It's the smell of the forest at night.

Collecting herself, yet feeling dazed, Jessa tries to catch the thread of conversation. What was her sister just saying? She wants to float away. That old feeling of wanting to get high courses through her. She wasn't good about dealing when things got rough.

She breathes again and adjusts Emma Jean. Holding Emma Jean makes her come back to the moment.

"What school?" she says, watching her sister stride ahead. They pass from the outdoor living area into a long hallway and then make two left turns. Jessa looks at the paintings that line the walls, mostly still-lifes. Jessa finds irony in the fact her sister collects art but misses everything that could be wild, beautiful, and original right under her nose.

Chelsea pushes open the door into her study, a magnificent room with vaulted, cream-colored ceilings and soothing, amber-colored furniture.

Smiling, Chelsea holds up a glossy folder and hands her a thick packet. "Ecole d'Humanité is where I've made arrangements...serving gifted children, though we don't know that yet about Emma Jean. Still, they'll take the money."

Jessa notices that her sister's eyes are the most animated and shiny they have been all afternoon.

Chelsea turns her back to Jessa and Emma Jean and looks out the large bay window. "It was once on the list of places we were to go for high school. Before you..." she pauses. "Decided to go another way. I would have loved it there, but Father said that I needed to be here watching out for you."

The regret in her sister's voice squeezes Jessa in a way that she has not felt before. *She's given up so much for me.* She thinks about the reckless way she has spent her youth; her stupidities striking her with pinpricks, as if she is being allergy tested. Yes, she thinks, I've been allergic to good sense so much of my life.

"Switzerland?" Jessa says, in a squeaky voice. As she looks at the happy kids on the cover, her stomach churns like she has to go to the bathroom immediately. Shitting fear, that's what getting clean felt like. That's what it feels like to face up to the lies and everything bad you've done. Your bowels just drop from under you, and everything goes soft. It's not polite. It's a run to the nearest bathroom. She clenches the lower half of her body.

"That's why you're here, so we could talk about this like adults—I think you're capable of that much. I've already explained everything to Cartusciello."

Jessa puts Emma Jean down, "Just sit down and stay for a minute," she says. "Don't touch anything. It's a special room of Auntie Chelsea's."

Emma Jean scampers over to a corner and looks at a big deer figurine sitting on a low table.

"I said, don't touch anything," Jessa repeats.

"Are you ready to hear my proposal? It's very simple. If you send her away, then I will say that you are fit and that you should inherit your share, as the will stipulates. As you've been waiting for. If not, it will be ten years before the money is released to you. Unfortunately, you'll get all the money then. Father figured you would have to have your act together by then. I wanted it to be longer, but he still had some hope in you."

Jessa's fear bubbles up into her throat. She automatically wraps her arms around herself and hugs. She's about to double over with the news. She feels small and powerless, like a white lab rat, running into corners, in a maze not of her making. *Please, oh please, not ten years!*

BabaJesusYemayaKaliArchAngelMichael...SOMEONE GIVE ME SOME GUIDANCE!

Peace Mind is strangely quiet.

For a moment, Jessa feels as if she has entered a surreal game show. Three white doors appear in her mind's eye. She believes that Jumpy Mind is making them all open and close rapidly. She sees glimpses of cars crashing down on trees behind Door #1. She wants Jumpy Mind to stop opening and closing that door.

What's behind Door #2? A door swings open and she sees Marcus, and for a moment she feels the delicious contact of his skin against hers. She remembers when he bumped into her by accident, in the storeroom. She lost her balance and fell backwards, her rubber clogs slipping on the floor. He grabbed her arm, steadying her. His caring grip made her blush and sent pleasant signals to every part of her body. Who could not want to sleep with Marcus? She had wanted to. Not because he was Black, but because he was grounded and beautiful and believed in her. She had met him two weeks after her recovery, when she had nothing. He gave her a job and a place at the co-op.

Her thoughts cloud together. Maybe she made up Faunus so that she could have Marcus? Maybe she was still high, making it all up.

Door #3 swings open and lots and lots of tiny pink pillows spill out. Behind the pillows, Jessa sees herself as she had been on the last day of her addiction. Tricking for food and for drugs. Dirty and poor. That last year on the street gave her a reality lesson on being poor...she couldn't take that again. The nasty looks from people, not being able to go where she wanted to go, diving in dumpsters. How did people endure it?

And then from behind all those pillows emerged another version of her, confident, clean and walking with a steady stride. Jumpy Mind said, "Step over that gutter rat. That was never you. You were never meant to live a hard life. You always knew you would be coming back, didn't you?"

Emma Jean bounces her doll up and down.

"For how long?" Jessa asks.

"At the school for a year or so, but ultimately you'll move to give her up for adoption. I'll make it as painless as possible," she says this turning around slowly, looking right into Jessa's eyes.

The eyes that Jessa sees now are very cold. Adoption? Jessa feels she is one step away from dog panting. Jumpy Mind doesn't miss a beat. "Make it easy on yourself," it says. "Yes, yes, yes, you can give her up. Just for a little while. While you travel on the boat. Don't forget about the boat!"

She feels a scratch on her foot. Emma Jean has unhooked a paperclip and is running it over her Jessa's foot, slowly.

She bends down and snatches it from her daughter's hand. "Don't play with that," she says harsher than she means to. "Go play with dolly while I talk with Auntie Chelsea," she says through gritted teeth and a fake smile.

She looks at Emma Jean. For half a second she thinks how easy it would be to release her. Novel, odd, strange. Of her body, but of something else. Wild.

"What about the truth?" Peace Mind offers.

Are you on another planet? she answers back. *Yes, of course you are, you're not even real! No, I must try to reason with her.*

"She's not Black, I can assure you that," she begins quietly. "If she was...Chelsea, if she was, what are you saying?"

"It's someone else, not Marcus?" Chelsea says as she pulls out a black chair behind her desk and sits down. Her face deflates and clouds over.

Jessa sees that it has not occurred to her sister that she could be wrong. She was not the wrong one.

Jessa swallows hard. "Yes, it is someone else," she says. *Something else.*

"It doesn't matter," Chelsea says. "It doesn't change anything." Her eyes harden into steel flints that seem to give off sparks. "You're bound to mess up again."

Jessa rushes to the desk and leans on it, "Just sign the papers saying I'm okay. I am okay. And, then you never have to see us. We can go away. It's like you won't have a sister." She smells her pungent fear radiating out from her yellow tank.

"All the years of what I put you through, I can't make up for that. Never. Never. Never, and I am so sorry. But, after today, I promise, I will be no trouble," Jessa says.

Emma Jean jumps up and runs over and assumes the stance like her mother. She places her small hands at the height of Jessa's knees and leans into the frame of the desk.

"If you don't put her away, it's ten years." Chelsea says.

"I am fit, and I will contest it," Jessa shouts and spit flies out of her mouth. "Spitefulness shouldn't be legalized! This is not what Daddy wanted," she says.

"Contest it with what?" The sneer is ugly and contorts her sister's face. "The $175 saved up in your checking account?"

Registering the surprise on her sister's face, Chelsea adds, "Yes, I've done some digging on you. Don't you see it is for the best?"

"Trust me, Chelsea, I've been paying for my mistakes."

"So you're admitting Emma Jean is a mistake?" Chelsea says, her eyes opening wide.

"Is that what you want me to say? That she's a mistake? I wasn't talking about her. I was talking about everything else…what I put you through and Dad through and everyone."

Chelsea's eyebrows arch. Jessa notices how she has the same look as when they were girls. Jessa can see now how she has always made her sister look good. Weariness creeps over her, like when she was coming down from a long high. Her throat feels dry.

"You've never believed that I could change, that I could grow. That I didn't need saving," Jessa says. "All of my 12-stepping, all of my reconciliation letters, everything I've tried and committed to. You've never believed me or in me."

"Addicts always lie," Chelsea says.

The finality in her sister's tone hits Jessa like a punch in the stomach.

"And you'll do anything in the name of family, won't you, even if it means becoming a monster?"

Jessa could feel in her whole body how she's been her sister's foil. *I always make you look good. The one who needs saving.* She sees herself locked in this struggle with her sister. Jessa takes two steps forward and wipes away the tears. She sees her sister now in a way that she has never seen her before. *Chelsea's never been interested in the truth.*

Jessa feels a cone of power rising inside of her that wants expression through her hands. "Maybe the spirits were right. They told me you never had the capacity to love. I didn't believe them. Maybe it was in *your* genes, you know?"

"I don't know what you're talking about," Chelsea snaps. "Your energy jibber jabber fails to impress me."

"Always so quick to protect what you didn't even earn. Always thinking you're better than everyone else," Jessa says.

Chelsea's face grows a deep flash of red. She shakes her head as if trying to shake off an insect.

"What happened to you when we were young? Was the good squeezed out of you?" Jessa says.

"The papers are waiting," Chelsea says pointing and then she scrunches up her face.

Jessa comes toward her sister, putting all her concentration on the middle of Chelsea's heart center, at her breastbone. Jessa breathes out the light from inside of her. *I'm sorry, big sister.*

"I need some some water..." Chelsea says trying to rise out of her chair.

Jumpy Mind and Peace Mind are, for once, speechless.

Could it be this easy? Her fingers tingle and her whole body feels awake. She's forgotten about the boat, the money, and the new life. She is high again, so high. This was the high she had been seeking, waiting for. The best high. All her attention is in this moment, surging forth with power. She sees the webbing around her sister's body and with her hands, she starts to direct it upward. As it unfurls, it lifts with it a faint outline of Chelsea's body. The outline rises slowly. Chelsea's body is fighting now; she's pounding the table and her face is a burnt autumn red. Jessa goes deeper, searching for the seed of her sister's heart, wanting to squeeze it, rupture it.

Emma Jean comes away from the desk and tugs on her, "Mama, what are you doing? Aunt Chel-Chel?"

I can't stop. I don't want to stop. Don't make me stop.

Emma Jean looks at her, and, for a moment, Jessa is back in the forest and there is the sound of water and the feeling of soft leaves underfoot. Something else is looking out at her from her daughter's eyes. Strange. Wild. Wise perhaps. She's not sure what she sees.

Looking at her daughter breaks her attention. Reluctantly, Jessa releases her focus from her sister. Chelsea falls out of her chair, heaving.

Emma Jean rushes over and places her small hands on her aunt's face. "Aunt Chel-Chel sick?"

Jessa goes into the kitchen and gets a glass of water, comes back, and sets it down on the desk. Her sister is sitting up against the bay windows looking wild-eyed, but the color in her face is normal.

Jessa lifts her daughter into her arms and adjusts her shoulder bag. Standing over her sister, she says. "Sign the papers, don't sign the papers. Your heart is still going to be too small."

As she walks toward the front door, Jessa notices that Emma Jean's hair has formed six new, long locks.

THE WISHING WELL
OFF FORDHAM ROAD

DEENA BANKS LOOKED OUT HER FIFTH-FLOOR WINDOW AT THE sunlight reaching over the tallest buildings of the neighborhood. Deena drank in the promise of the day. It was not quite time to take the U4 train from the Bronx to Dr. Milton's veterinary clinic in Manhattan. Deena was up earlier than usual because she was nursing Mr. Chester, a skinny, gray, droopy-eared, lop rabbit, back to health. She was also keeping an eye on the wishing well and its resident—both of whom were smack in the middle of her block. She looked in the direction of the wishing well, anticipating the line that would soon form.

Over the last few weeks, these early hours were the dangerous ones. Delinquent school kids, drunks, and other desperate wish-seekers would come along, making noise and harassing the wishing well creature. But surely, Deena thought, that thing brought all this trouble on itself.

As usual, Calvin and Milo, two teenage boys who lived on the block, were down there making trouble. They were trying to get the wishing well creature out from its hole. *What do they think they'll do with it if they succeed?*

Calvin gripped a baseball bat, occasionally swinging it above the hole.

A head bobbed up from the murky water.

Calvin swung but missed his target.

Deena roared out the window into the quiet morning, "You leave that thing alone. Don't you boys have something better to do?"

Damn delinquent kids, the same thing every day! How this neighborhood has changed.

"Mind your own business," Calvin shouted.

But it was the tallest boy, Milo, who was trouble, in his patched denim jacket, dirty white jeans, and short dreadlocks. He looked her in the eye and said, "Suck me off."

"Oh, I'm ready for your mess today." Deena yelled.

Ignoring her warning, the boys circled the hole taunting what lived there with their insults.

"Pull your ass up out of the water, you rotting fishman," Milo said. He splashed his foot in the water. "You smell like something dead."

Oh, I'm going to fix you, she thought while pulling out her prize from a Woolworth's shopping bag. Gesturing toward the rabbit's cage, Deena said, "Mr. Chester, I hope this doesn't hurt your ears."

The rabbit scrunched its nose and, seeming to understand, flattened both ears and awkwardly hopped to the other side of his metal cage.

Leaning halfway out of the window, Deena shouted through her brand-new bullhorn, "WHAT DID I SAY? I'M TIRED OF YOUR ANTICS! DAY AFTER DAY OF SUCH NONSENSE!"

Simon, the morning security guard hired by the neighborhood to watch the wishing well, came running out from the bodega across the street throwing a donut onto the curb. The powdered confection rolled on the street and over to the well. In a blink, the wishing well creature rose and grabbed it, taking it underwater. Deena saw a blur of black hair, a furred face, and a long arm covered in red scales.

Calvin swung, but the creature was too quick for him.

Holding the bullhorn tightly, Deena yelled at the top of her lungs, "Simon! Why aren't you doing your job?"

Other lights in buildings across the street clicked on. Bleary eyes peered from blinds, curtains, and stained, ratty sheets.

Waving his stick, Simon yelled at the boys. "Don't make no more trouble for yourselves. Go on now. I'm tired of having to constantly get with the two of you."

The boys, having their revelry interrupted, spoke quickly to each other, and Calvin reluctantly threw down his bat. They strode away, Calvin giving Deena the finger.

"It's a freak," Milo shouted.

Calvin turned, pointed, and said, "And, Simon, you're a rent a cop."

"It can't come up with no wishes. It's a goddamn hoax!" Milo added.

Scowling, Deena put her head back inside. That wishing well hasn't been anything except a problem. Miserable boys, just miserable. Miserable neighborhood. *The wishing well is the worst thing that could have happened to us. Other neighborhoods in the city get their buildings fixed. Or new mailboxes that can't be broken into every other week. We get a useless wishing well from God knows where.*

She snorted and ran to the stove where her morning breakfast of fried mackerel and eggs was now smokier than she liked. Though Deena worked for a veterinarian and knew that rabbits did not eat mackerel and eggs, this fact did not prevent Deena from mixing some of her breakfast together with fresh spinach and commercial rabbit food pellets to give to Mr. Chester. She trusted her instinct when it came to animals. "Vets don't know everything," she often said behind the back of Dr. Milton. Using her instinct with people made no difference—Deena knew they were no good. However, she knew animals were precious, and a smidgen of intuition with them went a long way.

"You're the only good thing in the world," she said, knowing that Mr. Chester had already seen the worst of it. She opened the cage and patted the soft hair on his head, letting her hand linger to caress his ears. His quivering cheeks let her know she was appreciated. A glance at his bandaged body still made her wince.

When she first saw Mr. Chester, a glaze-eyed white girl smelling of stale apple juice, urine, and sweat had brought him to the clinic wrapped in aluminum foil. Blood stains soaked her clothes. She said nothing, plopped the bundle on the counter, spun on her heel, and left. Deena, upon inspection, discovered the previous owner had poured some kind of corrosive liquid onto his right eyeball, and had hacked off the rabbit's right leg. Deena wondered about the girl, her environment and what could cause someone to act so cruelly. That day Deena cleaned and tended to Mr. Chester. Even though Dr. Milton kept saying that Mr. Chester wasn't going to make it, she persisted.

On impulse, she asked Dr. Milton if she could take Mr. Chester home.

"It's kinda quiet in the house now without my mom."

"If you want to play Florence Nightingale…go right ahead. He won't last more than a few days," Dr. Milton warned her.

That was six weeks ago, near the time the well appeared. "Dr. Milton doesn't know everything," Deena said aloud while picking out the bits of blackened mackerel bone.

❧

On her way to work she bumped into Simon in the bodega. He had replaced his lost donut with a larger, plumper one, purple filling oozing from its core. Thick white sugar flecks were caught in his beard and mustache.

"You should patrol more in the morning. That's what we pay you for."

"What's eating you?"

"Those boys are a nuisance and are getting worse every day. Don't you think sooner or later they are going to hurt that thing?"

He shrugged. "They might, but boys will be boys."

"Don't hand me that crap about boys," she said. Deena adjusted her purse and glared at him. "I should have told those boys what adults used to say to us kids, 'If lil snake want grow big, he must keep a'gras canna.'"

Simon looked puzzled. "Come again?" he asked.

"We say that back in Guyana—that means if kids want to grow up, they must be cautious…like a little snake who keeps covered in the grass and does not call attention to itself."

Simon gave her a blank look.

"Forget it," Deena said, irritated that she even mentioned it.

The stout shopkeeper with bad dentures called out from behind the plastic booth, "Hey, mami! Guyana, that's where you from? All these years I never knew."

"There's a lot of things you don't know about me." And will never know, she thought.

Clueless as usual, the shopkeeper continued, "So many people moving in and out. What can I do? It's hard to know anybody anymore."

Shaking his head, Simon said, "What do I care about the kids…about the wishing well? And what do you care?"

"Because it's on *my* block, and I get woken up by their and everybody else's hoopla." Her back and shoulder muscles tensed, and the inside of her hands became damp.

"You're the only one on the block that cares," Simon sighed. "Everyone else ignores it or goes to visit it."

A question edged into her mind. *Deena, why do you care?*

Deena wanted to slap Simon. "This used to be a decent neighborhood, and Fordham Road was once the main thoroughfare for the Bronx. Do you know what a thoroughfare is?" Deena stood tall.

"Thoroughfare, smoroughfare," Simon snorted. "I get my dollars regardless. Anyway, I want to go back to my job at Madison Square Garden. I liked seeing all the stars come through there. Man, one time I saw Carly Simon…that is one tall bitch." He smiled, showing a huge overbite and discolored teeth.

The shopkeeper laughed.

"Don't worry Deena. You ever seen it all the way out of the water?" Simon paused, tweaked his mustache, and got closer to her, whispering like they were friends at a party and he had a juicy tidbit of gossip to share. "It was doing some tricks a couple of days ago and it flipped out of the water. It's hefty. No one is really stupid enough to mess with it." He folded his arms and nodded, as if to say, "That's all you need to know."

Not reassured by his comment, Deena paid for a package of Hostess cupcakes, turned, and made her way out the store.

⟲

"Damn construction men fixing things that ain't even broke," Deena had muttered to herself when all the commotion first began. One day the construction men were fixing a pothole the size of three cars. Then, overnight, a larger, deeper hole with water emerged—with the creature in it. Everyone stayed away from the hole at first, until the creature boldly put out a sign that read *Wishing Well*.

Old Mrs. Hernandez with the gout problems, who lived in a building directly across from Deena's and had a daughter who was in jail for murdering her boyfriend, said a prayer over the well, talked to the creature, and now she was living up in a mansion in the Palisades. Or was it the Hamptons? Deena couldn't remember. Since then, swarms of people had come to check out the creature and make wishes, but not Deena. For all she knew it could be some prankster midget man in a suit. *Still, whatever it is, those obnoxious boys should be leaving it alone.*

Deena carefully walked past the well on her way to the #4 Fordham Road subway stop. Curiosity had gotten the best of her, and she had peeked at the well last week; it seemed to go down to the core of the earth. Sometimes the water looked murky, and sometimes it was as shattering blue as the rivers were in Guyana. She and her friends swam the summers away in those rivers until she was ten.

"Thank you for looking out for me. It's a rough crowd here," the wishing well creature said. His face resembled a cross between a man's and a tapir's, with long black hair that began at the top of his head and covered the sides, red eyes, and a flexible snout. Black tufts of fur dotted his cheeks and chin. His neck was scaly, and since only his head and neck were barely out of the water she could not tell what the rest of his body looked like. She imagined it tough and leathery.

Deena paused for a moment; the wishing well creature had never spoken to her before. Its voice struck her as human sounding, clear and on the higher side but pleasant to her ear. She turned away and kept walking, determined not to give it the satisfaction that she had noticed anything about it.

It called out to her again, "It was nice of you."

Deena kept a steady stride.

"You're the only one in this whole neighborhood, possibly in this whole city who hasn't come to visit me yet. Don't you have any wishes?"

Wishes?! Deena stopped in her tracks. Swinging around, her thick, waist length, black braid almost snapped to attention. How dare it interrupt her peace, the only peace she had during the morning before she got on the train (full of smelly, rude people) to her job! How dare it remind her of the world! Its presence had already brought camera crews, churchgoers, fanatics, merchants parading their wares (like T-shirts with *I swam with the Wishing Well Man*) through her neighborhood, and even the desperate and despised. She wasn't trying to be *nice.* If her mother had lived to see this spectacle, she would have been appalled. Now, now she could give this thing a good piece of her mind.

"Oh, get back in your hole; you're a sham," she whispered, her tight voice squeezing out the words.

"Give me a try," he said sniffing the air. His nostrils expanded, horse-like, and then contracted. "I'm better than those cupcakes." "I'm not going to fall for that." She dropped down on all fours, not paying any heed that she could rip her stockings. *Let it smell my breath today.* "I've seen you gulp down people's pennies, and I'm really not very impressed. Now go *away.*"

Impulsively, she threw her cupcakes in the hole. They bobbed for a minute and then sank without a trace.

The creature submerged its head in the murky water and swam off. Pleased with herself for insulting it, she stood up and straightened her jacket and skirt. She breathed deeply, and her eyes took in all that she saw.

To Deena, the designation of wishing well was generous. People called it a wishing well; the thing called it such. But there were no faux bricks, rocks, or hanging plants like she'd seen at other wishing wells. It was really just a large hole in the ground. But when Deena looked inside the hole with her head cocked to the side, she spied iridescent colors. The shimmery colors swept up and created a rainbow off the water, making her feel as if she were standing under it at the edge of the world.

The edge of the world is where light shimmers, she thought. In the colorful arc, for a moment, she saw her mother, a petite woman holding a green and gold-colored suitcase in one hand and irises in the other. *Mom, oh Mom.*

At the same time that she saw her mother, secret wishes whispered to her. Old wishes she had forgotten existed, extinguished years ago. The deepest wish. *I wanted to be a veterinarian.*

She savagely beat the wishes back before they could be spoken or granted. In two blinks, the colors of memory were gone—the luminescence of her mother's suitcase, the crisp purple of the irises—all gone. Her head throbbed, and her voice felt raw like after she yelled at the boys. This thing, its presence made her angry, bringing to the surface the searing bundle of disappointments her life had been.

She looked at the objects placed around the edge of the hole. Why the hell would someone leave the Bible, Dr. Seuss books, gem stones of hematite, quartz crystals, rosaries, Barbie dolls (in various stages of undress), vanilla incense burning from cones that resembled brown nipples, stuffed animals (a giraffe, three cats, two rabbits, an old Snoopy doll), Victoria Secret and Macy's catalogues, dirty envelopes stuffed with requests, a can of Spam, an empty Big Mac container, a vase of roses, a computer flash drive, burning candles in glasses from the local botanica, a bag of subway tokens, a home pregnancy kit, a placemat that said "Jesus, I need you," piles of lottery tickets, a container of Johnson's Baby Powder, a brown cane with a fake ivory handle, and a gyro stick with thick lamb cubes turning green at the edges?

From the magic of this spectacle, Deena turned and faced her neighborhood. *Why can't anything ever really get better?* The tattered, sagging awnings of the bodegas, the glass in the street, the calcified (human or animal—it was hard to tell) shit piled up in clumps on the sidewalk. She saw lethargic proprietors opening up the two $1.99 Stores for a day's work with baby clothes, fake flowers, cheap sneakers, pink plastic bottles of nail polish remover, and toilet paper all jammed together and displayed in the windows.

Everything is becoming the dollar ninety-nine store. These were not the same streets she had loved when she and her mother had first moved to the neighborhood decades and decades ago.

◎

On the #4 train between Fordham Road and Manhattan, Deena thought about the tapir-faced creature. What was a wish anyway? What could she wish for? There was nothing to have. She sighed. Everything was bad: her heart with its irregular beats, her neighborhood, her job with Dr. Milton, who annoyed her to no end. No, she stopped herself in mid-thought. No, the little brown eyes and soft yielding coat of her beloved Mr. Chester came to her. He was good.

Deena was wedged between a Black man who wore a Yankee's jacket and a redheaded pale woman who smelled strongly of perfume that was heavy on wood and citrus notes. The man had started out near her and had moved his pelvis closer with every subway stop. He was now rubbing up against her backside, slowly and lewdly.

Turning slightly, Deena jabbed him with her elbow, "Move the hell off of my butt. If you want that kind of attention from a woman, go down to 42nd street!"

The redhead with the cloying scent looked away.

"Don't flatter yourself, your ass don't look *that* good," he said. He glared as if he was going to kick her, but he just sucked his teeth and moved back a quarter of an inch.

Two teenagers exchanged smirks, but most everyone else found the floor an interesting place to look. Deena ignored the man. The train was packed, and the intense smells of sweat, perfume, and foot odor lulled Deena back to the image of her mother as it had visited her at the wishing well.

How different her mama looked in that vision than in her last days. Her mother had sacrificed organ after organ until she was a jaundiced, shrunken skeleton who was always cold and craved Fig Newtons and chocolate milk. Her mother wanted none of the hot curry dishes of Guyana. *I wish I hadn't seen my mother die in my house.*

Throughout the sickness, Deena often clipped her mother's fingernails. She could never understand why they grew so long. They had reminded Deena of the claws on some of the rare birds she occasionally treated in the clinic. She'd finished with the right hand and took a break. "I'll be back Mama," she said. When she came back and put their dinners down and saw the line of drool sliding down her mother's chin, she knew her mother was dead. All Deena could think about for months after was her unfinished task. She felt ashamed. She didn't believe in God, but her mother did. How was that to go to Heaven with only one set of nails clipped? Would God mind? Did the physical form match the soulform that God saw?

Deena shook her head. *Why am I remembering this? Things that I wish for can't be given to me.*

Seething, she almost ripped the handle off her bag trying to yank it through the crowd when her subway stop came.

As she approached the turnstiles to leave, she felt a pull on her elbow.

"Miss, Miss."

She turned around. It was the redhead.

"You have something on the back of your jacket."

"What?" Deena asked.

"That man. I think—look on the back of your jacket."

The woman shook her head, blushing and walked away. Deena pulled the back of her jacket toward her and touched a sticky wet spot.

"What I would wish for is to kill all the fucking scum of the world!" With tears in her eyes she rummaged around in her purse for a tissue. She had lived in New York almost thirty years of her fifty-eight-year-old life. *I should expect anything and everything from this fucked up city.* This fresh indignity left her feeling bruised.

℘

Deena opened up the office. Within minutes she had her lab coat on and for the first hour went to work cleaning out some the animals' cages and checking on others. At ten o'clock she gave a skin treatment to Sheena, an uncharacteristically friendly Siamese.

Dr. Milton, a short white man of about forty with pockmarked skin, came into the second examination room where Deena was working.

"Good morning."

"Yes, and the same," Deena said, preoccupied with the events of the morning.

He put down *The New York Times*, went and fetched his lab coat. "You look tired," he said, coming back into the room.

"Yeah, those boys that I've told you about were up to their antics again. And you know how I *hate* the train." She methodically rubbed the white paste on the shaved areas of Sheena's skin. Deena liked the morning, though disliked "morning" people, a group of people to which Dr. Milton belonged.

"Who doesn't?" he continued amiably. "I've got to go up and look at that wishing well. Probably some hoax. God, I used to love going to Fordham Road. I remember when my mother took me up there to shop at Alexander's. Hah," he laughed, "Alexander's, what a dinosaur."

"Alexander's doesn't exist anymore, Dr. Milton. Caldor is there now," Deena said flatly.

"You're kidding? I just never get a chance to get up to the Bronx," he said.

Of course not, why would you? Deena wanted to say. *You probably wouldn't know how to find your way back to your condo on East 92nd Street.* She absentmindedly petted Sheena and checked the length of time the skin treatment had to be left on.

Changing the subject and forcing a smile, she said, "I was standing at the edge of the well, and I remembered things that I had forgotten. Like stuff about my mother and," she hesitated, "Well, like how I wanted to be a vet years and years ago."

He got quiet and shook his head. "Uh, huh, it's too bad. It would be hard for you with no science background, and of course your age."

I might be old but I'm not dead.

He smiled and gingerly opened two sugar packets and poured them into his mug of coffee. "Is the Henderson cat doing better than yesterday?"

"Yup, he is. He had a bowel movement this morning." She gently picked up Sheena and went downstairs, not waiting for his response.

∽

Let this whole silly thing go, she admonished herself. *There are animals to weigh, samples to send out, and water and food to distribute—a full day of work.* But still something poked at her. The thick coil of feelings, hidden behind anger and indifference, was unrolling.

Finding a quiet time in the day she sought out her employer. She had the Henderson chart with her for protection. All day she had resisted the desire to talk more about being a veterinarian until a pressure settled in Deena's chest that she could not ignore. When she breathed in, it felt as if someone was dripping hot wax on her chest.

Dr. Milton sat in his main office at a mahogany desk, looking out the window at the endless parade of busy New Yorkers going by.

She knocked and then fidgeted at the half-open door.

"Yes?" he said looking at her.

"I have what the lab sent us on the Henderson cat, and the chart." She sat down in a comfy, brown chair farthest from his desk.

Deena mustered up her courage, and blurted out, "Dr. Milton, if I wanted to try to pursue the vet thing there *are* places in the city…"

"Cornell is the best place to study veterinary medicine, and you wouldn't get in."

"Maybe, I could go to the Animal Medical Center," she continued, unable to make herself be quiet. "They have some classes, or even back to the ASPCA. Maybe, I could take some time off for classes or something."

Rising, he came toward her. He made a motion to take the chart and then stopped. He began rubbing the back of his neck, which he only did when he was annoyed. She had seen this gesture often when his son, Timothy, a lanky young man with a parrot tattoo on his neck, came to the office to bum some money.

"Deena, we've talked about this before when you first got here. You need some post baccalaureate degree in the sciences. I hired you because you had read extensively and had some volunteering background at the ASPCA. But you don't even have a *correspondence* course to be a veterinary assistant. You know Sally Struthers and all that?" he suppressed a laugh.

She watched his lips flap about. *Fuck Sally Struthers on late night TV commercials.*

"You've let me help before on surgeries," Deena added, a defiant tone creeping into her voice.

"I've let you help, but...I want my clients to know that they are getting professional service. That's why you've done nothing more than help."

All she wanted him to say was, yes it was possible. Why couldn't anyone say that to her about anything?

He shrugged, "The money, God, where would you ever get the money to finance school?"

She shrugged too. *This was a mistake.*

"Unless you could get some kind of minority scholarship," he added casually.

"I'm not an American minority, I'm Guyanese."

Dr. Milton looked as if seeing Deena for the first time, taking in her long hair, light complexion, laugh lines, the deep wrinkles around her mouth, and big eyes.

"That's a minority in this country."

I've been working here eight years. He doesn't even know anything about me. Does he think I say things about Guyana because I've vacationed there?

"Deena." He placed a hand on her shoulder, intoning the words, "There are some dreams we all have to let go of when we mature. Now, I've got to call some clients." Taking the chart and lab report from her and gesturing toward the door, he signaled the conversation was finished.

Deena swallowed her anger and left. She had bandaged, wrapped, and stitched everything from cats to iguanas. She did overtime *all* the time because he was too cheap to hire another assistant, or to go into practice with someone else. What about when Dr. Milton was away on vacation and she handled everything, she asked herself?

Didn't that count for something? Throwing away the cupcakes had been a mistake—it was going to be a long day.

༉

Her mother is in the bed next to her. She is scraping her fingernails along the wall. Her mother moans, "They are not done. They are not painted. They will not let me into Heaven with these." Her mother yells, waving her hand back and forth. Her mother's hand is grotesque with the growth of the nails. Looking at her hand, Deena is reminded of women with the longest fingernails in the Guinness Book of World Records. Her mother's hand is useless with its hardened spiral appendages. She becomes silent and Deena quietly lies there.

There is a pimple on Deena's face. It grows as big as a kiwi. Her fingertip touches it, exploring it, and the pimple explodes pop, pop, boom rah. White pus flows out of it onto her face smelling like spoiled yogurt and stale potato chips. Deena quickly gets up and rubs her face on a hot towel. The towel is scalding, angry steam rising from the towel heating the bathroom mirror. The heat flattens the pimple, and it shrinks to a normal size. She lies in bed again, and slowly the pimple grows, filling out with pus again. It becomes so big that this new pimple-presence rises and sits up on her face. She infers that it is self-impressed with its full-bodied amoeboid shape, and it is unremorseful at the pain it's causing her. The pimple-presence laughs at her, spilling white pus down its front. Its laughter wakes her mother, who begins scratching on the wall again.

Deena bolts awake with the echoes of the pimple-presence's laughter and her mother's wailing in her ears.

༉

A week later, on her way to work, the wishing well creature rose and said to Deena, "Let me introduce myself. I am Rivkinsommer- sabat. You can call me Rivi."

She looked at her watch, noting that she had a minute or two to spare. She bent down to shake the outstretched mungy hand. A mildewed smell, with a strong hint of birch, crept up through her nostrils.

"I am Deena Banks." *He is a curiosity.*

"Do you want to talk about your dream?"

"No, it's too scary." She could feel him reaching out to her and wondered why; she wasn't as startled or angry as she was before. "And don't try to read my mind," Deena said, almost as an afterthought.

"I can't help it," the creature said, confirming her suspicion with a nod. "Though, I often forget it as soon as possible, if that's any consolation."

Changing the subject she asked, "What do *you* dream?"

He said without pause, "I dream of suppertime in 17th century Paris, of milkshake waterfalls, of gold crucifixes inlaid with ivory and jade, of dervishes that have lost their whirl, of fuzzy-headed dandelions, of folded up love messages in bottles that float, of whale sperm that shoots out into the ocean, of wheelbarrows full of peonies, of English fedoras, of things pedestrian and grand. Deena, I dream the forevers of tomorrow."

"Those are big dreams for living in a hole so small," was all Deena could think to say.

"I know about your dreams, Deena."

"They're private," she said with an air of finality.

"Not as much as you think."

"There's so much misery and decay in New York," Deena said. *And I feel it all.* "I don't know how you can stand it here."

"As opposed to St. Paul, Minnesota? Misery, Deena, that's the human condition. I bring hope for those who want it. That's my job."

"People are junk on the inside," Deena said plaintively. "I have to be going now."

She left before he could reply.

⌒

Deena needed Dr. Milton's advice about the parrot that wasn't eating. She had run every test she knew of and remained stumped. His office door was slightly ajar, and she lifted her hand to knock but paused when she heard her name mentioned, and Winnie's animated voice. Winnie Chang, a tall, chatty veterinarian, worked at a larger clinic a subway stop away. She and Dr. Milton had been having an affair as long as Deena had worked there. Winnie was a regular fixture every other Friday, usually dressed in a red leather jacket, a pair of jeans, and black pumps; they would leave the office for an hour and a half. Where they went for their trysts, Deena neither knew nor cared. Dr. Milton had at first made awkward explanations for Winnie's visits. Noting Deena's disinterest, they continued a steady, openly affectionate affair.

She leaned forward to hear.

"She's always edgy," Winnie was saying. "God, she has no idea how hard professors would be on her. People think just because you work with animals that it's just some kind of fun carnival ride all the time. I worked my ass off in vet school. Didn't you tell me she was on welfare once? God, she would get eaten alive."

"I wouldn't say that you worked it completely off."

Winnie giggled.

They whispered something that Deena couldn't hear.

"…talent, and handles herself professionally. But she'd never pass the exams to get into vet school. She's a high school drop-out I think."

"With her background, and her age, God, she's lucky she's even employed at a place like this. Joshua, you're so much nicer to her than anyone else in this business would be—"

Dr. Milton interrupted, "Can you believe she's Guyanese? I thought she was Cambodian or something."

Deena slinked away from the door. She took refuge in the bathroom. Making sure the door was locked, she rubbed her face and held onto the sink. Pressing her teeth into the right side of her tongue, hard, kept the tears away. Although she didn't cry, her body registered its sadness through its throbbing, reminding her of every ache and pain in her aging body. *I'm an old woman. Why don't I just give up? I don't belong here anymore. Where do I belong then?*

❧

There she was, in the middle of a busy intersection. Deena carried a glazed black bowl made of clay. In her bowl, gravel and bits of tar were mixed in with her morning mackerel and eggs. A golf ball rolled toward her and hit her foot. It then rolled in another direction, and she followed its steady roll into the street and over to a golf course.

A table in the middle of the golf course was laid with a feast. Three men stood around the table, one resembled Dr. Milton but she couldn't be sure, his face kept blurring. One man, the shortest of the three, took her bowl and handed her another one.

"Get yourself a good seat, it's going to be an excellent game," he said.

"Thank you. I'm not a big golf fan, but it's such a nice day that I think I'll watch for a little while."

There was food cooking, she could smell it in the air; a meat smell mixed with garlic and fresh oregano. Enticing. A game of golf was underway, and Deena sat on the grass to watch. As the tallest man brought his club down, she noticed that the ball was not white and had a strange appearance and shape. She was about to call out when the club struck down on the ball, and Deena realized it was the head of Mr. Chester.

"Stop it!" she screamed.

"What's the problem?" a man who she confirmed was Dr. Milton (the bad skin gave it away) asked, carrying another bowl.

"Where's my baby?" Deena demanded.

He pulled out a little barbecued drumstick with a rich red hue.

❧

It was the first warm night of spring, and Deena slurped on a delicious, fat, dark green pickle. She had taken her phone off the hook for the day. She hadn't been to work for the first time in eight years, and she knew her job was in danger if she wasn't fired already.

She could hear Milo's voice outside her window. She tried to ignore it but there was urgency in the voice, something was wrong. *Can't I have peace for one night?* Deena threw her pickle into a bowl, cursed, and put her shoes on.

Before leaving she checked on Mr. Chester, who was sleeping. Deena examined his eye bandage and turned on the classical music station for him. "Okay, I'll only be gone for a minute, you hear? Don't you worry about nothing."

She went downstairs and walked across the street. Milo was yelling his head off over the wishing well. "Come out here you fucking animal face freak!"

Deena heard whimpering from nearby. Where was Calvin? "What's going on here?"

Milo looked up and his face softened. Strangely, he seemed glad to see Deena.

"It's Calvin." He pointed down the street.

Regretting her decision to leave Mr. Chester and the quiet of her home, Deena folded her arms and said, "Yeah, what kind of mess has he gotten into? It's always something with you two."

"This freak did something to him." The boy shook his head and paused like he was trying to remember, "He was there and then he was…" As if punched in the stomach, Milo doubled over.

"What is it?" Deena said. She instinctively reached out to touch him but pulled back.

"I didn't wish *that*. I wouldn't have wished *that*. This creep show thing better turn him back. Fix him. I'm not playing. I'll dive into the well if I have to!"

"Milo, you're not making any damn sense." Although she didn't grasp what he was talking about, she sensed none of Milo's irritating bravado. Deena looked over to the shadows that seemed to gather at the end of the block.

"Look at him! Will you look at him?"

"Calvin, is that you? Are you okay?" Deena called. "Calvin, come here." The block was quiet for this time of night. *Where was Simon when you needed him?*

Milo was at her side in an instant. "At the corner," he hissed.

Frowning, with every step she took she wondered if this was some kind of prank. She wouldn't put it past them.

Over her shoulder from the well, Deena heard Rivi rise up out of the water and speak. His voice sounded calm, nonchalant. "Maybe you can explain it to Milo, Deena. An answered wish alters what you know. Remember that you wished to be a veterinarian a long time ago? If you had become that, everything you know would have been different. You would have walked into a different reality."

"What?" she said, turning. "My reality would have been different?" She was having a hard time following Milo *and* Rivi. *I need to get back to Mr. Chester.*

"Look, you two can talk about philosophies and shit later! What about Calvin?" Milo was wild-eyed, visibly scared, his chest heaving under the light blue windbreaker.

Her throat tightened and felt pricked by needles as she noticed Milo's agitated body language. She didn't know what he was capable of. *I don't know what any of us are capable of.*

"We're not talking about me," Deena answered the creature firmly. *Would that have solved everything? Would my life really have been different?* Shaking those questions off, she brought her attention to the matter at hand.

When they arrived at the end of the block, she exhaled with relief.

A fancy candy red painted car was parked at the corner. She'd seen one of those on TV but couldn't recall the make.

Her relief evaporated when she heard Calvin's voice, whimpering, nearby.

"Calvin, come out here in the light, so I can really see you," Deena commanded, looking around.

For a moment, she thought she glimpsed Calvin sitting in the passenger seat of the car. But that couldn't be him. She squinted. His face. There was something undeniably wrong with it, as if it had been stretched out and mashed back together. Lopsided cheekbones. A forehead jutting out more than she remembered. His head home to many patchy areas; his tightly curled hair looking like puffy black islands on his scarred scalp. Dull, ashen skin.

Milo pounded on the hood of the car, "No, no, no."

She rubbed her eyes. No, she told herself. *This was an illusion, just like when I stood in the arc of colored light.*

"We were standing together, right here," Milo said, pointing at the car, spittle flying from his mouth. "My beautiful car. We were looking under the hood, we close it and as Calvin touches the car he…it just absorbed him."

Although she could not see him, Calvin's whimpering had become a mix of barks, deep sighs, and shrieks. They boomed from the car.

"It happened slowly and it sure looked painful," Milo added. "I tried to hold onto him but that didn't stop anything."

Blinking, she looked from him to the wishing well creature.

Pointing to the car, her body shaking, Deena asked, "What have you done?"

"Milo now owns a beautiful, top of the line Corvette, full of fuel. That is what he wished for."

"Rivkinsommersabat, I don't know what your game is or how you did this, but you *can't* do that to Calvin, he's a child. A hoodlum, yes, but in all reality, still a child," Deena said, shaking her head.

Calvin's sounds of distress from the car stopped. Deena shivered.

Rivkinsommersabat motioned for Deena to come closer. She crouched down, her knees making a cracking sound.

"Secretly, didn't you want to make him disappear?" he asked.

"No!" she protested. "I—"

He held up his hand, interrupting her, "When you saw him peeing against the mailboxes in your hallway? When he intentionally bumped into your mother on the way to the hospital, causing her to fall? When he chased away the kids from school selling cookies? When he called you 'old high yellow bitch'? You detested everything about him. You wished for this and *worse.*"

"Hush up! I did not wish that on Calvin!" She fell silent for a moment as the partial truth of his words wrapped around her like a noose.

Milo flattened himself on the hood, opening his arms wide. "It's going to be okay, bro. You hear me in there? Wherever you are in there, Calvin, hold on," Milo said.

"It's some kind of trick that you're playing and it's gone too far. Calvin's parents will be upset. You must undo it."

"Calvin's parents are gone. He lives with his grandmother, she's super old and don't leave the house," Milo said with a resigned tone.

"Do you wonder what kinds of wishes count and when?" Rivi continued.

"This is madness," Deena said, recoiling. "You keep up this nonsense and the police will come. You'll be pulled out. You're going to get hurt."

He shrugged his massive shoulders. "No one cares about Calvin."

Milo jumped up and yelled, "This is some fucked up ass shit. Somebody do something!"

Deena startled. Milo's confusion and anger were palpable.

The wishing well creature held up his webbed hand, "Milo, all that screaming is extremely irritating. There is an old book that I use to help me make wishes. Anyway, sometimes you have to use your judgment to approximate things. In this case, I used my judgment."

"A book? He's got to be fucking joking, right?" Milo said, his eyes rapidly blinking. "Someone's got to be fucking joking. This doesn't make any sense. I just wished for a car so I could leave outta here. Take Calvin with me." He stood, clenching and unclenching his fists.

Deena backed away. *This is wrong. I don't want to get involved.*

Looking at Milo, the creature said, "No one will remember Calvin as he once was but you and Deena. He'll always be with you, Milo. You can go anywhere you want. He's now a part of that stunning car. Keep up the car, keep his spirit alive. I dare say this whole situation will build character for you, Milo. I suggest you find a place to keep the car safe. Lots of people around here who would love to have a car like that."

Through tears Milo sputtered, "I'm so sorry that we were bothering you. Please turn him back. I'm sorry."

"I'm so glad that you're here, Deena, to admire my handiwork. This is the other side of hope and wishes," he said.

Now whispering to either her or himself, Deena wasn't sure, he said, "That I can do such a thing to Calvin. I didn't think it was in me."

"You must stop it. You must change things." Pointing at Milo and then the car, Deena said, "This is not hope. This is not what you said you gave."

He cocked his head to one side, with an almost human expression and said, "Ever wonder what *I* wish for? Ever think about who I go to for wishes? No, you probably don't."

Watching him slowly sink, her mind swam from the boys to her own tangle of needs that kept rising to surface. *Why is he letting me see what he has done?*

She called to him, "How did you know that I wanted to be a veterinarian?"

"It's a great job for humans who dislike other humans," he said. His long lower lip curled up, giving his face a mocking look.

"But..." he popped out of the water. "You do care, don't you? That's it, you *care* too much."

"No, I don't," she said defiantly.

"Look about you, the neighborhood you used to love, the animals—the way things *used* to be. It is *I* who doesn't really care anymore," he said. "I love animals, too. You're lucky now aren't you, Deena? Lucky, that animals don't have wishes and they don't dream like we do?"

Tired of his puzzles and secrets, she said, "I don't care about that or Calvin. I don't want to be a part of this terrible game."

Deena barely heard the wishing well creature before he submerged completely. "I'll be seeing you soon."

Milo stood, looking at her with his puffy eyes tinged with red, tight mouth, hands clenched at his sides.

Deena held up her hands. "Maybe he will change his mind but, he's right that you need to find a safe place to park that car. Now."

Deena left Milo and went back to her apartment and bolted all four locks on her door. As the evening settled into the deepest night, she found herself awake muttering…"I care. I care…I care."

☞

Mr. Chester hadn't moved around his cage, passed urine or stool in two days. Nursing him, Deena was anxious and irritable. Gritting her teeth, she considered her options. Dr. Milton could help, maybe?

"Okay," she said. "I'll go back."

Bursting into the waiting room she ignored Winnie's questions (she was seated behind the front desk) and went to find Dr. Milton.

"Please, it's my baby. Please, look at him, Dr. Milton. I know I haven't been acting right. I'm sorry. You can even fire me if you want…just look at him," she pleaded.

With pursed lips Dr. Milton silently opened the yellow blanket that was wrapped around Mr. Chester.

After examining him, he said flatly, "He'll probably die tonight."

"What?"

Sternly, Dr. Milton began, "Deena, about your behavior…Winnie and I are both concerned. We don't know what is going on with you. If it is drugs, I have little tol—"

Deena grabbed hold of Dr. Milton's arm. "Look here! He's all I got in the world. I'm not much to look at. I don't have a penny to my name, and I don't have any kin. I don't have anybody. I love him, please, help me." Deena's salty fat tears dropped and spread across the white protective lab paper that covered the table.

"Get a hold of yourself, quiet down," he said with pursed lips. "You've seen animals come and go. There's nothing that I can do for him. Too many traumas have been inflicted upon his body. I told you not to take him in the first place. What made you think you could save him? You're not a vet and won't ever be a vet."

"I can't...I love him." She bundled him up and ran out the office, past Winnie and through the door. She hailed a cab back to the Bronx.

૭

As she approached the well, Deena knew that this was where she would have to come. To come to him. To be brought to her knees.

She pushed past the small crowd, stepped on open-toed shoes, barking at people to get out of her way. "Let me through now!"

Upon seeing her, the creature wiggled himself out of the hole, the now muddy water sloshing about. He hoisted himself up on a piece of concrete. She no longer had to guess at what the rest of his body looked like. His torso and split tail were the color of black sand, but his legs were a deep blue. Ignoring his odd appearance she asked, "Can you save him?"

"You can save him."

She dropped her head. After a moment, he asked, "Is that your wish? For the rabbit, Mr. Chester, to live?"

"Yes, damn you. Yes."

"You know that it must alter everything that you know?"

Chester's body was stiff; he looked small in her hands. He had lost so much weight his ribs showed.

"Look, there is no more time for games," Deena said.

"You have to be informed of the rules."

"Please hurry."

He opened his mouth and then stopped.

"What is it?" she asked impatiently.

"I haven't had a real wish, one of love and sacrifice, in almost three centuries. I don't quite know what will happen."

She took a long look at the wishing well creature, and he at her. Up close, she took in the dark red eyes. He's old, Deena thought. *He's older than anything I've ever seen before.*

"Let's try," she said.

"Make a wish to me, three times," he said.

She said it to him and grabbing her, he said, "I've waited for you all this time." He waved his arms wide, "All this was to find you."

Mr. Chester moved his ears and made a face like he understood what she was about to do. She heard noises and people pointing, but her attention was fixed on the rainbow arc rising up, meeting her expectations and fears.

All along, life was preparing me for this, she thought. *The absurdity of her mother's death, Dr. Milton, even the $1.99 stores was all for something else. I know about a rabbit's heart. I even know about the human heart. Most are ragged and torn, but somewhere in greasy underused arteries are sugar packets of wonder and deep desires.*

Rivi's tired head drooped, and his hand felt light in hers. She nodded, knowing he needed this rest and knowing she was fresh for the journey. For a moment she was in the arc where the light shimmered.

❧

Deena floated around in the well, adjusting herself. Her facial skin was leathery, her hair just tufts around her turtle-like head; she possessed an otter-like torso, with human arms and blue legs. Her voice, when she exercised it, was deep. When she peeked out, she saw a line of people, with expectant faces, forming at the well, and she felt eager to begin her new task. The life she had lived fell away as a line loosens from a dock: identity, human meaning,

THE WISHING WELL OFF FORDHAM ROAD

dates, times, and situations. What she had been before was gone; all her loves and worries were gone. She understood the human condition, but she was not part of it anymore.

Rivkinsommersabat had lied about the spiritual book; there was no guide. However, he had shown her how she could read real wishes in the prism of the heart, starting with her own. And, maybe, she surmised, just maybe, that sly thing knew her wish was larger than being a veterinarian. *I can repair the world.*

ℂ

In uptown Manhattan, a trim, well-groomed man with inky dark hair took the next patient waiting to see him. A man with punkish green hair and a green beard approached with a cocker spaniel puppy under his arm.

"Hey bunny," the man said in passing to the lop rabbit sitting in the cage on a small table near the reception desk. The rabbit looked with its clear healthy eyes back at the man, holding his gaze for a moment before hopping to the other side of the cage.

The man shook his head as if to clear his thoughts and then began. "Bessie's tongue has been this bright orange color for the last three days. I think she ate something weird."

"Please, step into my office," Rivkinsommersabat said.

GRINDING DISNEY

I HAVE A MEAT GRINDER AND I HAVE BROUGHT IT TO THIS forest. Invitations were sent and, as the light fades, I see them twirl in, oblivious to danger. Leading the way is the fairest of them all; the one who keeps losing her shoe, the one who went from mermaid to human, and the rest of the princesses and common girls assemble. Alice is last, the girl of elixirs (can't we just admit that she likes to get high?). Oh and to my surprise, in floats Tinkerbell, the wannabe, more insect than fairy girl. I tell them that the meat grinder is a magical stagecoach that will transport them to a special realm called Immortality. They trill at the lie. Longevity has made them a trusting bunch. I tell them they must disrobe (the grinder will be hard enough to clean without shards of glass and cloth). They shed capes, headdresses, tiaras, and ribbons like the obedient girls they are. I confiscate Alice's flask. It's a tight fit, but I get them all in. Just when I am about to turn the crank, Tinkerbell sticks her head out and asks, but why should we go to this land of Immortality? They love us, they'll always love us here. *Are you sure?* I say. I don't have a beef with her and am about to tell her to fly off, but then someone pulls her down and she disappears. For a moment, I hesitate. Then, I remember how sharp their candy-tipped swords were when they plunged them into our soft young bellies, before we knew our own dreams. They are smarter than they appear, which has always been key to their survival—and their ability to adapt with the ages. Adaptation takes brains. I grind away and ignore their pleas for rescue. I watch. The grinder extrudes neat mottled pinkish ribbons occasionally streaked with iridescent shimmering scales. And, with a pop, yellow fairy dust spurts out in place of the meat. Enjoying this more than I can say, I have not noticed that a crowd has gathered. Hungry. They know I do not belong to this forest. My spell casting falters. Hitting a dark beast on its snout, we fight for the fairytale meat.

WHAT THE SLOTS HOLD

LADY LUCK, KNOWN BY MANY NAMES, CAME TO CLAIM HER own in Atlantic City. She stalked past the drunk, slack-mouthed men at the blackjack tables. A cocktail waitress holding a platter of drinks looked up, screamed, and fled. Casino alarms blared and men that from her twenty-five-foot height looked like children ran toward her from every corner. They yelled and fired their guns at her. Annoyed, she plucked coins from her dress, dropped them, and watched as the golden disks smashed the men's heads.

With a magical axe given to her by Ares, she hacked at row after row of the garish Greek God slot machines. As she worked, she remembered the handsome face of the mortal she had met so long ago. Pierre, whose skin tasted like pure rain. He was a descendent of the greatest magicians to have ever lived. A secret visit from Olympus to see the earthly realm had tempted her. She, a daughter of Aphrodite, a natural lover, fell so easily for his charms. He said he would build palaces where men would whisper her name. She might never have known that her magic was stolen, corrupted, used to kidnap others. Not until she overheard a joke about casinos from Zeus. She would show both gods and humans what happens when Lady Luck is angry. The last blow split the largest slot machine in two. In a burst of orange light, her cousin Fortuna emerged from the rubble. Lady Luck cut the golden bindings holding the goddess. They hugged. She threw more coins from her dress and watched as they sprouted legs, arms, and hands holding daggers and chased the remaining humans. Taking Fortuna's hand, Lady Luck said, "Vegas next."

THE LINEUP

RICKY DRAGS DEREK OUT OF HIS HIDING PLACE, INTO THE lineup with the other neighborhood boys. Derek's armpits smell sour, like vinegar. Last time he ran out of lineup, Ricky tackled him, left bruises. Ricky's the biggest teenager on the block. Have to stay still. Derek hears the engine squeal. Ricky's been obsessed with Evel Knievel for months. No barrels or Greyhound buses for Ricky's stunts. Young boys are the next best thing. Derek tries not to think of his head split like a watermelon on the street. Tight as sardines now, all holding their breath, not moving. Someone faints. Dominoes.

MISS BLACK LITTLE HILL OF 1965

ISABEL FINGERED THE TEARDROP EMERALD EARRINGS WHILE waiting for her husband to open the passenger door of their car. Two weeks into their marriage, and his gifts kept coming. And he promised more! She smiled at her good fortune.

He'd caught her eye at church. Strangers at church always do. He said he was visiting his distant cousin. Smooth dark skin, wavy hair, a fine new peanut-brown cashmere coat. Ruby rings on his fingers. From Pensacola, the big city.

A smarter woman would have noticed different things about this man, asked pointed questions. But she didn't need to be smart, did she? She was, after all, recently crowned Miss Black Little Hill. 1965 was her year, she could feel it.

Some in her town wondered how this well-dressed city man made his money.

"I love a man that can cook," her mother said a few weeks into the courting.

Isabel winced. She wished her ninny of a mother would shut up. "Mama, he said he was in the restaurant business. He co-owns several restaurants. Isn't that right, Derek?"

"That's right. Other people handle the cooking. I have the ideas."

"A coloured man with vision," Isabel said.

℗

"When am I going to get that surprise you keep talking about?" she asked, stepping out of the car.

"Soon," he said, squeezing her hand a little too tight. They walked toward the restaurant.

Her mind travelled the length of all the things he had promised, including a chinchilla fur coat! What had her prospects been in Little Hill anyway? Marrying one of the local boys, breaking their backs, working in the orange juice business, and living in a place one step up from a sharecropping shack?

The restaurant's drooping red and white awning read, *Neighborhood Pizza and Pasta.*

She hid her disappointment. The outside didn't look like much: one large window and a simple black wooden door. He held the door open for a woman with a scarf on her head, carrying a pizza box. She nodded at them as she passed by and into the night. As they entered, Isabel wondered about his other restaurants.

"You didn't think I could do Italian, huh?" he said.

He had talked little about his restaurants, or food, or much of anything at all. The wedding, honeymoon, and move from Little Hill to Pensacola had kept them busy.

"But we already ate," she protested.

He pulled her along, his grip stronger than usual.

Two young Black men greeted them, and he introduced her as his wife, but no one took her coat or offered to get her a glass of water.

Instead, Derek hurried them through the small, shabby main dining room. No white tablecloths, she noticed.

The restaurant narrowed into a gray, dimly lit hallway.

"Where are we going?" she asked.

She paused in the hallway's shadow, sensing the balance of her youth was about to ebb away. She rested her hand on the wall, finding it cool and pebbly. The scent of her mother's biscuits came to her then. This moment surprised her. She had been so eager to leave everything behind. She thought about turning around. That was stupid, she knew. Where could she go? She was his wife now.

"C'mon," he said.

Walking in, the restaurant's brightly lit kitchen assaulted her senses. Pots gleamed back at her. On every wall, bunches of basil and oregano hung from hooks. She had never been in a restaurant's kitchen.

"What's back here?" she asked, folding her arms.

He didn't answer but strode ahead. Two doors faced them. He pushed open the one that read, *Employees Only*.

The large room they walked into looked like a small department store gone awry. Movable racks of clothes stood in each corner. Coats were piled on pallets, mounds of ladies' handbags slumped next to a table where a large woman in a red polka dot dress sat. Gleaming toasters stood next to small televisions and electric mixers. A cornucopia.

Two men and the woman looked up and smiled.

"Evening, Derek," the younger of the two men said. He was clipping beige department store tags off pairs of men's trousers.

Derek opened his arms toward the group and said, "My business partner Robbie, cousin Tico, and Portia."

"Pleased to meet you," Isabel said in her most polished voice, with a slight dip of her head.

Robbie, who looked like he could be in high school, offered a shy grin. Tico looked back at her with the deadest eyes she had ever seen.

After their initial greeting, the men went back to their sorting and clipping. James Brown belted out "Papa's Got a Brand New Bag" from the radio on a nearby shelf.

She gaped at her husband as he removed his coat, loosened his tie, and rolled up his sleeves. The room felt hot, and she wondered if she should remove her coat, too.

"What is this?" she said.

"This is home, baby."

"I don't understand," she said.

"She thought your bullshit was real," said Portia, the woman with a contraption over her right eye that Isabel had never seen before. Portia used this tool as she bent over a tray of jewelry, looking at a stone. Was that a diamond Portia held?

Her husband put his large hand on her head, clamping down on it, flattening her lustrous curls. "You didn't think I *bought* all those fine things now, did you?" he said.

She tried to move her head up and down to suggest, *yes, that is exactly what she thought*, but he turned it slowly side to side.

"No, no, wrong answer," he said.

"She did think that," Tico muttered.

Derek lifted his hand and gently pushed her into the middle of the room.

"Mondays and Tuesdays we get the stuff in," Robbie said. "Wednesday is processing day, and Thursday is when people come visit after our dinner rush. We need a pretty face for the ladies. They don't want to buy stuff from guys. And Portia there ain't fit for no one to look at, and she's got an even worse personality, but she knows her jewelry."

Unfazed, Portia said, "Rocks is much nicer than people. Figured that out a long time ago."

"You steal it all?" Isabel squeaked. She thought of the cops-and-robbers shows on TV and wondered how he broke into so many homes.

Throwing his head back, Derek made the loudest laugh she had ever heard him make. Guffaws erupted from his body.

"They put that crown on your head a bit too tight," Derek said when he finally caught his breath.

"She country, what can you expect?" Portia said, shaking her head. "Most of the stuff is stolen before it gets to the stores; some things belonged to someone else before they got to us. We got fences all over town."

"Inventory," Robbie said.

Isabel crinkled her nose, put her hands to her throat, feeling as if she might gag. "Whatever this is, I…"

Her husband snarled his mouth, those delicious features knotting up. "Miss Little Hill, we go shopping for things we like, just like you go shopping. Oh yeah…that's right," he said, slapping his hand on his thigh with a flourish. "You don't go shopping because you're too piss-poor to shop."

Derek leaned toward Tico and shook his head. "You know her town didn't even have a Woolworth's nearby?"

One of the young men from the front of the restaurant appeared at the door. "About twenty people here."

Derek nodded, then pulled Isabel close. He whispered, "You get to keep one thing from every haul. One thing. Should keep your greedy ass happy. That's why you married me, right? So, you could have the finer things in life?"

His words bit into her. Isabel, squeezed her butt muscles, drawing on her pageant training to keep herself erect, and resisted collapsing onto the floor from fright.

Without waiting for an answer, he let her go, turned, and walked out the door.

"Show time, honey," Portia said. "Better sit down and get familiar with what we got."

Robbie snorted, and Tico held her gaze briefly with his cold flat eyes.

She sat down next to Portia, noticing the woman's cracked lips.

Portia added, "Did he tell you that his first wife, Miss Black Lincoln Bridge 1961, ran away? But she didn't get very far."

"Miss Black Long Bay 1963, had an accident, didn't she, Tico?" Robbie said, his voice dropping an octave. She trembled as she saw the look that passed between the two men.

"Tragic," Tico said.

Isabel shook her head and then recalled the feeling of being on stage in front of the judges for much of her life. She would watch and learn everything about her captors and the people they served. She may not have been smart, but she had taken to heart the main principles of all successful beauty pageant winners: be confident, no matter what happens on stage, and project a winning attitude. They would regret underestimating her. Putting her hands in her lap and hoping they didn't notice her leg twitching under the table, she smiled wide and said, "Pass me some of the dresses. Modeling is one of my talents."

THE INVISIBLE SON

"NO ONE SUSPECTS YOU'RE A DEALER WHEN YOU'RE IN A LIMO,"
Brian said to Cara, his school's social worker. When he talks with
her, Brian feels time slow down, melt, and thicken, allowing him
to think, and recently that had loosened his tongue. She appears
now in his mind's eye for a moment—a brown giantess, who wears
spectacularly large gold hoop earrings, loud orange vests, and
sometimes even a jumpsuit. She looks kind of hip for an old Black
lady, especially when she wears combat boots. Not like the others
over the years.

Now, he closes his eyes for a moment and leans against the
leather headrest that fits him perfectly, letting the music of Marvin
Gaye reach through him. His dad's favorite. He likes it, too.

"Three stops." His father turns down the music.

Brian nods. They've already done five stops (three girls' night
out trips, and two anniversaries), all legit rides, and when Brian
looks out the window, he sees late night. The stars are out.

He has his father's mop of dark blonde hair and at fifteen is
almost as tall as him. His dad is bulky, he fills out a suit; Brian
is wiry, he can live on protein shakes like his dad, lift weights
constantly, and maybe gain two pounds.

How long have you been working with your father?

Since I was twelve, after mom died, he wants to say out loud, but swallows instead. *Stupid, you're letting her creep in.* He wants the social worker's voice to be quiet. Cara's not here with him in the night.

First Stop

The Lincoln Mega stretch limo eases to a stop behind a row of apartment buildings. A man emerges from the shadows. His father makes the tinted passenger side window slide slow, just enough so it's level with Brian's eyes. *Dad looks out for me just fine.* Brian reaches down and carefully peels away a small white packet that's taped behind his belt buckle. He knows his father's right hand rests on a Glock 17, but there won't be trouble here.

The man slips in several neatly folded hundred-dollar bills. Brian uses just the barest touch of his thumb and forefinger to take it. Sometimes folks are so jittery, they fling the money in Brian's lap and it takes him forever to count it. Their eyes are the ones he remembers when he's tired, too tired to eat his dad's undercooked oatmeal and runny eggs.

Hardest job there is. One wrong move and you're gone. But it's a good job, you know? And, I'm inside most of the time. Cara's large brown face, dotted with nubby moles, stayed smiling even when he told her more. No arching eyebrows or shocked expression. Had he ever gotten this far with the others? No, they believed he fell asleep in his classes because he was dumb, lazy, maybe even "developmentally delayed." He wonders if high school will be different. Is there a point to keep coming to classes, sitting in the back, and listening to teachers who know nothing about his nights?

Second Stop

They round a corner near a warehouse district and park. His father gets out and smokes a cigarette while leaning against the limo. This is Brian's cue. He's got to cut the rest of the stuff up. Never at home, always around some corner. *Worst part of the job.* He opens a compartment next to his seat and reaches for the mirror. A small plastic bag of brownish powder is underneath. He dumps out a little on the mirror. This is heroin, and, unlike coke, it needs to be cut some so it's not too strong, so that his father can make it last longer and make more money. From under his seat, Brian grabs a small bag of powdered sugar. He unsheathes the razor blade in his wallet and moves the blade into the thick powder dividing it into columns. He adds a bit of sugar, divides them further. He is deft with the blade. Brian looks to his left and makes sure his father is still taking a break. Then, a quick taste. Pinky finger to nose, and a deep inhale. Only way he can stay calm now. His secret. Besides, Brian learned in his economics class about the importance of quality control in running a business.

Third Stop

This stop always makes Brian tense. He opens the glove compartment and chomps on his stash of Reese's Peanut Butter Cups. One after the other. His father pulls behind a Hummer limo and a black Audi.

His body shakes to the beat of the music from the club. He's got to be on now. These are the classy buyers, dopers, and addicts. They will run in and out of the club to buy and then some will want to hang out in the limo. He will soon turn into clean-up boy, watching to make sure no one scratches the upholstery, breaks the champagne glasses, leaves lipstick tubes or keys behind, or takes stuff out of the limo that doesn't belong to them. Sometimes, his father tells him to get in the main cabin and serve them drinks. Usually, he's tending to rowdy fuckers who spit, curse, and spill everything, sometimes on purpose, he thinks. *Some like to see me scurry.*

Later tonight, if he's lucky, he might see rich women's legs straddling their guys. Tiny sparkly dresses hiked up around their butts and their backs undulating to secret rhythms. *You haven't told me about that perk,* Cara says. He ignores her. *What would she know about anything sexy like that?* He has to be careful though not to remind those in the back that although a screen divides, it does not fully conceal. He is supposed to be invisible. The invisible son. He has not told Cara about how invisible he could be as a pretend chauffeur apprentice. "My apprentice" is what his dad says to people when they look at him in that "What's your kid doing here?" kind of way. "My son can work in Vegas or LA. He's had the best training," his dad would say.

The chocolate and heroin surges through Brian's body and everything feels RIGHT NOW—the stars coming at him from far away, the crimson stockings that girl wears as she goes into the club, the feeling that he knows all about the night. He holds on to that delicious moment knowing it will fade in just a few more seconds. There it goes.

His dad stretches, loosens his tie, and reaches into his pocket to light up his usual at this hour—an atom bomb—marijuana mixed with heroin. In a moment he gets out, opens the back door of the limo, and changes out of his formal black jacket and hat to an electric blue double-breasted blazer. It's a ritual Brian knows well. Although his dad will sell and score later in the night, he knows that now is his dad's time for fun. To party with other limo drivers who deal. He watches his father walk and wonders what it will be like to fill that electric blue suit someday.

Throughout the night, Brian takes money with his two-finger touch. Good colognes and perfumes waft past his nose. He imagines they have names like Destiny, Mysterious Pleasure, and Seductive Nights. He's not supposed to keep the engine on, but he does so to listen to music. To stay awake. He's not allowed to listen to music on his phone; his dad's quick right hook made sure that mistake wouldn't be repeated. He is supposed to look out for the police or rival dealers.

A giggle erupts at the edge of Brian's consciousness, jerks him awake. The screen is down because no one has come into the limo for any additional fun. He turns and sees a woman in a red skirt and black, low-cut top kissing his dad's chest.

"What you got for me tonight? Hey, hey, hey," the woman says. Her lips are pouty and for a moment Brian wonders what it would be like to be next to those lips. Or, any female lips. He never gets to meet girls. Too tired during the day, too busy at night.

"Calm down," his father says to the woman Brian recognizes now as "Pris," a local gal who likes to hang with the high rollers. Sometimes she asks how school is going and what music he listens to. No big deal.

Pris turns, leans forward and Brian sees how lit up her dusty brown eyes look, like a character in a video game, how her usually put-together face looks lopsided, as if someone had come and wiped half her makeup off.

"You okay?" Brian asks her.

His father jerks his face up from Pris' ample cleavage, "Of course she's okay."

Is there anyone special in your father's life?

No. Not like my mom. He sometimes brings girls to the limo. Party girls, you know.

What do you do when he's with them?

I walk around. Dad's dates are always okay with me.

Brian gets out of the limo before his father gives him another look. He didn't know that Pris was one of his father's regular dates, but whatever they were doing, he leaves them to it. Not a show worth watching. But he lingers near the limo, a jittery feeling coming over him, as if he might vomit up his congealed peanut butter cups right there. He has a bad feeling and decides to distract himself.

He walks the length of the block and back twice. A bouncer he doesn't know gives him the once over, so soon Brian heads back to the limo. He knows something is wrong when he sees his father, disheveled and looking around for him. Brian knows that look. He's seen it before. Once when his mother died in a car accident, and last year when they were stopped by the police after finishing a drug run. His father's hazel eyes dim to gray for a moment. Then, as he breathes in, Brian sees them spark awake. Brian wants to retreat, feels the ball of his right foot housed in a black sneaker lift up slow. He knows this anger is a rope waiting to choke him.

"Get in."

Brian obeys and moves to the passenger side.

"Idiot! In the back, on the other side," his father explodes, stabbing the air with his forefinger several times.

Brian hustles over and opens the door. Pris is stretched out on the beige couch, face down, bleeding from a gash on the side of her head.

"That stupid bitch tried to steal from me," his father yells, starts up the limo.

"She's bleeding," Brian says into the cold night. Brian looks around searching for what she might have hit her head on.

"We can't take her back into the club," his father says.

What are you going to do if your dad really hurts someone? Cara had saved that question for last.

In all our years in the limo, my father hasn't ever hurt anyone.

"We have to take her somewhere. To a hospital," Brian says. He dabs at the gash with a wad of cocktail napkins.

"Right." His father looks at him in the rearview mirror. Brian pretends he does not know that the direction they are heading is not in the direction of any hospital. He feels something rip inside of him. His thoughts lead him to the razor in his wallet. Could he catch his father off guard? Would using it help Pris? He wonders what he will do when they arrive.

Brian can't hear Cara's voice anymore. He tells himself it didn't matter as after tonight he wouldn't be going back to school again.

NEW EMPLOYEE ORIENTATION GUIDE FOR SNATCH DAY

We are pleased you have chosen Troll Bridge Senior Homes as your employer and will join our colleagues in enriching trolls' later years. Our mission is to empower senior trolls to live healthier, more active, and more joyful lives through lifelong learning and integrative health and wellness practices. This guide explains the protocols for one of our most popular events—"Snatch Day."

"SNATCH DAY" IS A TIME-HONORED TRADITION AT TROLL Bridge Senior Homes and well-attended by all our residents, their families, and friends. Prospective clients may also visit during Snatch Day. As with everything else at TBSH, we aspire to provide a quality experience in every aspect of an aging troll's life. Our residents miss the feel of grabbing and scaring humans, and while we can't provide humans, we can recreate a pleasant moment from their youth.

ATTITUDE

WE EXPECT OUR EMPLOYEES TO EXEMPLIFY OUR HIGH STAN-dard of hospitality on this day. The residents look forward to this day, so do your best to act cheerful through the inevitable accidents which are bound to happen because many residents refuse to wear their diapers on Snatch Day.

A new employee will certainly be asked, "Are the diapers made of baby goat skin?" This ugly rumor has circulated since the founding of our home. You must answer a definitive "no."

Remember, all employees are paid time and a half for working during Snatch Day.

BILLY GOATS

OUR COMMUNITIES VIEW SNATCH DAY AS A RITE OF PASSAGE, and unfortunately, so do the Billy Goats. The teenage Billy Goats begin to assemble around dawn. We don't have enough staff or volunteers to keep them out. They are often harmless and do little more than annoy us with their screaming while our residents shuffle by.

LOGISTICS

ON SNATCH DAY, ALL EMPLOYEES WILL REPORT AN HOUR earlier than their regularly scheduled shift.

You will take potential clients interested in TBSH to our display cave with the crystalline floor. Do not take them into Tunnel 23.

The staff will set up three teams of eight young volunteer trolls; boys will most often volunteer. You will mark a big white "X" on their backs. You will find paint in Tunnel 12.

The residents in better condition residing in Tunnel 22 can be helped into small holes near the large oak tree out front. They will lie in wait for the "unsuspecting villager."

When all are gathered, the supervisor will clap their hands, stomp their feet and yell, "Go Snatch." The volunteers will allow themselves to be snatched. Family members will cheer from the stands.

You will need to guide some of our residents. This can take a long time. Residents will want to boast to you about the number of volunteers, over the years, that they have snatched. Patience is required.

The oldest among our residents tend to favor the more human-looking volunteers. We are an inclusive community and can't change deeply held prejudices. Direct a resident to the nearest volunteer snatchee.

Snatch Day also means courting for the teenage troll attendees of the event. As their parents will socialize at our most generous snack table boasting beer, grub sauce, fish, and other foods, the teenagers will want to socialize. This is natural. You may be required by the supervisor to locate any young couples who have wandered off in the woods.

Everything winds down around 3 p.m. At this time, you will round up residents and awaken the ones who fell asleep. You must account for every resident on your roster! Some of our residents can still shape shift, using glamour, although only for a few minutes. Notice any unusual-looking logs, rabbits, or snakes around the opening of TBSH. They can't hold a different shape for long, but it only takes a few minutes for one of them to escape and grab a human in the next town over. We must ensure that Snatch Day is as safe as we bill it.

ADDENDUM

IT HAS COME TO OUR ATTENTION THAT IN PAST YEARS SOME staff members created life-size human looking trophies made of grain and livestock to give out on Snatch Day. This is not an appropriate use of staff time and such trophies can harm residents, causing them to fixate on their prior experiences with humans. Any employee engaging in such behavior will be immediately terminated.

AND THEY WILL RISE FROM THE OCEANS

ISABELLA COULD NOT BEAR TO SEE PASCAL IN PAIN. HER FIANCÉ writhed at the table as the water spirit occupied his body and disrupted what had been a peaceful and uneventful séance. He had never summoned a non-human spirit before, and Isabella didn't know why he had now. Sweat ran down her back, the cold rivulets dampening her elegant flapper dress dotted with intricate blue beading. Moisture pooled at her hairline. Miles' and Elliot's tight brown faces looked as bewildered as she felt. For once Miles was speechless while they sat at the table. Her lips trembled watching her beloved's face contort. Pascal's eyebrows knotted together, the veins in his prominent forehead bulged. His mouth tightened and his skin took on an oily sheen. *Why would he open himself to this spirit? Why would he possibly invite something like this?* Ever since his trip to the wild places of Egypt, Tunis, Arabia, he had come back unsettled. He spoke of the mysteries of rivers, great water spirits, and the power of oceans. As water in the crystal glasses on the table gently bubbled—another manifestation of the spirit's presence—she felt a chilling fear toward Pascal's obsession with water. *It will lead to no good.*

The humidity in the parlor was the first thing that alerted her senses. Instead of feeling like a crisp October evening in Manhattan, it felt like June, air so heavy and moist it felt as if a damp cloth was wrapped around her head. The spirit arrived late into the evening after the usual affair. Pascal, working as a medium, summoned a few deceased souls, and shared their specific messages for some of the bereaved guests. Miles and Elliot laid their hands on the sick. Miles was especially good at stomach ailments.

Departed souls, ghosts, "the ancestors" as Pascal called them, showed up and announced themselves with a potent scent or a sound like the dropping of pennies. They left clues and sometimes teased the person seeking their guidance. This possession was nothing like that.

Pascal's eyes rolled back in his head and spittle formed in the corners of his handsome, full-lipped mouth. What should she do? She squirmed. She was not a medium or a healer but a believer in the unknown and unseen and Pascal's champion. She possessed no spiritual talent but had insisted on being at the table with Pascal and the other men. Earlier that evening, Pascal finally, grudgingly, assented. *I've earned my place. That small victory distinguishes me from the rest of his followers.*

When Pascal's arms twitched like a puppeteer pulled at them, someone gasped. Isabella was barely aware of the small crowd, followers of Pascal who stood a few steps back from the circular table where she and the others sat. Their séances and spiritual meetings drew curious Black socialites, artists, and everyday seekers. The tension and growing fear in the room felt like a belt tightening against her ribs, making it difficult to breathe.

Pascal's shuddering jerk brought her attention back. She noticed his eyes watered.

"What have you come to tell us?" she said, finding her voice at last.

"What's your name?" Miles interrupted.

It's here for a reason, with or without a name. She clamped down on the irritation that this man brought out in her.

"He who has roamed many lands," the spirit began, its voice sharp and clear like a pin prick on her skin, "and now seeks the waters, knows my name. He wants the secrets of my brothers and sisters."

Pascal's face was a wreck of light and darkness now, his eyes clouding, rheumy as if he suffered from too much drink.

Elliot muttered the Lord's Prayer loudly.

"He wants to go down to the bottom. Arrogant man," the water spirit continued.

Isabella drew in her breath. The other men shifted and stared.

Pascal turned his head toward her, blue spirit eyes fixed on her. *Those eyes!* For a moment it was as if it submerged her in dank water, a foul place where dead creatures rotted in the dark.

The heavy oak table shook, and she gripped Pascal's hand harder. The glasses of water shattered, scattering shards and droplets across the table and into the crowd. People near her shouted. Many backed away, some turned and fled the parlor. Flinching, she forced herself to tighten her hand. *I will not let you go, beloved.*

"Spirit, release Pascal. Go forth from here," Isabella commanded.

"We show you back to the light," Miles said, standing, still gripping her and Elliot's hands.

Her hand throbbed from Miles's grip and from the wet heat of Pascal's hand.

"We are tempted!" the spirit roared.

After a moment, all was still in the room. Isabella's heart galloped as Pascal slumped over to her side. The chamber felt dimmer although no one had touched the lights.

She released her hold. Taking Pascal's face in between her hands, she rubbed his cheeks.

Eleanor, a woman of means and a newer regular attendee, rushed forward. "Is he alright?" she said.

Eleanor was from a well-known family in D.C. and had gone to Spelman College, not Howard University, as Isabella had. A socialite now in New York, she moved as if surrounded in a layer of delicate cloth and softness. Her voice seemed softer still, a squeak, but a determined squeak. Isabella noted the other differences between them—Eleanor was tall and busty, blessed with perpetually dewy-looking skin and medium-length hair held by a simple barrette, which looked nothing like Isabella's sleek pageboy wave.

Isabella reminded herself that she, not Eleanor, was engaged to Pascal. *He has chosen me for special things.* Feeling protective nonetheless, Isabella whispered, "Darling, how are you feeling?"

Pascal's face was losing the coloring and harsh expression the water spirit etched on it. He opened his large eyes. She loved those dark, fearsome eyes. They complemented his face, showing the complexion of dual parentage, just like hers. She was a tad lighter shade of tan. He was darker, caressed with reddish undertones in his skin. Some called them mulattoes, but she liked the word colored, as was the fashion of the day.

"Pascal, what was that?" Miles asked in a clipped tone. He leaned on the table, wiping himself with his familiar blue handkerchief.

Pascal bolted up. "Was the Old One of the Ocean here?"

"Yes, it took you," she said.

Pascal pulled out a handkerchief from his gray and blue lounging jacket. "You *made* it go away. I could hear you."

She recoiled at his tone, color rising quickly to her face. Had she been wrong to make the spirit leave? She thought he knew little of what was happening during a trance. "Darling, I was worried."

He waved a hand and turned to Elliot and Miles, "What did it say?"

"It was fearsome and noxious," Elliot said. The tall man stood with his arms folded.

"Not much," Miles said with a shrug. "It didn't seem friendly."

Isabella twitched her nose. A musty smell clung to Pascal.

"Tell me what it said," he demanded. They told him in detail. Pascal pursed his full lips, sat back, and said, "This is good."

❧

Pascal's butler and driver, Middy, an older man with a limp, brought towels and cleaned up the mess. In a short time, Pascal assured everyone he was fine. "Please everyone, head to the parlor. I'll be there shortly."

Pascal motioned for Isabella to follow the others. Baffled, she tried to shake off the feeling of doom as she reluctantly left him. She followed the crowd, now speaking in hushed tones, from the small room where the séances were held through the adjoining hallways that led to the large parlor.

There were extravagant signs of Pascal's successes displayed throughout the building, one that he owned outright. She had not seen so many beautiful pieces of art in any home. He was richer than any colored man she would ever hope to meet, cultured, comfortable in his own skin. Her thoughts turned toward the few whispers she had heard about him when she met him last year. Rumors swirled around him when he arrived in New York's colored circles. There were tales of him using sex magic in Louisiana. Some said he poisoned his white father and that was how he gained his wealth. Isabella knew that rumors and gossip often twined around successful colored men. *I believe in him and I love him, that's what matters.*

Everything in the parlor overflowed with beauty and elegance except the newest object that stood on a pedestal on the far side of the room. *That awful thing!* The vessel Pascal brought back from Egypt—a large, four-foot urn. Old, chipped on one side, with intricate carvings all around. And there was something else. She could not help noticing how the squat, slate-gray figures carved into the urn had wide mouths that seemed to leer and grimace, lifelike. They looked as if their forms could step off the jar to greet her. They struck her as ugly and mean spirited. *Isabella, you are being silly.* Pascal said little about it on his return except that it had once been used for sacred water rituals.

She moved away from the urn and thought of more pleasant things. When troubled, she returned to the comfort and anticipation of her future wedding. *If only Pascal would commit to a date.* Although she had long ago vowed not to be constrained by the strictures for colored women of the day, she did want to be married. He was twelve years her senior, but as an unmarried twenty-four-year-old, she was not a young girl either. *Several of my friends have been married for years!*

Every time she was near him, she ached, and his slightest touch sent waves down her body. Oh, how they could travel together and see sites that she'd only read about! She did not want to pester, it would not be her place to do so, but how she wanted to share a wedding date with her friends and rejoice.

She made small talk with the guests, about thirty in all and more than half were women. More and more women were coming to their meetings. Although many spiritualist meetings had faded in the past years, Pascal's arrival had revived them in Harlem. Besides Eleanor, she liked most of the women there.

"What the hell was that?" Miles asked.

"I don't know. Pascal looked quite surprised," Isabella said.

He snorted and took a long pull from his glass of brandy. A muscularity in his mustached face, volatile, he always seemed ill at ease but nonetheless a powerful healer.

"He's never attempted anything like that before. Was this your idea?" He leaned in close enough that she could smell the sweet whiskey on his breath. "Water, such a feminine notion, connected to birthing…" he said, with only a thinly veiled sneer.

Her face flushed for the second time that night. Vexing. A bit too vexing given the scare Isabella had just kept her head through. As if her womb did the summoning, even opened the door for Pascal.

Isabella held up her head, narrowed her eyes and gave him a cool look that she usually reserved for obnoxious men who called to her on the city streets. "I can assure you that I had nothing to do with this evening."

"What do you make of it, his fixation on water?" Miles pressed.

"I can't say, Miles."

Elliot joined them. She smiled at him. Cooler in temperament and more pleasant in every way than Miles, Elliot seemed not to resent her connection to Pascal.

"Does he seem different to you?" Isabella asked.

"No," Elliot said.

"Horse shit," Miles said. "Since his trip away, I rarely see him anymore, except for these meetings. He's holed up here. Really, Isabella, you should try to get him out more. Work your feminine wiles."

"I do try," Isabella stammered.

"He's trying to build something good and powerful here," Elliot said, his eyes gleaming. "Maybe he has better things to do than spend time at the private drinking clubs you so often favor."

"He never drank much anyway," Miles said with a shrug. "Plus, he's moody and sullen most of the time. He's given up on so many things we used to like to do together."

Isabella felt the small man's rising frustration. It's true, she thought, although Miles had known her beloved much longer than Elliot, they didn't seem as close anymore.

"Great men have to put their time into building great things. Things that last," Elliot said with a smile that showed slight dimples in his long handsome face.

Miles shook his head. "Tonight was almost a disaster! What disarray he was in. We go from a healing to—"

"To something beyond our wildest expectations," said Pascal stepping up behind them, startling Isabella. He stood open armed, his hair perfectly waved and looking even more fetching than before. He had not come in from the main entrance they were facing, but from one behind them.

"Pascal," she said, moving toward him.

Caught off guard, Miles opened and closed his mouth.

"I called that powerful spirit because I wanted to know about the ocean. So many secrets float in its waters and are buried at the bottom of its vast expanse."

"It felt foul. If Isabella hadn't stopped it, you may not be standing here right now," Miles said.

Isabella could hear the challenge in his voice.

"Isabella is a woman of fine intentions, but I needed no help. I need *believers* if we are to do something great, not naysayers. I thought you understood that, Miles."

I am a believer, Isabella thought. *I have been guided by your hand and your light.*

"I confess confusion. I haven't understood much this evening," Miles said, shaking his head.

"Let's make it an early night then," Pascal said, his voice louder. He stood aside, "Middy has your coat and will show you out."

Murmurs shot through the crowd. Middy stood silently next to Pascal.

Anger flashed in Miles' eyes, but instead of making a scene, he took his coat with one hand and gave the butler his empty glass with the other.

"Isabella, a pleasure. Elliot," Miles said, giving a curt nod to each.

She wasn't sorry to see him go. Did she see a brief smile cross Elliot's face?

Pascal went over to stand near the urn. Surveying the crowd, he said, "We must probe the unseen mysteries to better help our people. We are over twenty years into a new century and what is the state of the colored man? He wants for everything. He wants for dignity, for work, for education, for prosperity, for industry. His women are forced to be maids and often face the hands of the white men who wish to mistreat them in the vilest kind of way. And my friends, many of the church leaders offer little except mind-numbing obeisance. It is upon us, friends, to take our vision into the world, soaring to new heights. That is what these sessions are about. Let us talk tonight of what may help the colored race. And of Africa, a place of deep mystery."

"Oh, Pascal, no, do not compare us to the deplorable savages of Africa," a woman Isabella didn't know scoffed.

Shaking his head, Pascal gave the speaker a withering gaze. "You speak from the comfortable vantage point of ignorance." As he spoke, the round woman moved a step back as if feeling the power of his rebuke, the weight of her transgression.

"We are a part of the dark mysteries of Africa, a continent which I have traveled. We must seek those motherly roots for guidance," he continued.

The small crowd swayed and nodded. Isabella did not like the way they stared at him. As if he was some deity. *But is that not true of me, too?* Knowing his accomplishments, she looked at him with awe, too. A man who has faced death, who can work the unseen energies, a man who can talk to spirits, who can heal. *And when he looks upon me, do I not also wish to fall down at his feet?* She could feel herself falling now into this delicious intoxication, feeding her senses, making her want only him. But when she opened her eyes, she saw the vessel, and it gave her such a fit of unease she did not hear the rest of what Pascal said. Did she see movement on the urn? No, it was a trick of the light, she thought. The last hour had been a strain on her.

"Is it always like that, like what we saw?" a stooped older man asked.

"No. Tonight we saw something special. We've had a very eventful night. We hold these meetings so we may help you and each other—that we may connect with our spiritual purpose and evolution. Now please, stay as long as you'd like and enjoy yourselves in the comfort of my home."

Interrupting Isabella's thoughts, he offered his arm. "Shall we walk?"

She nodded.

Being this close to him erupted a fire through her belly. He moved through the crowd and chatted with people as they made their way out to a small balcony. The fresh air helped clear her thoughts, though, this close, she noticed a sour, mildewed smell still clung to him.

"What's on your mind?" Pascal asked.

"Everything that I saw with my eyes. Why would you summon such a being?" she asked, feeling small and unsure.

"I have my reasons. Do you trust me?"

She nodded.

"Have I not been worthy of your trust?"

She nodded.

"Did I not choose you above all those who would seek to be at my side?"

She felt the spark of their meeting a year ago ignite within her. Isabella had never dreamed she would meet a man who shared her own interests in the unseen world. Most of the colored men she met were church-raised and suspicious of, if not hostile to, any notion of the spirit world. She found it difficult to hide her curiosity when they had met at one of the American Theosophical Society's lectures. They couldn't stop talking to each other during the reception held after the lecture. She was entranced then and smitten after their first date.

"Yes," she said, letting the memories fade.

"So believe that you'll know all the pieces at the right time." Pascal lifted her chin to look at him. "We must grow, Isabella. We must challenge ourselves. I have to challenge my talents."

The October night air was cool, but being this close to him caused goosebumps to ripple across her skin.

"What else, Isabella?"

It was as if he could look into the very core of her and know what she was thinking.

"Our wedding date remains—"

"Do not worry, we will set a date. I have much on my mind now."

"Although I don't have family, I would like to inform my friends—"

"I can't worry about frivolities," he said, a steely look in his eyes.

She drew back. He had never spoken to her that way. She noted his sharpness, just like after the séance. *It was like looking at a double of him. Pascal but not himself.*

He took her hands in his. "Soon we will go beyond these heal-ings and the common complaints of our people. Beyond 'help me talk to my deceased grandson' or 'help me with a new job at some terrible factory.' We must work toward a grander vision. I need someone who can see that, Isabella, someone who can share that. We can't get bogged down in the everyday. We, of course, will get married. I would not have asked for your hand otherwise."

"Yes, of course," she said. *I should not doubt him.*

They walked back into the house. A few people remained, sitting on the sumptuous chairs and settee. She paused and picked up her favorite object in the room. It was a baby blue, circular music box, about four inches high and a handspan wide, last year's Christ-mas gift. It played notes from "Blue Danube." She had saved for months to purchase it and she was proud that he kept it visible in this room with so many other prized treasures. A small token of her deep love for him.

"How are the arrangements coming for my meeting with Swami Asokonanada?" he asked.

"I should know soon. There are many people that want to meet with him."

"That's why I donate so much money to that organization, so I can leapfrog over other people," he said with a wry smile. *"And that's why you work there."*

And because I studied world religions at Howard University. "I must not seem to play favors when setting up his schedule."

One of the benefits of her job as a secretary for the American Theosophical Society was that she helped schedule all the meet-ings of guest speakers from around the world. It filled her with a great deal of excitement and purpose. Sri Sri Asokonanada, a noted healer and teacher, would make his second trip to the US shortly. He advocated yoga and meditation and wanted to meet with people who were open to spiritual teachings and esoteric ideas. Pascal had made large donations to the New York chapter of the ATS and had asked for nothing in return, until now.

"I met many swamis and gurus in my travels over the years. Strange, powerful men. I am eager to meet this one."

"I know," Isabella said.

His eyes glowed as he continued, "Some have developed powers, siddhis, beyond our current imagination. Men that can shrink themselves, sit in the middle of a snowstorm and melt snow around them. Some can stop their hearts. This one follows the way of water—water spirits...Shiva."

"Yes. I will make sure it happens," she reassured him. The feverish glow in his eyes unsettled her. She changed topics. "I'm so looking forward to seeing *Cleopatra's Night* tomorrow."

"As am I, dear one," Pascal said.

"My mother always wanted me to go to an opera, but we weren't able to. Philadelphia's ethos of brotherly love never much extended to coloreds and the arts."

"Opera was the only one of my father's loves that he shared with me," he said, the creases in his face softening. "How the enjoyment of music can make louts and scoundrels into men."

She smiled, forgetting the labors of the night. "You're exposing me to the opera. Sometime, I would love for you to come with me to the Negro Baseball League. They are in town."

His face soured. "I'm not interested."

"I enjoyed playing softball when I was at Howard. I haven't played for fun in so many months," Isabella said with a sigh.

"There are forgivable things when one is a *girl*," Pascal reprimanded. "It is not fitting for a woman such as yourself to play any kind of ball. Jumping, sweating, and running are not suitable for ladies. It's undignified." He turned up his nose. "You are better served to use your energies elsewhere."

Chastised, she lowered her eyes and said nothing. *I like using my mind and body.*

"It is late. I will have Middy drive you home."

"Thank you," she reached up to kiss him, holding her breath to avoid the lingering fusty smell.

֍

They arrived at the opera house in their finery. Pascal presented the tickets, but the glassy-eyed man at the ticket booth glared at them. "There must be some mistake," the clerk said.

"There is always a problem when a man is being robbed in front of everyone," Pascal said. "I have paid for a private box and am being denied."

The clerk stalked off to get the manager. Several white patrons, dressed in gay clothes, swirled around them. Isabella's stomach lurched. She wanted to melt into the floor.

The manager arrived. The clerk by his side stood straighter and tightened up his boyish face.

"Edward must have sold them," he said addressing the manager, a tall older man with an erect posture. "He must have thought this man picked them up for his employer.

Pascal puffed his chest out, "I work for myself. I know that such a thing might be hard for you to believe, young man. We want to see the show."

The manager said nothing more than, "I see."

Isabella's throat went dry. *I knew this was too good to be true.*

After a moment, the clerk's face fumed, "Go back uptown with your own kind."

"You do not know what my kind is," Pascal snarled.

Isabel's eyes widened. She had seen Pascal deal with situations like this before much more calmly and even with a hint of humor. Not how he was acting tonight.

"A light-skinned monkey is still a monkey in a suit. Get out of here before there's real trouble," the clerk said, clenching the tickets. The manager took the tickets from the young man.

"We will refund the cost to you," The manager said in a low voice. "There's clearly been a clerical error."

"Is there a colored balcony?" Isabella said, her voice trembling.

All three men ignored her.

"I do not want a refund. There's been no error!" Pascal's face and neck flushed.

She tugged on Pascal's arm as the crowd gathered around them. The crowd was behaving itself, momentarily, but dread creeped through her, making her breath shallow. The patrons, anyone, could turn on them. She knew their heads could be bloodied in the next few minutes and then she would *never* get to be Pascal's bride.

"Shall we get an officer of the law?" Pascal's voice boomed.

She could see the rising anger in Pascal's twitching eyes as if he were forgetting the rules that they both abided by. Rules that made no sense. Rules that washed away dreams and tore into their psyches. But by forgetting those rules, he was abandoning them to chaos.

"What did you say?" the manager said, dropping the tickets.

"Pascal," she said, shaking his arm. "Let's go now. We shall walk back up to Harlem." She reached out to him with all the mental energy she could muster, trying to will him back to reason.

The coolness in the lobby evaporated and Isabella felt a sticky, cloying, pervasive heat envelop her. The tangy smell Isabella noticed from last night choked the air. Pascal's right arm twitched. As if someone controlled it from afar, it lifted, moving toward the clerk.

"We're done. Get out of here," the clerk yelped, but, as Pascal advanced, the clerk fell to his knees. His face reddened. The young man's glasses slid off and he clutched at his throat.

The patrons scurried away from the four of them. Someone cried out for a doctor and another for the police.

Pascal stood over the clerk and said, "A time is coming when such a thing will never happen again to any colored person. America will be washed of its sins. I have seen it."

"Pascal, we must go," she said, grabbing his arm.

He looked through her, his eyes a shimmering spirit blue, and shoved her. Isabella slammed into the manager who pushed her out of his way.

Isabella righted herself and watched as Pascal towered over the man and chanted. *Pascal is possessed!*

The clerk vomited eel black fluids. The oily liquid that spewed from his mouth oozed across the lobby floor. On instinct, Isabella took her purse and knocked Pascal across the head. "Spirit, leave this body!" she yelled.

She heard Pascal's neck crack. He blinked many times. People had come to help the clerk who now moaned and writhed on the floor.

The manager locked eyes with Pascal and walked backwards, as if in a stupor. His thin lips trembled and his hands shook. "A demon is among us. God help us!"

Isabella snatched his hand, pulled him toward her and they ran out of the lobby and kept running for a few blocks. When they stopped, Pascal said nothing, as if still in a daze. They found a phone booth and she called Middy to pick them up.

They rode in silence. She thought about Pascal's behavior and strange comment about America being cleansed of its sins. Her stomach knotted as she thought about her troubled beloved. When Middy arrived in front of her building, before leaving, Isabella reached over to kiss Pascal. As if far away, he barely moved his head to acknowledge her. Her lips pressed into a cold, damp cheek.

And there was no telephone call from him that evening or the next.

☙

I shouldn't bother him after what happened a few nights ago. She paced up and down the block for ten minutes before finally deciding to call on Pascal.

Pleased that she convinced Middy to let her in after she told him she had urgent news for Pascal, she walked down the hall to Pascal's study. She opened the door, walked in, and saw several open books on the table. Isabella rifled through them. Most were about the slave trade. They made her shiver. Such a cruel history her people sprang from. Such difficult reading.

Well, where was he?

She climbed the grand stairwell to the second floor, drawn to the parlor. She entered from the door at the far end of the hall, the one Pascal had used after the séance.

"Pascal, dear, I'm here with a surprise."

The smell caught her attention. Damp. Musky. Oceanic.

Pascal lay on the floor on his side, shaking.

The urn had been taken down from its pedestal and rested a few inches away from him. It was different. To her surprise the carvings of the ugly figures were gone! The chipped urn's "face" was blank. She rushed toward Pascal and then stopped. Everywhere the squat gray figures surrounded him. The forms before her were real, not shadows. Their wide mouths gaped. They jerked, hopped, and leapt. They pulled at his ears and at his fingers. Unintelligible, guttural sounds erupted from them. As if sharing one mind, they froze and collectively turned to look at Isabella.

In a flash, they formed a circle around her as well. She jumped and yelped. Isabella stomped on them, but like rubber they bounced off her shoes.

She screamed for Middy. Grabbing an ashtray off an end table, she threw it at the dancing figures. They scattered, disappearing.

"Oh God," she moaned as she lifted Pascal's legs and attempted to drag him over to the couch.

Middy ran in.

"Middy, oh thank God! Please help me lift him up."

They pulled him up on the sofa. Middy shook Pascal and repeatedly called his name. "Mr. Clay, Mr. Clay. Come back."

Middy pulled a vial from his trouser pocket, opened it, and pushed it under Pascal's nose.

Pascal snapped awake. Feverish and drawn, he waved away any more of the salts.

She paced around the room and stopped in front of the urn. It now looked as it always did. The figures were there once again. She rubbed her eyes and shook her head.

Middy lifted the urn with effort and placed it back on its stand.

"Middy, when you walked in…did you see?"

"Nothing, Miss Randall. I saw nothing."

"I think—"

"I'll bring something up for you and Mr. Clay to eat. He'll need it."

"Can you tell me?" she said, drawing close to him. Her eyes searched his tight face for answers.

"Ma'am?"

"Have you seen him like this before?"

An unreadable expression flickered across his face. "Yes, Ma'am. Yes, I have. He pushes himself with his work."

The faithful manservant turned and left.

It took a full half hour for Pascal to rouse. To her dismay he awoke angry, directing much of it at her.

"Pascal, what's going on? I saw—"

"He should have never let you in here." He sat up but had not risen from the couch.

"Don't blame Middy."

Pascal folded his arms and said, "I employ him, and I can and *will* blame him. I gave him strict orders not to disturb me under any circumstances!"

"He didn't," Isabella said.

"What are you doing here anyway?" he said in a tone that cut.

"Pascal, please…I only meant—"

"I'm sure you've heard that the road to hell was paved with good intentions."

She was trying hard to blink back tears. "I came to give you good news. The swami is coming earlier than expected. I wanted to surprise you. After the other night, I—"

His brow softened, those beautiful lips upturned and the few lines around his eyes relaxed.

"Go on," he said, studying her.

"That's it, something changed in his schedule. He'll come next week."

"That is welcome news."

The morning's unusual events caught up with her. She felt faint. *When was the last time I ate?* She grabbed one of the sandwiches Middy left and took two big bites. The act of chewing helped slow her breathing, she concentrated on the texture of the bread, the sharpness of the cheese. She focused on all the sensations of the food, willing herself to focus.

He patted her knee. "You saw a type of water sprite. Harmless."

"They live on the urn?" she asked, her brows arching. "Why were they surrounding you?"

"They are protectors of it."

She swallowed and then said, "They didn't look protective at all. Not at all. Please don't lie to me, Pascal."

"The urn connects to the great spirits of the ocean. The sprites act as intermediaries in a way. Under the right conditions, the spirits will grant requests."

"What request?"

"That is none of your concern."

Isabella locked eyes with Pascal, searching them.

"Do not look at me like that!" he snapped.

"What do you know about the power of those spirits? Like the one you called on?"

Pascal rose from the couch and turned his back to her. Steady on his feet, he seemed recovered from the earlier incident. "I am a seeker."

Isabella swallowed another bite of her sandwich. "I don't understand what's happening to you. You've traveled so many places, but I swear that your recent trip," she sighed and hugged herself. "You're different now…All those books on slavery in your study," she said, her voice trailing to a whisper.

He turned around, his face now a scowl. "No one will teach us *our* history."

"I don't want to think so much about the past."

"Don't be a ninny. There are already enough of those in the world."

Isabella laid the half-eaten sandwich back on the plate. She got up and wiped a tear from her face. "I shall call on you when you are more civil." She felt unable to stop trembling.

He rushed over, grabbed her, and kissed her deeply on the lips. "Forgive me. I am not myself today."

Or many days of late, she thought.

Their lips pressing together, however, made her forget everything in that moment. The tingling of his tongue and the groomed waves of his hair, and the outline of his manhood that she could feel pressed up against her, caught her breath. He pulled away and walked toward the end table and picked up the music box. The music played and he wrapped his arm around her waist and waltzed her across the room.

As they danced, she thought of Robert Louis Stevenson's troubled characters of Dr. Jekyll and Mr. Hyde. Had she been so enamored by Pascal's charm, his determination and ability to rouse a crowd, that she had overlooked his less flattering traits? She felt her thinking about him was increasingly muddled by his ongoing involvement with strange spirits.

He kissed her again with passion. She stiffened. After a long moment, he released her, stroked her hair, pet-like, she thought, and sent her out the door.

"You'll know everything at the right time, Isabella. Trust in me."

℗

She had only met one swami before and he had barely spoken to her. She felt none of the peace and sense of calm then as she did now, riding in the car with Sri Sri Asokonanada. The older Indian man had been solicitous and courteous. She felt sorry though for his assistant, Kamal, a young pimply looking monk, as he seemed ill at ease in all social settings.

Middy had picked them up from the American Theosophical Society office and they rode in companionable silence. She did not tell the swami that he was going to meet her fiancé. No one at the Society knew she and Pascal were to be married. Pascal was just another wealthy donor interested in the occult. They did not seem to care what color he was.

When they arrived at Pascal's, she was surprised to see Elliot but didn't let her face betray that anything was out of the ordinary. She introduced him after Pascal, "Mr. Gibson, is also an organizer of the monthly healings."

Pascal and Elliot greeted Sri Sri Asokonanada with warmth and then led him upstairs. She and Kamal waited in a receiving room for guests on the first floor.

Isabella had brought a newspaper with her and hadn't gotten to the society pages when the swami appeared with Middy at their door.

"Miss Randall," the swami said. His angular, thin face sagged.

The young monk who had been dozing, jumped up.

It's been less than twenty minutes!

"Sri Sri Asokonanada, is something wrong?" she asked.

"We must leave now," he said with a determined and fixed brow, but not unkindly.

"Of course," she nodded. "This is the last appointment of the day. Middy will take you and Kamal back to your accommodations."

The swami nodded.

After she found Middy in the kitchen and saw them off, she took the stairs two at a time, eager to find Elliot and Pascal.

"What happened?" she asked Pascal. She noticed his face looked drained, as if he had added years to his life, like after the séance.

"There is a time for everything, Isabella," Pascal said curtly.

They looked at each other, and impatience twisted in her core that she couldn't hide. "Well, did you find him pleasant to talk to?" she blurted.

"It is none of your affair," Elliot said with such ferocity that she felt punched in the stomach.

Isabella could not stop herself from releasing the frustration that bubbled inside. "I worked hard to arrange that meeting. If there is something unpleasant that has happened, then it could affect my job—"

"Stop thinking of yourself. Enough. Leave us. I will call you," Pascal said. She noticed his eyes had the hint of derangement and rage she had seen at the opera house.

She drew back.

Elliot didn't bother to look at her as she scurried from the room.

℗

The days went on without her hearing much from Pascal. When they dined, he looked as if sleep had eluded him for days and he was terrible company. He wouldn't say another word about the swami's visit. She gathered it had gone badly. She so wanted to know what transpired between them, though she knew she shouldn't ask.

Taking a break between appointments, Isabella and Swami Asokonanada walked in Central Park on a beautiful fall day. Kamal trailed behind, periodically sneezing, a victim of seasonal allergies.

She had gotten used to the swami being silent unless spoken to. Today they made small talk about his schedule and the foods he had sampled on this trip. Swami Asokonanada was in love with glazed donuts, even though he declared Americans had too much of a sweet tooth. Her thoughts circled as they walked, and her gaze bounced from place to place.

They sat on a bench, and she rubbed the back of her neck several times. She crossed and uncrossed her legs. *If Pascal will not tell me how it all went, I'll have to ask.* She looked into the yogi's eyes. "I was surprised to hear you and Mr. Clay spoke so briefly."

"Yes, one of my least favorite visits," he said, shaking his head.

"He does good work with his healings."

"Indeed, that is a fact. He has opened many doors to the other side and is an earnest seeker. But I could be of no help to him, my child."

"Why?"

The swami paused before speaking. "Miss Randall, is there something I should know?"

No one at the Society knew about her and Pascal. She bowed her head. "Please don't say anything. He is my friend, and I am worried about him. He's been acting strangely for some time." *Like a different person.*

The wise man's face clouded over. "He wanted me to teach him. I said no. He wanted to know some of the most sacred rites of water to commune with and try to command energies that know nothing of human sensibilities. Not only could this cause madness in him but it would disturb elemental forces that could not be easily controlled."

"Oh," she said. More confused than when she asked.

He rose. "I would advise caution in your dealings with him, Miss Randall. He has an unbalanced mind, ready to topple."

ᑫ

The next night, she was relieved to hear Elliot's voice on the phone asking if he could meet with her and Miles at a café to talk about Pascal.

The booth seated all of them comfortably. She was surprised how glad she was to see Miles. The past few weeks had felt anything but normal.

"Thanks for coming," Elliot said.

"Hummpf," Miles said and took a sip of his soda.

Elliot looked around before he spoke. "I'm worried about our teacher and friend."

Her breath caught. *Me, too!*

"He isn't so much of a friend to me anymore," Miles said.

"Please, Miles," she said, placing her gloved hand over his.

"He's been entertaining wild ideas," Elliot whispered.

"I told you he was acting strange. But he clearly doesn't want my help or else he would have called," Miles said looking away.

"I've been watching him, and I'm worried. He sought a spiritual teacher. The swami said no to him. It messed him up," Elliot said.

"What swami?" Miles raised his eyebrows.

Isabella filled him in on the last few weeks.

"I need your help," Elliot said.

"What is it? What can we do?" *Anything*, Isabella thought.

"We need to bring the teacher to him," Elliot continued. "I'm worried that if he doesn't get some guidance, he will do something that could harm someone or himself."

"Nonsense," Miles said, shaking his head. "Pascal would never hurt anyone."

"Isabella, haven't you seen some things recently that have scared you?" Elliot asked.

"Yes," she said with a slow nod. "I have. Miles, he's right. This is not the normal Pascal."

Elliot smiled then and said, "I know it's been hard for you."

She took a deep breath. *Maybe Elliot does understand.*

"What do you propose we do?" Miles said.

"Can you bring the swami back?" Elliot asked.

"No," she shook her head. "I don't think that I can. His trip here is concluding. He has very little time."

"Do you love Pascal?" Elliot said.

The dark-skinned waitress smiled at them, refilling Elliot and Isabella's coffee cups.

What kind of question is that?

"Don't question my loyalty," she said, the words tumbling out fast. She felt her cheeks grow hot. She sat up straight and took a moment to compose herself. "He has other appointments, and it would look strange for me to request a change in his schedule."

Elliot paused and shook his head. In a flash that made Isabella jump, he leaned across the table and grabbed her hand. "He wants to make a deal with the ocean spirits to open sacred portals."

A shudder went through her as Miles spit out his soda. "That's crazy! Impossible!"

"I don't know whether or not it is, but that's his goal, part of his plan," he said, releasing his grip.

"Why does he want to do that?" Isabella asked.

Elliot shrugged. "Once those portals are open, he believes he can help more people in a new way."

"Nonsense," Miles tutted. "How could he think such a thing?"

Isabella looked at Miles, "I fear that he is working himself to death."

Elliot gently placed his hands over hers, "Put another meeting on the swami's calendar, please. Take charge. Find a way."

◌

She had gotten lucky scheduling another meeting with the swami in that Kamal had come down with a bad cold (and not allergies after all), in the last few days. Isabella happily stepped in to attend to the swami's needs. And she had brought him the best donuts in the city. He agreed to meet with her "troubled friend" once more to see if he could provide some temporary comfort. Middy said nothing to her or Swami Asokonanada in the car ride over to Pascal's or as he opened the parlor doors. She thought that strange. As soon as they stepped in the parlor, Isabella knew she had made a grave error. The air in the room felt charged and thick like the night of the séance. One look around the room plummeted her hopes that the kind man next to her would be able to reach her beloved. He was supposed to have a private audience with Pascal. Instead the room was full of people.

Pascal stood with Elliot and some of their followers, Eleanor among them. An obnoxious giggle escaped her lips. The urn stood in the middle of the room. Miles lay sideways on the couch, his hands tied in the front. Blood dribbled from gashes on Miles's forehead and chin. Miles must have fought with Elliot and others once he realized that something was wrong. Terribly wrong.

"Pascal," he shouted, "You must stop. This is madness."

"What's going on here?" Isabella demanded.

Miles spoke in a halted voice, "Do you know what he wants to do? He wants to raise *all* the African souls from their ocean grave! All who died on the way over!"

"Our people who were taken from us! They will avenge us from their imposed watery graves!" Pascal said. "All who take part in this ceremony will rule the earth with me. The greatest ocean spirits are joining in—we will wash this earth clean and begin again."

This could not be her beloved's plan. He was possessed. Tricked by a powerful spirit. Maybe more than one!

Pascal motioned for two of his followers to grab the swami.

Swami Asokonanada maintained a calm demeanor. "This is not what I expected tonight."

Pascal strode over to the slight man and said, "I ask you again, transfer your powers to me. I do not wish to take your life to obtain them. Your great wisdom can help me rule."

Isabella rushed toward Pascal but Elliot grabbed her arm and jerked her back. "He doesn't need you for this part," he hissed.

"Nooooo, no, no. You must let them go, Pascal. I need you. What about our life?"

Pascal turned to her, "I give you one chance, to reign with me in the new place, a place cleansed of America's sins. So many sins against so many peoples."

"Elliot! He is being controlled. Look at his eyes!" Isabella said. Indeed, Pascal's eyes had turned a hazy blue.

Eleanor squeaked, "You don't need her."

Elliot's grip tightened. She twisted, and they locked eyes. How she hated seeing his smug grin. "You lied to me," she said through gritted teeth. In that moment she wanted to extinguish the trusting part of her that had been so disastrously misled.

"You're playing your part," Elliot said.

"These spirits are manipulating him. Can't you see that?" she implored. "*They* want power, they want to be free to cause chaos," she cried.

The swami spoke. "Pascal, you do not know what you seek. You have been misled. If you open those portals, no souls will come, but the ocean spirits will enter and destroy the world. Do you understand? This world. There is no way you can control them."

"Your imaginations are all so terribly small," Pascal bellowed. "How can they do worse than what we have all already endured?"

Twisting in Elliot's grip, Isabella said, "As you have said so many times, we are here to plumb the mysteries of life in ways that further our goals of justice. You can do that my love, *we* can still do that, but not like this."

"Shut up," Elliot said as he tightened his grip on Isabella, causing her to wince.

Pascal shook his head and laughed. "You had your chance to be part of this. Of something great. Now you will be my sacrifice."

A terrible cracking noise burst from the urn.

"We must get to the heart of the issue. We must come back to our ancestors." Spittle flew out of Pascal's mouth. He chanted, and slowly the gray figures on the urn, the water sprites, transformed. Isabella, transfixed, shuddered as if something plucked at each of her vertebrae. Gasps arose from some of his followers as they watched the static images on the urn undulate and then, with little effort, peel themselves off the urn and drop to the floor.

Pascal nodded to the men holding the swami. They pushed him to the ground.

Water shot out of the urn. Frogs jumped out. An earth splitting noise erupted. Many fell to their knees and covered their ears. Elliot almost lost his balance and Isabella dropped into a squat.

"Now! Sacrifice him now!" Pascal screamed.

I must destroy the source. Isabella seized on this thought.

Elliot, distracted, had loosened his grip. She took her chance. She had been a pitcher in her college days. Fast, accurate. A talent so long buried. Isabella shot up and grabbed the object closest to her, the music box. Her fingers wrapped around the cold object. The memory of Pascal dancing with her, twirling her around the room, passed through her. Their love. Her desire. Gripping it with precision, she hurled the music box toward the urn.

Contact. The urn shattered. An unholy guttural scream from Pascal engulfed the room. Pascal collapsed. Pascal's followers rushed over to him. She made her way over to the swami who was unhurt. Dead frogs of various colors and shapes were strewn everywhere. It was impossible to avoid stepping on one. They both worked to untie Miles.

In the middle of the room, Eleanor helped Pascal sit up. He bled from the nose and he bore strange marks that ran the length of his face. He opened his eyes with effort, and when his gaze landed upon her, she saw little gratitude in them. Motioning to Miles and Swami Asokonanada, she made for the parlor door.

CEMETERY SISTERS

THE CEMETERY NEVER SCARED WELCOME SPARKS, EVEN AS A child. Cutting through it to get home provided the quickest route and allowed unrivaled use of her imagination. She would make up stories about people, looking for the oldest headstones. Most days after school, before it got dark, she'd pick an interesting gravestone, settle in, and strike up a conversation. She'd share things that didn't sit right in her mind.

She might say, "Ana Sterling of 1950, if you were here, I'd show you around Thistleview. Not that there's very much to see. In your day, I bet you used to go into that old city called Tulsa, not too far from here. It's not there anymore now, Ana."

Or, "One day the preacher's wife slapped me for not wearing a slip. After service, she asked me to come in the back to talk to her, and before I knew it, she had her beefy hand on me. The preacher's wife said, 'Welcome, can't you see your breasts are falling out that dress? Do you want to end up like your mother?'

"Mama never said I had to wear a slip, Ana. I don't even have a slip. I stopped going to church after that. The preacher's wife doesn't bother me anymore. She doesn't even speak to me at all. She just looks right through me as if I'm some piece of old cobweb.

Were slips big in your day, Ana? I bet they were. People had money back then from what I've read. They went places that needed slips."

On this day, seventeen-year-old Welcome made her way through the forested part of the cemetery, where the red cedars were thickest and some of the oldest headstones lay. She paused and sniffed, noticing the coolness in this part of the cemetery. She then heard words sung by a female voice:

My funny valentine

Sweet comic valentine

You make me smile with my heart

Goosebumps pebbled her pale skin, and she hunched into her ragged coat. The phrases repeated, and Welcome looked toward the nearest stand of trees. She darted behind one and then another, thinking some of her stupid classmates had followed her. After a few minutes of frantic searching and finding no singers—she knew no one in town that sounded as good as that voice—with every vein straining in her face, she listened.

Another female voice rang out, this one deeper in tone:

We're trying to come throu …

Come to us!

The moment seared her, like when she waited for the once-a-month afternoon train. On most days, Welcome dreamed of getting on the train to leave town. She imagined holding a bag of butterscotch candies in one hand and an old suitcase in the other. Wherever Welcome stood or sat, she sensed the trains, every part of her alert and yearning.

Pricks of excitement and danger bit into her, making her hop from foot to foot. She couldn't make herself stand still. Nothing she had heard so far in her life sounded as good as these voices. They made her feel as if her favorite butterscotch candies were melting on her tongue. No, it was as if she floated in warm butterscotch candy. She ran up and down the stretch of the cemetery. Welcome overturned rocks, peeked behind headstones, climbed a small tree, and searched for the origin of those voices until she could barely see in front of her.

Exhausted, she remembered her responsibilities. *Mama will wonder where dinner is.*

"Please, whatever you are, come to me," she said at last, the frustration catching in her throat. On the rest of the walk home as the sun sank, a feeling of utter sadness swept over Welcome. *Maybe everyone in town is right. I'm going crazy, like Mama.*

☙

The next morning, she let herself believe that the voices were real. She had heard something; she couldn't be crazy. Yet.

As she approached the thicket on her way to school, she observed and listened. She concentrated on every robin that flew by, every thrush that skittered through the fallen leaves, and noticed now how this part of the cemetery made her feel as if she walked through a cool mist, despite the warmth of the sun. She gaped at the way the light weaved in and out through the red cedars' conical branches. When she knew she could tarry no longer, she forced herself to move and touched her right hand to every tree as if to leave a sign for something that perhaps waited for her.

☙

Mrs. Dori Gavey jolted Welcome's attention when she said, "Welcome, I think that you are very talented. You are my best student and the only one that I want to talk with about life outside Thistleview."

Welcome stared at her teacher with the warm smile, trying to understand why she was asked to stay behind. The school day had dragged on, as it often did for Welcome. She sat watching and waiting, looking at the clock every few minutes, willing the hours to pass. The only time that she felt awake enough to say or do anything meaningful was in Mrs. Gavey's design and implementation class; known as "dimps" among students. Tall, shapely, red-haired Mrs. Gavey came to Thistleview about the time Welcome began the sixth grade. She was the only person Welcome knew who had come, in recent years, to Thistleview to stay. Mrs. Gavey's hire was the last attempt by the town to provide students with classes about cities in case someone wanted to go "out there," which increasingly no sensible Thistleview resident desired. Welcome often felt sorry for her as no one seemed much interested in Gavey's specialty subjects of building, design, or city history. Most of the girls begged out of it and decided to go to the domestic arts classes instead, but Welcome enjoyed learning about urban design, architecture, mechanical drafting, and how the great old cities were constructed and what they were like many decades ago. They sounded like made up places—Hong Kong, Oakland, Venice, Brisbane—but through Gavey's lectures, Welcome imagined herself traveling to them. However, today even the talented teacher's lecture on "Cityscape Leisure Activities Prior to the Great Separation" felt remote.

"Let me get to the point," Mrs. Gavey said, sitting back down at her desk and motioning for Welcome to pull up a chair.

"I want you to apply to a college. I believe there are several that would accept you, especially in New Orlando. Has anyone talked with you about your future, Welcome?"

Cities! New Orlando! Of course, she had heard of it, but no one in Thistleview talked openly about cities. One didn't talk of much in Thistleview, period. They had everything they needed here.

"No, Ma'am," Welcome said, her mind spinning from the mention of New Orlando. New Orlando wasn't even one of the places the trains from Thistleview traveled to!

"Well, it's time that someone did, as you're graduating soon. I've taken the liberty of reaching out to a few contacts outside of here about travel permits. I should have more to share in about a week. We'll start making a plan then."

Welcome nodded as Mrs. Gavey walked her to the door. She couldn't stop smiling.

Welcome scratched the name New Orlando over and over again in her mind as she walked home. *To ride the train out of Thistleview!*

That night, she lay on her stomach with a map made from hemp showing the towns like Thistleview that were part of the Great Separation, which had sprouted up about fifty years ago—the towns that had separated themselves from the remaining, functioning cities after the virus and war. Connected to the rest of the country by a rail system, these towns advocated for self-sufficiency and a way of life that was simple and traditional.

What a wide world there was outside of Thistleview! She could go any place if she could just make herself get on that train.

❦

Day after day, color and definition leaked out of her world. She still could find no voice and no music. She *had* imagined it all!

"Welcome, come here," her mother screeched.

Welcome rose from her bed to see what her mother wanted.

Her mother sat in the bathtub with several candles lit. Her cup of amber liquid was still full, which told Welcome that she had only been soaking for a short time.

"My back needs a scrub," her mother said, closing her eyes and pointing.

Welcome avoided looking at her mother's pale naked body as much as she could. She, however, could see her mother's breasts well in the candlelight. They looked fallen to her, and not just flat as she'd seen of long-ago primitive women in ancient magazines in the Knowledge Centers. Fallen, as if all the life that lived inside her mother had given way.

At least she's not lifting and playing with them, like she usually does. Mama doesn't know she's crazy. She hears voices, talks to them. Maybe that's the way it will be for me. At least I won't lift my dress in public.

I'm reminding myself right now to not do that to myself. Maybe I'll be a funny old crazy woman.

She grabbed the old and worn loofah, picked off the moldy spots, and began. While she scrubbed her mother's ruddy colored back dotted with moles, she occupied herself by counting how many ants crawled around one claw foot of the tub.

"I'm thinking of your daddy tonight," her mother said.

"Yeah," Welcome said, trying not to show undue curiosity, which would require more scrubbing, but hearing anything about her father was always of interest.

"He brought me to this house and said, 'Welcome home, you're mine.' And we lived just fine. And I fixed him eggs and Spam when we could get it, almost burned, 'cause that's the way he liked it," she said. Her mother grunted as if the memory poked at her now. She continued, slightly above a whisper, "He'd go away with a crew and scavenge in the worst of the old cities, make his money, and come back to me. No matter what people in town said about me, he never cared. He never cared. He didn't even care that I started to hear the voices soon after being with him."

Welcome's attention drifted; she already knew this much about her father.

"But one day, he got dressed as fine as I'd ever seen him. Nice black pants, a red shirt, and black jacket, and I said to him, 'You up and put your clothes on. You leaving and can't say goodbye?' He looked so strange that day. I remember looking at his lips, they looked like they puffed up to make a kiss and then like he bit into something sour. Those lips! His lips always looked swollen, like someone had punched him. You got those swollen type lips, too."

Her mother absentmindedly picked at the skin on her arms and looked up at Welcome. "Your father said, 'Why say goodbye, when welcome is so much nicer?'"

"He left like he was going to take a walk right into town, like he was going to see someone. You were due soon. I didn't even ask him to get me anything; I wasn't having no cravings for nothing except to get you out of me. You were tearing me up with all that kicking and moving. I thought I was birthing a banshee," she said, her dry laugh cutting the air.

"He never came back. You were born three days later, and I named you Welcome."

Welcome shook her head; her father couldn't have left. It couldn't be true. Her mother was making it up. As she made up most things.

She felt punched. "You told me he died traveling to salvage." Welcome let the heavy, dirty loofa drop into the water.

"You're growing up now. I thought you might want a taste of the truth."

Her mother drew her knees up to her large chest. "Go and boil me some water for tea."

As Welcome got up to leave, she held onto the door with her back to her mother. "Mama, I'm sorry that he did that to you. But I don't understand. You named me Welcome because that's the last thing he said?"

"Don't be sorry and no!" her mother said, splashing a hand in the water, "Your dad was a fool. I named…I named you Welcome so I can look at you and think of something good and inviting and so that you can never say goodbye to me. Never."

Welcome closed the door, feeling as if she was a toy that her mother picked up and played with occasionally. *Mama never makes any sense.*

Later that night, Welcome dreamed that her father was a gray-haired giant who lived in the biggest ditch at the end of the world. He owned pretty things and ate them one by one, with a large fork and knife, and wore red and black shoes.

༄

After several weeks of exploring every perimeter of the cemetery, yet still not hearing anything, Welcome wanted to up her odds of finding the mysterious melodic voices, especially that first voice she heard. She took matters into her own hands.

She knew she would need to see Mr. Applegate, the caretaker of the cemetery. She knew Mr. Applegate to be a solitary widower, and that he was the son of Lily Applegate, buried in the cemetery. She saw him in town from time to time and thought he always smelled good for someone who worked at the cemetery.

The wind blew hard as she made her way round to his house at the northwest edge of the cemetery. As she walked along, huddled in her thin coat, she looked down and saw a trapped water bubble under the ice. She squatted so that she could get a better look at it. It was waiting for something to turn it into the rigid structure that it will be if the cold continues, or if a warm turn of the weather has its way it will stay water and merge into other puddles, she thought. *That is me, that trapped little pancake size of water. What will become of me? Will I thaw or will I freeze?*

Holding this question inside, she knocked on the blue door of Mr. Applegate's house. Another knock brought her face to face with Mr. Applegate. His brown face with a deep bronze undertone had a slack appearance as if he were about to smile but then decided against it. He looked twice her mother's age in the face, but Welcome saw how his chest bulged under his beige long-sleeved shirt and how his muscled arms hung down, loose.

He looked around her and then fixed his gaze on her.

"Welcome, you with anyone?"

"No, Mr. Applegate, I've come by myself to see you."

He paused for a moment and then opened the door wide. "Come in."

Grateful to be asked in, she rubbed her hands against her arms, stamped her feet, and took in the dark house and the framed pictures on the wall of him and his deceased wife, Wilhelmina. For a moment, her mind conjured up the best piece of lemon meringue pie that she had ever tasted. His wife had made it for a church event when Welcome was very young. Her tongue oozed saliva responding to the memory of it. Her mother never baked and everything in town was rationed, including sugar.

They stood in the hallway looking at each other.

"Something wrong with your mother?" he asked.

"No," she said, casting her eyes down. "She's fine."

"Take your coat? Get you something to drink? The cold made me not want to get out of bed today," he said, attempting a smile through tobacco-stained teeth.

"No, I can't stay long. I wanted to know if I could help you tend to the cemetery after school on some days."

"For pay?" He belched and then put his hand to his mouth, "Excuse me."

She shrugged, "I guess." She shifted some to not look directly at him. Her mother had showed her how to lean to one side and look slightly past men's shoulders. Her mother made her get up and practice all sorts of things at night after hearing her voices. Sometimes the voices told her useful things like what plants to grow in the garden to use on burns or cuts or teas to make when Welcome was sick. Looking off at an angle helped right now though because Welcome's heart raced, and her head pounded with such force, she could barely think. And what would she do if he said no? She needed to know she wasn't crazy. Finding the voices would help.

"Not much extra work right now as it's winter," he said.

She saw him taking her in, her hair, unnaturally and prematurely gray in the very front and the rest jet black. Her mama always said, 'Thick gray and black hair like some wild raccoon." Her head dropped slightly, and her expression seemed to give him pause.

"But, I could use a bit of help around here every now and again, especially when it gets warmer. Your mother says it's all right?"

"Yes." The lie fell from her lips before she could even think about it. *Mama don't need to know everything about my life. Won't matter to her if I'm crazy or not, long as I make her dinner and take care of her.*

"I guess you're pretty strong—you're bigger than me when you stand up straight," he said, then laughed.

She smiled though she wasn't sure if she should. Welcome pretended not to notice how he looked at her, stared now in a different way, a way that made her feel like she should flatten and roll herself out thin, like a piece of dough, and slide backwards under the bottom of his door. Like he knew there rested a wild energy in her that could get stirred up. Maybe it comes from being with so many dead people; maybe he's forgotten what it's like to be around girls, she thought.

With her round face and unusually long eyelashes, Welcome knew she was growing into an attractive, if not beautiful young woman. Boys no longer called her "gray slime" even if they didn't ask her out and thought her mother was strange. She was five feet, eleven inches in bare feet, and three inches taller in the hand-me-down heels her mother made her wear from time to time and that Welcome chose this day. Before leaving school, she made sure to go to the bathroom and wash her face, removing all ink stains, around her mouth, from chewing on her old pen.

"So, I can come by when the weather gets better?" Welcome asked.

The question broke the staring spell and he nodded, "Sure can. You want something warm to drink before you leave?"

"No, Mama's probably wondering where I am. Thank you very much and I'll be around soon."

❧

On her rounds, that spring, Welcome discovered that the cemetery was a busy place. There was always a dead body to help dig a grave for, flowers to place at headstones, and cleanup after the kids who loitered about on weekends. She was honest and returned wallets, lost keys, and other minor items that occasionally turned up near the graves. She mowed and watered the grass and helped Mr. Applegate trim trees.

Through the lengthening of light, she waited for the voices to return. She whistled to keep occupied, continuing to make up stories about the deceased. To test her own limits, she used the headstones as hurdles when she knew Mr. Applegate wasn't around. She'd spring up and unfurl her long legs and let mud splatter onto her face. Running around breathless, she'd collapse on the ground.

"Did you like that?" she said to no one in particular. "Here let me try again."

"Talk to me, someone or something," she whispered into the night before locking the front gate up, feeling loneliness webbing inside of her.

∽

One day at the cemetery, while contemplating if she should take some flowers home to cheer up her mother, she heard her name spoken clear as a bell.

"Welcome, over here. Look up."

Directly across from her the faint impression of a young woman sat high in a tree. She waved.

"We did it! I should know to trust you, Millicent," the woman in the tree said, a trill of breathiness evident.

Welcome dropped the flowers and stiffened. It was one thing to hear voices and another thing to see what? An apparition? A hallucination? Now that the moment arrived, Welcome didn't know what to do.

A second voice, deeper than the first and familiar sounding said, "Yes, you should. But I'm afraid that we're scaring her half to death."

"Sister, will you hush, she's looking at us. She's so pretty."

Welcome stared. The woman in the tree became more visible now. She sat with her legs crossed, dressed in brown, high-waisted trousers and a white linen shirt. Black, peep-toe heels graced her feet. The young woman looked to Welcome to be in her mid-twenties. There were no lines on her heart-shaped face. She held Welcome's gaze with a wide-open smile that made Welcome feel special and blush in a way she never had before. And then, in a moment, the woman disappeared, everything except her delicate hands with slim tapered fingers.

"Oh, goodness, I thought I had it right," the second voice said. Welcome stared as the hands kept gesturing about. "Well, this is most distressing," the tree woman said. "I'm here, but I'm not here." In a moment a second figure appeared right next to where the other one had been sitting. She looked like the first figure except her hair was darker than chestnut brown and not as wavy as the other woman's, and she had a prominent mole under her nose. She wore a blue, button-down dress, with distinctive shoulder pads, that came to her knees and a pair of loafers.

This second figure said, "Please Welcome, do come close. We've been trying to come through for such a long time."

Welcome knew that she couldn't be intoxicated. Welcome had never had a full drink in her young life. On one long ago Christmas she appeased her mother by sipping some hideous concoction that her mother put before her. "Drinking always makes me feel better," she had said to Welcome. "I can drown out the voices that way."

Maybe I should run. But, in the moment, Welcome reviewed all the fun things that had happened in her life without her causing them. After taking that depressingly small tally, she pulled herself up to her full, impressive height, wiped around the edges of her mouth, and stepped toward the tree.

∽

Welcome could tell no one about her new acquaintances. She looked over her shoulder as she approached what the sisters called "the Grove," the area of the forest that they appeared in. She'd meet them after school. A week in and she couldn't remember a more special time in her life.

They were the Pontey sisters, Grace and Millicent, born and raised in this area during the early 1900s, more than a century before the Great Separation. They told her scraps of their memories:

making a roast duck with crabapple stuffing, sewing buttons on a coat, playing with porcelain dolls when they were girls, and listening to records. Grace, the younger sister, was her favorite. She was the singer. Her face was dimpled, clear-skinned, and when she came through, she smelled like lemons. Welcome had guessed correctly: when Grace died, she was in her early twenties. Her laugh sounded like a tinny tinkling bell. She was shy and quiet, not like Millicent, older at least by ten years. And Grace called her "dumpling" from time to time. Grace was getting good at materializing, but sometimes she'd get confused and only her slender hands showed, wildly gesticulating. Sometimes she could not maintain her image, said that it was too tiring, and just talked instead of materializing.

Sharp-faced Millicent asked questions and without warning might chafe at something Welcome said, her mood souring.

"The living don't understand anything. They don't take advantage of what they got right under their noses," Millicent said one cold spring afternoon.

"Don't say that. What do I have here?" Welcome said.

"You feel the sun on your face, right? When your mother fries fish or bakes something good, it stays in your nose—right?" Millicent asked, impatiently.

"My mama don't fry fish and her baking will make you sick."

Millicent tutted. "Dead is dead. Bad cooking one can live with."

"Millicent! There's no need for rudeness," Grace said.

Millicent disappeared then.

A silence tightened like a cord between Welcome and Grace.

"I don't think that she likes me," Welcome said, standing up and stretching her legs.

"My sister often takes getting used to," Grace said and then cocked her head. "To be fair, she's not been herself lately."

"What do you do when you're not here with me?"

"We think about our lives. Regrets, choices, losses. We argue. We mourn. Millicent roams and experiments with her abilities."

They waited for Millicent to return, but after a bit Grace said with a wink, "More time for us."

After Grace sang a song for her, they explored the creatures of the Grove—the moles, foxes, and birds, and Grace showed her how to see the glow around animals. "If you are very calm, you can see the light that is around all living beings. And, if you know what you are doing, you can ride that light."

"What does that mean?"

Before Grace could answer Millicent appeared then and with a grin that showed all her teeth.

"Did you miss me?" she said, her grin growing wider.

Before Welcome could answer, Millicent waved her hand, "Forgive me. We should not talk of sad times and the past; it is a joy that we can be together." And then, floating close to Welcome, she looked into her eyes and said, "Tell us everything about you, Welcome."

An icy tremor twisted Welcome's insides as she tried not to notice how Millicent's super wide, uneven-teeth-pressed-tightly-together grin unnerved her.

∾

Despite her reservations about Millicent, Welcome always wanted to know more about their lives. They had been raised in a family with plenty, one of the wealthier families in the town.

"What did it feel like to be free? Have money?" Welcome said.

"I wasn't free, Welcome," Grace said. "Yes, we had money and nice things, but our father dictated much of our lives."

"Yes, he was a bore, wasn't he?" Millicent said.

Grace nodded. "You made it fun though, sister. Millicent always begged father for more parties, and when I was married, she came over and cheered me up."

Welcome paid attention. This was the first time Grace had mentioned a husband. And the thought of parties made Welcome swoon inside. Parties were rare in Thistleview.

"I married young, as my father wanted. My husband was a doctor." Grace shook her head and Welcome could feel a deep anger ripple through the ghost. Grace's presence faded some, but she kept talking. "Although he was supposed to be devoted to healing, he was cruel and small-minded. He tried to dictate everything I did." Grace shook her head, a frown clouding her face. "Oh, in those days, that was the way it was." She smiled at her sister who was looking up at the sky.

"What did you do all day? Did you work?"

"We were healers, in a way," Grace said.

"Nurses," Millicent corrected.

"Healing was a talent," Grace said, her face brightening.

And as Grace opened her mouth to say more, Millicent waved a hand. "Hush, you always talk too much, dead or alive."

Welcome jolted back. Grace's shimmery smile instantly disappeared. A look that Welcome couldn't read passed between them.

Millicent's pinched face spat though she possessed no saliva. "The men then were small-minded and cruel, and most women were sheep-like, scared of their own shadow. Not much has changed."

"That's not true," Welcome said, feeling heat rise in her face. "Mr. Applegate is kind and Mrs. Gavey is the smartest person in the town."

"My sister is right, I do talk too much," Grace said with a wave of a hand. "What is in the past needs to stay there, right sister?"

Grace is the peacemaker between them. Welcome noticed with interest that although Millicent changed the subject to talk about her favorite music from when they were young, she never answered Grace's question.

Her mother spooned out the semi-burned tuna, sardine, and sauerkraut casserole. "Sorry about the edges, they're always so hard for me."

Welcome nodded and forced a smile. *Be grateful as Mama hardly ever cooks.* She looked down at the gray and white almost square shape on her plate. Her mama really did try. She did. She dragged her fork through the block of casserole and steeled herself. Mrs. Gavey had kept her promise and talked with Welcome at length about her prospects and the risks and challenges of leaving Thistleview. Their conversation had settled into Welcome and had made her even more aware of what it meant to leave. In her small room at night as she was going to sleep, she would imagine that the train was coming for her. For a few moments, the roar of the train became her second pulse, her life dependent on its metallic vigor. The approach of it vibrated the small pile of books and the old wooden hamper in her room. Welcome would imagine every object near her, animate with possibility, as if the rusty clock on the wall and the makeshift bed also yearned for their own adventures. She'd twitch, bite into her pillow, and yelp as she felt the imaginary train arrive full blast past her house. After the shaking, she'd shrink, knowing that she still lived in the same squat house, her mother's light snoring next door lulling her back to sleep. She'd awake in the morning, disappointed that her ghost train hadn't taken her away.

It's time for me to say something.

⟨∅⟩

At breakfast the next day, Welcome waited for her mother to get halfway through a cup of tea before and said, "Mama, Mrs. Gavey said that I was good at studying the old cities and building things. You know, with my hands. That I might be able to go to college. She said she would help me apply for the special requests needed."

Her mother's eyes fixed on Welcome, but she said nothing. Welcome continued talking, her words spilling out in a rush. "Daddy was good at building things."

Her mother nodded. "Yes, he could put his hands upon something and change it. Like that table," she said pointing.

They both turned to look at the old oak table topped with a vase of dying flowers.

"But girls don't know how to make things but trouble."

"Girls can build things!" Welcome felt the heat rising in her face.

"You're not going anywhere. You are going to stay right here and take care of me when I become old," her mother yelled, her eyes narrowing with defiance.

Welcome flinched then steadied her gaze. "When is that Mama? When will you get old?"

"Well, I'm already old."

Her mother shrugged and leaned both elbows on the table looking into her daughter's face. Welcome noticed that, for a moment, her mother's blue eyes looked clear, clearer than the sky. Her mother dipped her head. "Some days I can't tell where I am, what the past is, and where now begins."

"I know, Mama," Welcome said. She could see how the anger had fled her mother's face, leaving a listless expression and a trembling mouth. Her mother started crying softly and rubbing her arms.

Watching her mother, all of Welcome's plans faded away. She got up and hugged her. Her mother's body went limp, and she slid out of the chair into her daughter's arms. They landed on the floor. Welcome rocked her, noticing how small her mother's body felt. In her ear, she whispered, "I'll stay, I'll stay."

Welcome found the sisters' talents amazing. Millicent was always eager to show off. They could conjure an item from memory, and it would appear for a few moments. And, as Grace had said, they had the ability to ride a creature's light and even subtly control its actions.

Welcome loved the birds that made their home in the cemetery's forest. She delighted in seeing the thrushes circle around and the talkative, iridescent grackles. On this day, they watched a grackle come close.

Millicent went silent, and Welcome noticed the bird's bodily glow change from a low to a brighter light, which she was used to seeing from Grace's lessons. The bird went about its activities, pecking at the ground, looking for worms in the moist earth.

The bird stopped and let out a shrill cry unlike any of its usual whistles and croaks. Welcome turned to Millicent whose face tightened and gaze was locked onto the bird.

Grace's eyes widened, and she leaned forward. "You have become quite advanced, sister."

Millicent ignored them, but a self-satisfied and spine-chilling grin spread across her face that made Welcome shiver.

The grackle shot into the air and Welcome caught her breath. She put her hand to her eyes as she followed the bird's rapid ascent.

"Millicent, that's enough, don't you think?" Grace said.

"I'm trying to get my spirit in," she said. Welcome noted a sharpness in her voice.

Up and up the bird flew. Welcome felt the hairs on her arms raise and she watched with puzzlement as a blue light formed and bubbled around Millicent. *That's new.* Welcome exhaled with relief as finally the bird descended. But something was wrong with the bird. It zigged and zagged through the sky. As it returned toward them, the bird's high-pitched cry blasted Welcome's ears.

"Oh, stop it, whatever you are doing. You're hurting it!" Welcome said.

"I'm almost in," Millicent said, her voice throaty and rough.

The bird came nearer, flying through the sisters and around Welcome's head. Its black eyes had a wild look and blood trickled from its mouth. Welcome could no longer see the bird's natural glow, instead it looked as if it had been coated with thick blue paint. Finally, the bird's distress ended, and it fell to the ground with a sickening thud. Welcome rushed over. She picked up the bird. Dead.

"What did you do?" Welcome wailed, cradling the dead bird.

Millicent frowned. "Tried to join into its body."

"That's not right, inserting yourself in." Welcome said, screwing up her face. Her stomach clenched. She didn't understand what Millicent was doing, she just knew it was cruel, wrong, and unnatural.

Millicent's blue image grew brighter and the look on her face was distant and impassive, her thin lips pursed. "What would you know about right and wrong? Do you know how long it has taken me to perfect that kind of experience? The grackle was going to die someday, and today it died being part of a greater thing."

Welcome had not seen this unfeeling side of Millicent.

"She's right," Grace whispered. "It's not becoming of our creed. You went too far."

Millicent disappeared abruptly.

"Come back, Millicent. Explain what you did," Welcome said. "I want to understand." She turned to face Grace. "Your creed? What did you mean by that?"

"Please do not press me. Millicent is already upset," Grace said, frowning.

How does Millicent act when she is upset? Welcome wondered.

"Keep your secrets then, I'm going home," Welcome said. She left to bury the sacrificial bird.

∽

For a few days, Welcome avoided the Grove, but she missed Grace. She felt even more alone at school as she had told Mrs. Gavey that she wasn't interested anymore in college and leaving Thistleview. It hurt her to turn away from Mrs. Gavey, but she knew she couldn't ever leave her mother.

When Welcome arrived in the Grove at the usual time, it surprised her to only find Millicent.

"Where's Grace?"

"She's away...resting." Millicent said.

This had never been the pattern of their visits, but Welcome was so troubled by the sinking feeling of being stuck forever in the town, she sat down and put her hands on her head.

"Something troubles you?" Millicent asked.

Welcome looked up, frowning. "You're not going to hurt another bird, are you?"

"No, I know how that bothered you. I'm sorry. Let's get your mind off whatever is bothering you. Want to play a game?"

She looked at Millicent for a long moment. "Maybe I should go, or we should call Grace."

"This game involves you and Grace, but really, it's a favor," Millicent said.

Welcome cocked her head. Her stomach roiled and she felt light-headed. *I should leave.*

Millicent came closer and Welcome could see the faintest outline of a bluish haze around the ghost. "She needs your help, Welcome. She's not doing well and there's something I want to try, and I need you."

She wondered how ghosts couldn't feel well but thought this was a question for Grace later. "I'll do anything to help her," Welcome said, sitting up with attention.

"Yes, I figured that you'd want to help. You're such a good girl," Millicent said softly, a human coo.

"Get settled against that headstone there. This won't hurt at all. It will feel like going to sleep."

Welcome did as she was told, and she could already feel her eyes drooping.

"I want you to think about Grace," Millicent said.

It felt to Welcome as if she were drifting far away, but when she opened her eyes, Millicent floated near her.

"Close your eyes and concentrate on Grace. Wouldn't it be nice if you could get closer to her? Wouldn't you like that?"

Welcome blushed. It was as if Millicent read her mind and knew that Welcome fantasized about the train and that sometimes she imagined Grace leaving with her. Her entire body relaxed. And, then she noticed a warmth creeping across her skin. After a short while, she didn't have the energy to open her eyes. Was Millicent touching her? Weren't ghosts supposed to be cold? This was a delicious warmth, not a coldness.

"I guess," Welcome finally answered, her mind fighting off drowsiness.

Strange symbols and geometric shapes appeared in her mind's eye. She saw a brilliant, pulsing blue light. And, then nothingness.

After several moments Welcome thought she heard her name being called through a long hallway. She wanted to rush toward it, but she was stuck somehow, pinned down. Why was it she couldn't move? The blue light was all around her, forcing her back. She felt a slamming against her head. She strained toward the voice that called her name. She knew that voice!

"Grace! Grace, where are you?"

"Follow my voice," Grace said.

With mental strain, she peeled herself away from the blue light that clung to her, the blue that threatened to ingest her. She dashed toward Grace's voice.

"Hurry!" Grace said.

She found a door where Grace stood and Welcome reached her hand out.

⌎

When Welcome opened her eyes, it was dark. She sat on the ground. How did she get here, near Mr. Applegate's house? Her head hurt. "Grace?" Welcome called.

"Welcome," Grace said. Welcome strained to see in the dark. Grace's voice was faint. She then saw Grace's hands. Something was wrong, Welcome could feel it.

"You're back here?" Welcome said, shaking off grogginess. "Are you better? Did I help?"

"Go home!" Grace croaked.

"I was with Millicent trying to help her, for you."

"Oh, Welcome, she…"

"What's happened to you?"

At that moment, Millicent appeared. "You did well, Welcome, thank you."

"Millicent, what did you think you were doing?"

"Shut up, Grace, you're scaring Welcome."

Grace let out a wail and Welcome covered her ears.

"Go home now, Welcome," Millicent ordered.

"Grace, are you all right?"

"I need to talk to Millicent," Grace said, her voice faint.

And then they were both gone, leaving her with a sinking feeling and a temple-splitting headache.

⟡

Welcome entered a small building near her school. The interior was decorated like a lodge with mounted animal heads against multiple walls. She hated having to come here, to talk with the Custodians of Knowledge. She walked to the back of the room where the ancient, frail, and never smiling Custodian Lawson sat.

"Custodian Lawson, I'm looking for information about the Pontey sisters…er…if there's anything about them."

Yesterday's encounter with them made Welcome curious about who they were as living people. She was going to have to lie to the Custodians, which she didn't like, and sweat dampened her armpits.

He coughed but did not move from his gargoyle-like position.

"Come again?" he said with a slow move of lips and raspy voice.

"It's for a class project. We need to find out information about people who lived before, before the Great Separation," Welcome said, her voice rising.

At that moment, a man with silver and black hair close to her mother's age emerged from another room.

"Hi, Custodian Lawson III," Welcome said, and dipped her head, a sign of respect. He was the one that came to their school to talk about the responsibility of knowledge and how the Custodians of Knowledge helped keep order. He had taken over for his father who had died suddenly of a heart attack. Mrs. Gavey never looked happy when he came to visit her class.

"It's always Troy for a pretty girl like you, Welcome," he said with a wink. Welcome exhaled and told herself to relax. He was the nicest of the three Custodians.

She repeated what she had told his grandfather.

Custodian Lawson III nodded and walked over to where his grandfather sat. "Grandpop didn't you know something of the Pontey sisters? I remember you talking about them when I was a boy. Something you heard from when you were young?"

The gargoyle-like man stared back "Come, again?" He coughed and Welcome noticed the thickness of his cataracts.

"Oh Grandpop," Custodian Lawson III grumbled. "I'll go in the back and check."

"Thanks," Welcome said.

And under his breath Welcome heard Custodian Lawson III mumble, "What am I going to do with you in a few years?"

It took what seemed like forever and Welcome walked around the room to avoid Custodian Lawson's stare. She picked her nails to avoid looking at him.

He softly mouthed the name Pontey, as if grinding it between his teeth.

Custodian Lawson III returned and brought out several boxes. He motioned for her to approach the long table, perpendicular to the large desk where his grandfather sat.

As they unfolded the old papers and yellowing materials, Welcome grew increasingly alarmed. Her insides burned. Her eyes took in that every paper screamed headlines about the "Murdering Sisters." Black and white photos of them reflected an accuracy as they looked now.

"God, Grandpop, now it is all coming back to me. These women went on a killing spree, right? Two upstanding men died by their hands; says here that they killed themselves," he said, pointing to an article.

Blood pounded in Welcome's ears. Welcome could feel herself swoon and placed both hands on the table for support.

Custodian Lawson III eyed her suspiciously, "You look like the world is coming to an end."

"I'm okay," she managed to say.

Hastily bundling up all the papers and placing them back in the boxes, he added, "You don't want to do a history project on them. They're not upstanding ladies. Hey, what about Mrs. Colby? Now there's a woman."

The preacher's wife? Welcome wanted to stamp her feet and say *not if you sent me to hell right now.* Instead, she kept her face steady despite the knot of thoughts that tumbled in her mind. "Thank you, I'll ask my teacher about it."

"Witches!" The gargoyle croaked so loud it felt as if the sound would burst her eardrums.

The sudden outburst startled both of them. Custodian Lawson III said, "What, granddad?"

His old dry lips repeated, "Witches. They were witches."

Welcome got out of there as fast as her feet would take her.

☙

As soon as she was out of sight from the Custodians of Knowledge building, she ran straight to the Grove. She didn't care about missing classes.

"Sisters!" She yelled, her voice thick and strong, surprising herself. She called several times.

Grace appeared first, as always. "What, what is it?"

"The Guardians, they said," Welcome dropped to her knees, the words choking in her throat. "I saw, I saw the papers. You killed them."

Millicent appeared where she liked to perch on an old gravestone, her eyes glittered.

"I told you she would find out. We should have said something," Grace said, her eyes dull and almost colorless. "Lying always makes things worse."

"Let her think what she wants. She's a big girl. Right, Welcome?"

Welcome noted the almost sneering tone of Millicent. *That's new and I don't like it.*

"It is true that we killed those men, but it didn't happen the way that you think," Grace finally said.

"What's wrong with you?" Welcome said, momentarily forgetting the shock of her discovery.

"I don't know. I don't feel like myself," Grace said.

I can't trust anyone. Everything tasted bitter in her mouth. Her secret friends were not friends. They had done something terrible in their day.

Welcome's heart raced and her open mouth narrowed into slit. In a low voice she said, "I must be mad to have believed you. You are evil and I am evil and probably crazy."

Welcome felt her head swim and as she turned away, she heard Millicent say, "She's too angry to listen now, Grace."

Welcome had avoided the cemetery for days now, using the more traditional path to school. Coming up the path to her home, fear shot through her. Custodian of Knowledge Lawson III was walking up to her worn porch.

"Custodian Lawson III?"

When he turned, she saw no kindness in his eyes.

She nodded to him. "My mother is probably asleep right now."

"I'm not here to see her, Welcome."

"Oh?" Welcome said. She stopped at the base of the porch stairs.

"I asked Mrs. Knox about your special assignment."

Welcome almost choked. She had not thought that he would investigate. *How could I be so stupid? Custodians always wanted to know everyone's business.* She should have asked Mrs. Gavey to cover for her. Would she have done that?

Welcome's hard-earned bag of candies slipped out of her hand, opened and the sweets scattered in the dirt. She made a move to retrieve them, and he stepped down two steps. She froze as she took in his hardened face.

"Lying is a sin, don't you know that by now, Welcome? Where'd you find out about the Pontey sisters? They're not buried in the cemetery."

She was truly dumbfounded. When she had asked the sisters about where their headstones were, they had said that time had eroded their modest headstones and since their family line had died with the there was no one to do upkeep. Welcome had wondered about that explanation but hadn't paid it too much mind. She never liked to press them about their deaths, figuring they didn't much want to remember.

"I just make up stories about people in the cemetery. It keeps me busy while I'm there. Pontey is an unusual name," she said, hoping the lie came out smooth.

He walked down the steps slowly, his voice lowering, "Maybe you shouldn't be working in the cemetery. You don't want to end up like your mama, all alone and crazy, now do you?"

She was about to defend her mother when the door burst open.

"Her Mama ain't alone and she ain't crazy, at least not today."

They both jumped as if shocked by a live current of electricity.

Mrs. Sparks, Welcome's mother, stood there in a disheveled housecoat and ripped maroon stockings. "What are you doing this side of town, Lawson?"

He curled his lip. Welcome knew that they had gone to school together long ago and there was no love lost between them.

"Oh hello, Lila. I was following up on some information for Welcome as she came for a visit a few days ago. Everything is settled. I'll be going now."

Welcome noticed that her mother had her right arm held behind her back.

Her mother's mouth quirked, and she charged at him. "That's the shittiest lie that you ever put your sorry mouth to. Get off this land...get out of herrrrrrrrrrrrrrrrrrrrrrrrrrrrrrrrrrrrrrrrrrrrrrrrre."

Welcome noticed the flash of metal a moment sooner than Custodian of Knowledge Lawson III did and moved out of the way.

Caught off guard, Custodian Lawson III flinched and ran down the steps.

Welcome's mother brandished a meat cleaver.

"Lila, stop it! I'm leaving," he yelled. "No need to get crazy."

"I'll show you what crazy does," Welcome's mother said, coming down the steps.

Once he had gotten into his old car and taken off, Welcome allowed herself a full breath. Welcome felt protected, but she saw the hateful look that he gave both of them as he drove off. He was not done with her yet.

Her mother stood looking at her daughter, a wheezing sound blowing from her lips every few seconds, "What trouble have you gotten yourself into, Welcome?"

"I made a mistake trusting someone," Welcome said and turned so her mother wouldn't see the tears forming in her eyes.

"Story of my life," her mother said, following Welcome and closing the door behind her.

Her mother didn't ask her any more about it, and that made Welcome grateful and sad at the same time.

∽

For a few days, Welcome tried something she hadn't attempted in a long time—to make herself interested in the other kids around her. Although they drew away from her, she observantly followed behind some of the girls and tried to show interest in their incessant chatter about boys and graduation. They wanted nothing to do with her, calling her "Graveyard Girl" and worse. Instead of feeling rebuffed, however, a relief passed through her. She wasn't like them and wasn't interested in them.

She found herself sighing when she reached the crossroads between the shortcut to her house through the cemetery or the regular route. She didn't want to let Mr. Applegate down. But the bigger pull to the cemetery was the emptiness inside of her. She missed Grace, despite everything. And she was worried about her. She felt a flush heat her face and creep across her chest. She was angry with herself for wanting to go back; they had lied to her. Welcome walked toward the cemetery. She would be responsible. Yes. She would go and do the job and ignore the Grove. It was possible to do. She would not give in to checking up on Grace.

After her tasks were done, she edged by the Grove, but didn't call out to them.

As she turned, Grace appeared in front of her. "Oh, Welcome! My dear, my dear, oh how I have missed you!" her voice tinkled. Her words flowed faster, "I know you are still angry with us, and I understand. But I must have a few moments with you. Oh, I must!"

Welcome was secretly happy to see Grace, but she made the sternest face she could muster. She folded her arms. "Five minutes, Grace."

Grace's face brightened and she nodded. "I can't bear for you to think we were murderers. Our aunt taught us the healing arts. Some people have a talent for that life and way of being. My sister and I practiced it, in a gentle and safe way."

"Witchcraft?" Welcome said, trying to hide her interest.

"Some would call us witches, though that was not what we called ourselves. It's what the men in our town said about us. Remember I said we were healers? We were. One day, my husband, the doctor, caught me helping one of his patients, and asked what I was doing. I had created a powerful salve and with proper spell work, it was very effective. He hated it, labeled it unscientific. So, Millicent and I went to nursing school to give ourselves some legitimacy. My husband hated that, too. Under the guise of being nurses, we created healing sachets and salves. People in town started coming to us to help with their ailments. Some of the more observant women wanted to know our secrets. We showed the women what we knew and formed a secret group. The power and influence of my sister and me grew, and my husband and his friends in town became envious."

Looking into her eyes, Welcome could feel the truth of Grace's words.

"There were eight of us in the group and over a year, they killed us. All of us."

Welcome's eyes bulged.

"One by one. Some were made to look like accidents, some just disappeared. They carefully covered up their tracks."

Chills raked across Welcome's arms.

"That's terrible. How did you know for sure that your husband and his friends were involved?"

"It took Millicent and me time to put the pieces together. My husband was a coward and never did the actual killing but planned them. His fellow partner was the one that came into the house and found me as I was packing to leave. Thank God, Millicent sensed I was in danger and came to the house. He was strangling me, Welcome."

Welcome shook her head and instinctively hugged herself as she listened to Grace's story.

"I looked into his hate-filled eyes while I struggled. And, then Millicent was there and clubbed him with a heavy lamp and pounded him until he was good and dead. Another one of my husband's cronies came to check if the deed was done and we took him by surprise. We ran after that and hid out in the forest. We wanted to leave but we had no car and not much money of our own. My husband organized a group of men to find us, which they did. They killed us and threw us in one of the ditches, on the land near your house.

Welcome walked to her and felt herself tremble. She yearned to touch Grace and comfort her. "What a horrible and cruel thing they did to you and Millicent. I can't imagine how afraid you were."

"Oh, it is so good to talk about it, to reveal it to someone else. The story shared with you lessens the burden." Grace said.

Welcome smiled, appreciating Grace's words and how the Grove again felt like a special place for them.

"There is something else, the more important thing. Welcome, you must leave here at once."

"Why?"

"Millicent is planning something, and you are to be part of it."

"What would she want with me?" Welcome asked.

"Do you remember that day when you woke up and Millicent and I were arguing?"

"Yes, of course. You seemed ready to tear at each other, but we never talked about it."

"She wants to become flesh again. That day, she put a marker on you."

Welcome raised her eyebrows and Grace as if in anticipation of her question rushed on. "She has created a connection between you and her. It is called impregnation of spirit. Something we were studying when we were younger. Like what she did with the bird. She is planning something terrible I fear."

Grace bowed her head. "She was always the more talented one. I've never been the strong one between us. I left so much to her. I regret that now. She's been draining my essence for years. Feeding off of me you might say."

Welcome's head buzzed as she listened to Grace's revelation. A bone-numbing chill spread throughout her limbs. Her throat tightened as she looked into the ghost's eyes, "I can't leave my mother."

"It's the only way, Welcome. You must, you must. You must leave and never look back. Or else, she will be able to move into your body and bind your will to her own. Once she controls your body, she can take control of others' bodies."

A thought pierced Welcome's heart and she sucked in a breath, bracing herself. "Was contacting me all part of her plan? Did you ever really want to get to know me?"

Grace's eyes grew soft. "You must believe me, Welcome, meeting you has been the very best thing. I thought you were the loveliest person I had ever met. I thought us lucky to have you. I have been here with my sister for a long time. She does not want to go toward the light and my love for her has blocked my chance of moving on. Her hateful heart will keep her here. I have hoped for years it would be different. If only it were different. I was lonely, Welcome. You changed that, and for that I am eternally grateful."

They heard the call of a thrush and Welcome drank in Grace's words and the feelings behind them. "I don't want to leave you," she said, choking out the words.

"There's not much more left of me. I have made my choices, and I know I will find peace soon. You have your whole life to live. You will always be my funny Valentine."

Welcome looked up in the darkening sky, racking her brain about what she could do to help Grace and herself. The train would not arrive in town for another week. One piece of Grace's story came back to her.

"You said that you were buried near the ditches by my house?"

"Yes," Grace nodded.

"I was always teased about where my house is. They thought my father was crazy buying a house so far from town, so close to the cemetery and too close to the train tracks."

Welcome had often pondered the position of her house. The railroad tracks sat kitty-corner to the road that led to her house. The edge of the town's large cemetery sat less than a stone's throw from the road behind her house. Parallel to the tracks lay six half-finished ditches, the smallest one right near the edge of the train track. During a grander and more ambitious moment in Thistleview's history, when her mother still talked to people and they didn't come away scratching their heads, Mr. Brooke, head of town services, initiated a plan to bring better plumbing to the house. She knew that her mother did something to scare the workers off and then soon after that the town ran out of money for those kinds of repairs. *Something changed for Mama after that time.* It was as if the dug up, moist earth beckoned to her mother. Sometimes on sunny days her mother, wide-eyed, wrapped in an old natty comforter, walked the short distance and talked to the voices who "knocked" that day. She said she could hear them better now. She'd walk around the depressions, pointing and muttering. Sometimes, she'd jump into one of the depressions, root herself into the earth and fall asleep. Welcome could never make any sense of it and was always grateful that no one saw her mother. But sometimes, after those times, her mother would wake with ideas about a plant to make a tea from.

"Grace, I've got an idea. I think my mother can help me."

☙

Welcome sprinted to her house. "Mama, Mama," she called as she opened the front door.

Her mother slumped on the old beat-up couch. She bolted up, "Jesus Christ, you are about to split my ear drums. What's wrong with you?"

"Everything, but I think you can help me. You have to help me."

Mrs. Sparks narrowed her eyes. "What are you talking about? I need my sleep."

At that moment, Welcome noticed a blue light penetrating the door. Her mind felt as if it was being slammed against a table. She shook off the feeling and focused.

"Mama, we have got to go out back, now!"

She grabbed her mother's hand and pulled her from the couch. She ran with her mother through the small house. "It's the voices, Mama."

Welcome tore open the screen door and dragged her mother down the short flight of steps.

"I'm the crazy one!" her mother yelped. "What's happened to my daughter?"

Welcome grabbed her mother's face. "Mama, you've always heard voices since we've lived here?"

They stood nearest the smallest ditch and Welcome could feel the heat from the ground snake its way up into her shoes.

"Yes, yes," Mrs. Sparks murmured. "Telling me their troubles and dreams. Terrible noise."

Pinpricks of fright dotted Welcome's consciousness as she looked back at the house, now encased in dark blue light. *Millicent must have been practicing all this time to leave the graveyard.*

"Together we have to call on them. A bad woman, a hurt woman is after me from the other side."

"You gone crazy, too," her mother said, voice raspy.

"No, I haven't. Please, you've got to focus. We have to ask them to help us. They have been trying to get your attention all my life!"

"Who?"

"The women who were healers. They all died here. Take my hands, Mama."

The woman did as she was told and clasped her daughter's hands.

"I think I have a talent to make the dead come through, to see them," Welcome added. "We have to work together."

Welcome could hear them already, whisperings coming from the earth.

"Call to them, Mama!"

"I don't know how. I'm crazy."

"You are not, crazy, Mama!" Welcome said, giving a shake to her mother's hand. "You can receive energy. You are a healer; you just haven't been trained."

"What? Those voices always talking a mish mash," her mother said, eyebrows raised, eyes questioning, disbelieving.

Welcome stomped her foot. *There's no time to make her understand.* She pointed as Millicent's cobalt form detached itself from the house and floated toward them.

"Look!"

Her mother's eyes grew big. "What's happening?"

"That spirit is coming for me. She's going to make me do bad things."

Her mother drew herself up, "The hell she ain't!" Her mother locked on to her daughter's hands. "What do I do?"

"Concentrate and call to the voices. Ask them to come through. They have wanted to for a long time!"

Welcome saw as her mother's face struggled to comprehend her daughter's words.

"Do it. I'll help you."

"Come through you tormenting voices," her mother shouted without hesitation. "Come through, I need you."

Mrs. Sparks rocked back and forth, keeping her eyes squeezed shut. Mother and daughter sank to the ground, shivering and holding each other.

Welcome heard her mother calling out names that she had never heard before: Jesse, Edith, Ruth, Susan, Delilah, and Patricia.

Welcome strained as Millicent was almost upon them. *No more time!*

Welcome gulped in a breath and, joining in with her mother, shouted, "Healers of Thistleview, come and claim your own. She has lost her way. She has broken and will continue to break the covenant of your ways. Bring her back into the earth and let her rest."

A shadowy female figure rose from the earth and Mrs. Sparks grabbed hold of Welcome. Mother and daughter instinctively drew back.

"You've got to take her away, you can't let her hurt my daughter, not my daughter. You been talking to me all these years. Help me for once. Please, please, please," Welcome's mother babbled. Halfway between standing and squatting, Lila Sparks pushed Welcome behind her.

Millicent's laugh boomed. "They are too late. This, Welcome is too late."

"Our sister wants revenge for what has happened," the apparition said, its voice grating and high-pitched.

"I know, but all those people are gone and dead and all she has done has been to pervert the very things that made you good while you were alive," Welcome replied.

"I have promised you a way to be free," Millicent's shadow said.

"She has hurt her sister, Grace," Welcome said.

"Grace is weak," Millicent said, and Welcome could hear the irritation in the ghost's tone.

How did I not see Millicent's cruelty and hatred of Grace before?

"She wants to be flesh for her own amusement. She does not belong here, in this time," Welcome said.

Welcome could feel other forms take shape around them. Soon they were encircled by female spirits, and for a moment, mother and daughter felt all the fear and pain that they had suffered at the end.

Her mother wailed and fell away from Welcome. "Too much!"

Baring her teeth through the psychic connection, Welcome continued to address them, shouting though her throat was raw. She would make the case for their lives.

"You have not been kind nor good. Your anger has seeped through our land. You have kept my mother's company long enough. You have fed on her but never gave her enough of yourself to make her see you! You have used her for all these years but have never taught much of anything that is useful. You have made her think that she is crazy. I thought I was also damaged. Is that the way of your kind?"

Her mother lay on the ground, her body curled into a tight ball, shaking and panting.

A cacophony of voices vibrated through Welcome.

"How dare you address them like that, you stupid child," Millicent said.

And, finally, there was Grace hovering above them, only a bare shimmer of her face visible.

Welcome rose. She pointed at all the forms gathered. "You must take your sister and keep her on your side. I promise that if you take Millicent away, my mother and I will honor you. We will honor your deaths. We will receive your teachings. We will share your teachings and help heal others. You will live through us. I offer you justice."

All went silent and then the dead women gathered together. First, they collectively breathed in and Grace's form disappeared. Welcome winced, her eyes fixed on where Grace had been. And then, as they chanted, Millicent's swirling blue energy grew fainter and fainter, though her screams were of such a pitch that both mother and daughter fell on their backs covering their ears.

❧

"That's it, Mama," Welcome said. She'd been encouraging her mother's efforts with the rabbit.

The rabbit a few yards away startled at Welcome's voice.

Her mother flopped onto the blanket they had spread out in the back yard a few hours before and wiped the sweat away from her brow. "There's nothing like feeling a creature's energy."

Welcome nodded. She patted her mother's shoulder, a feeling of gratitude washing over her. It had been a good day. Not all of them were. The healers had warned Welcome that her mother's progress would be slow. She had a lot of healing to do. But that was fine by Welcome. Each day her mother got stronger. Each day her mother absorbed the lessons the healers gave at a faster pace. They laughed more and talked in ways they hadn't ever before. She would stay here with her mother for a while, building something new. The cities could wait for a few years.

Welcome heard the knock at the front door. Her mother bolted up, her gaze unfocused.

"Are you sure about this?"

Welcome squeezed her mother's hand and nodded. "There is strength in numbers."

"Can we trust her?"

"Yes," Welcome said. "She can choose."

As she walked through the house to answer the door, she felt the rightness of her decision like a hum inside her. She would gather some women here. In secret. They would honor the healers and learn from them. They would help her mother and each other. *They might help me see Grace again, too.*

Smiling, she opened the door and greeted Mrs. Gavey.

Earlier versions of many of these stories have appeared in a variety of publications:

"Nussia" appeared on www.BookSmugglers.com in July 2018.

"Etta, Zora and the First Serpent" has appeared in *AfroMyths* 2, 2020, Afrocentric Books; audio drama *NightLight*, 2021.

"Cemetery Sisters" appeared in *Witches, Warriors and Wise Women*, Prospective Press, 2020.

"Urban Wendy" appeared in *Red Clay Review: The Literary & Arts Magazine of Chatham Community College*, 2013; audio drama, Black Women Are Scary, 2021.

"Family Line" originally appeared in the anthology *You Don't Say: Stories in the Second Person*, Ink Monkey Press, 2012; reprint in the anthology *Stories We Tell After Midnight*, Vol 2, Crone Girls Press, 2020; audio drama, *Black Women Are Scary*, 2021.

"Doll Seed" appeared in *FIYAH: The Magazine of Black Speculative Fiction*, 2019; 2020 winner of the Carl Brandon Kindred Award for best short fiction that tackles questions of race and ethnicity; reprint *Apex Magazine* 2021.

"The Curl of Emma Jean" appeared in the anthology *Uncommon Origins: A Collection of Gods, Monsters, Nature and Science*, Fighting Monkey Press 2016.

"The Wishing Well Off Fordham Road" appeared in *Midnight and Indigo*, 2020.

"What the Slots Hold" appeared in *Thing E-Zine*, 2016.

"The Lineup" appeared in *100 Word Story*

"Miss Black Little Hill of 1965" appeared in *Blood and Bourbon*, 2020.

"The Invisible Son" appeared in *Flying South*, 2014.

"And They Will Rise from the Oceans" appeared in *Nevermore*, Falstaff Books 2024.

BIO

Michele Tracy Berger is the Eric and Jane Nord Family Professor in the Department of Religious Studies and director of the Baker-Nord Center for the Humanities at Case Western Reserve University. She has a secondary appointment in the Department of English. Her short fiction, poetry and creative nonfiction has appeared in *100 Word Story, Apex Magazine, Glint Literary Journal, The Wild Word, Blood and Bourbon, FIYAH: Magazine of Black Speculative Fiction, Midnight and Indigo, Oracle: Fine Arts Review, Carolina Woman, Ms.*, and various anthologies. She is the 2019 winner of the Carl Brandon Kindred Award from the Carl Brandon Society for her story "Doll Seed" published in *FIYAH: Magazine of Black Speculative Fiction*. Much of her work explores psychological horror, especially through issues of race and gender.

OUR MISSION Founded in 1982, Aunt Lute Books is an intersectional, feminist press dedicated to publishing literature by those who have been traditionally underrepresented in or excluded by the literary canon. Core to Aunt Lute's mission is the belief that the written word is critical to understanding and relating to each other as human beings. Through the centering of voices, perspectives, and stories that have not been traditionally welcomed by mainstream publishing, we strengthen ties across cultures and experiences, promoting a broader range of expression, and, we hope, working toward a more inclusive and just future.

LAND ACKNOWLEDGMENT We, Aunt Lute Books, acknowledge that we do our work of uplifting marginalized voices and striving toward justice via the written word on the unceded ancestral homeland of the Ramaytush Ohlone who are the original inhabitants of the San Francisco Peninsula. As the indigenous stewards of this land and in accordance with their traditions, the Ramaytush Ohlone have never ceded, lost, nor forgotten their responsibilities as the caretakers of this place, as well as for all peoples who reside in their traditional territory. As Guests, we recognize that we benefit from living and working on their traditional homeland. We wish to pay our respects by acknowledging the Ancestors, Elders and Relatives of the Ramaytush Community and by affirming their sovereign rights as First Peoples.

For more information, please visit our website:

www.auntlute.com

aunt lute books

P.O. Box 410687
San Francisco, CA 94141
books@auntlute.com

This book would not have been possible without the kind contributions of the Aunt Lute Founding Friends:

Anonymous Donor	Diana Harris
Anonymous Donor	Phoebe Robins Hunter
Rusty Barceló	Diane Mosbacher, M.D., Ph.D.
Marian Bremer	Sara Paretsky
Marta Drury	William Preston, Jr.
Diane Goldstein	Elise Rymer Turner